Grace Will Lead Me Home

GRACE WILL LEAD ME HOME

KATHERINE VALENTINE

Image Books · Doubleday
New York London Toronto Sydney Auckland

AN IMAGE BOOK
PUBLISHED BY DOUBLEDAY
a division of Random House, Inc.

IMAGE, DOUBLEDAY, and the portrayal of a deer drinking from a
stream are registered trademarks of Random House, Inc.

Book design by Michael Collica

Cataloguing-in-Publication Data is on file with the Library of Congress:

ISBN 0-385-51194-9
Copyright © 2004 by Katherine Valentine
All Rights Reserved

PRINTED IN THE UNITED STATES OF AMERICA

July 2004
First Image Books Edition

5 7 9 10 8 6

To my beloved granddaughters . . .
. . . Ashley, Chelsea, Megan, Taylor Brooke,
and Tori Lee.

And to my dear Marissa who now plays
among the angels. It is your face I hope to see
first when the Lord finally calls me home.

ACKNOWLEDGMENTS

I now celebrate a brand new chapter in the ongoing Dorsetville series with the advent of Doubleday as my new publisher. To the entire staff of the Image imprint division, I wish to extend my heartfelt appreciation for your relentless enthusiasm and dedication to making Dorsetville both a great place to visit and a great read. Special thanks to Michelle Rapkin for her fine editorial direction. Also a hearty thank you to her assistant, Frances O'Connor, for working so hard to keep us both on track.

I also wish to thank Barbara Delinsky, fellow writer and dear, gentle friend whose encouragement and support I cherish, and for the priceless gift of introducing me to agent extraordinaire, Amy Berkower, Bless you.

And dear Amy . . . your faith in me as a writer continues to be a source of great comfort. For every kindness we extend, a blessing is bestowed. May your cup overrunneth. Thank you.

Grace Will Lead Me Home

GARNER CORRECTIONAL INSTITUTION

The prison gates swung open slowly. Stephen Richter stood poised, ready to step through, yet somewhat hesitant. For eight years—two thousand nine hundred and twenty-five days—he had waited for this moment, counting down the days, hours, and minutes until once again he would be free.

He had been twenty years old when these gates had closed behind him, locking out a world that for just an instant had held a spark of great promise. What if that spark had been forever extinguished? What if he could no longer remember who he had intended to become before fate commandeered by his two brothers had taken him on a giant detour?

And what about the girl? Her memory alone had kept him going all these years. He had loved her with all the love that had been sealed away throughout his youth. He had grown up in a home empty of affection. Any love his parents might have held for him had been exchanged long ago for drugs and booze.

On their last night together, Stephen had confessed this love and felt a release so great that he had cried. She had cried too as they clung together and made promises. They would get married, they pledged. Build a family where home was a place of refuge.

But before the dream could take root, the storm clouds had gathered, and then the gale had come, leveling his vision.

He had been charged as an accessory to murder. He was innocent, but weren't they all? the prosecutor said dryly. His brother Amos, who had actually planned the robbery and pulled the trigger, had gotten away before the cops had arrived, leaving his older brother and him to take the rap. He supposed he should hate Amos, but he didn't. He simply wanted to forget.

"Are you planning on staying?" a uniformed guard asked, his voice edged in sarcasm, standard prison fare.

He had yearned for freedom, prayed about it, dreamed about it, yet now that it was finally his, he found the enclosed walls offered a safety that the outside world without boundaries could not.

Two cars were parked by the front entrance.

"Hey, man. Over here," Amos called. He was seated behind the heavily tinted glass windshield of a Chevy

Suburban, his side window rolled halfway down. There were three other guys in the backseat.

He hesitated. Should he get in, although he had pledged never again to allow his brother back into his life? As he stood on the tarmac, his resolve began to weaken as he realized even the worst choices can feel better when familiar.

"Stephen! Over here!" the priest called. It was Monsignor Casio, leaning against a car, a little grayer at the temples, a little more of a paunch. There was a sense of welcome, of homecoming in that call. Stephen smiled at the warmth of it.

"Don't go that way, brother," Amos said. "He's got nothing that you want. What's he going to offer you? A life filled with hard work? A few lousy dollars at the end of a backbreaking day? Listen up. Nobody wants an ex-con. Come with us. You've done the time. You might as well enjoy the crime. We know a man who can set us up. There's big bucks in it for you."

Stephen headed toward the priest. He was certain the choice would be infinitely harder. His brother was right. Not many people would want to help an ex-con regardless of his innocence; yet he had a feeling that whatever the price, it would be worth it.

He wasn't sure what he was supposed to do with the rest of his life, any more than he knew the reason behind the eight years he had spent in prison for a crime that he had not committed. The priest always said that God's ways were a mystery, yet always superior to man's, and that we must learn not to question but simply to walk by faith and trust in His divine love.

In his storm-tossed world, Stephen had held onto

that knowledge like a lifeline and practiced not asking why, but submitting to His sovereign plan. It had not been easy, but then Stephen had learned a long time ago that nothing worth having was easy.

There were times, however, when he fell victim to doubts. Late at night as he listened to an inmate's soft cries of despair, his faith in a loving God wavered. Had these other men also been wrongly accused? Were they to suffer for the sins of their parents who had brought them up in a world of violence?

But then he would remember the priest's other words.

"Use faith as your compass, my son, not feelings or reasoning. God has a plan for everyone's life. Have faith in that plan and in God's unwavering love no matter how hard the trial or rocky the road. Trust. His grace will lead you home."

God's blessings rained down on the small community as its members prepared for today's celebration. It was a halcyon spring day. A soft breeze, tipped in a warmth portending summer, flowed like a silk ribbon off the river. But even its gentle caress could not assuage the high anxiety of the citizens involved in today's rededication ceremonies. It was an event that everyone had been anticipating for several weeks. In preparation, they had scrubbed and polished the little town until it looked as clean and tidy as a freshly bathed child. Folks wanted Dorsetville to be at its best since guests would be arriving from all over the state.

Winter debris—fallen branches, bags of sodden leaves

masses of twigs that had been hurled about by various winter storms—now laid in neat piles awaiting the highway department's annual spring pickup, an event that Mayor Roger Martin had pushed ahead by three weeks in deference to various state representatives who had agreed to attend the festivities.

"I want them to see for themselves that Dorsetville is the jewel in the state's crown," the mayor said. As soon as the words had left his lips, he felt a town slogan had been born.

The Congregational Church had been one of the oldest in all of New England and the town's pride. But that was before it had burned to the ground. Because of its historic significance, its rebuilding had been heavily financed by the state's historic preservation program. No doubt those in government wished to be in attendance today to make certain their constituents had gotten their money's worth. They would not be disappointed.

Chester Platt's construction crew had outdone themselves in rebuilding the church. Nearly everyone said that it was almost impossible to discern between the old structure and the new one. And although Chester should have been applauded for his fine craftsmanship and attention to minute detail, many said that he had help from the good Lord Himself.

Shortly after the fire, Tom Pastronostra, Dorsetville's building official, had been clearing out a bottom desk drawer when he discovered the church's original plans. He called Nigel Hayes, the town historian, who confirmed the find.

"It's a marvel they've survived without proper preservation," said Nigel, studying the document closely with a magnifying glass. He estimated that the yellowing piece of brittle parchment was nearly three hundred years old.

But Tom thought it was more of a marvel that he had sat at that desk for over a decade and a half and never once had come across it. In fact, he could have sworn that the plans had "just appeared."

But the miracles that helped to reconstruct the old church didn't stop there. In fact, from the very first day, whatever was needed seemed to appear magically.

The small paned arched windows (which matched the originals perfectly) were discovered by the church's pastor, the Reverend Frederick L. Curtis. Stalled in traffic on I-95, he had idled the time away by watching a demolition crew dismantle an old church in preparation for a new highway extension. Suddenly it hit him. The windows they were removing were exact replicas of the ones in his church.

For the next forty minutes, as other trapped motorists sat inhaling fumes and cursing the delay, the reverend, as excited as a child at Christmas, called highway department officials on his cell phone. By the time the traffic started moving again, he had made arrangements to purchase the complete set of windows.

When banisters were needed, Rochelle Phillips, head Sunday school teacher for the Congregational Church for more years than she liked to remember, discovered a perfect match while rummaging through Stanford House Wrecking, where she had gone in search of a new mantel piece. Chester later discovered that the railings had been turned by the same craftsmen who had designed the original spindles for the church's balcony.

The oak pews, which now shone like copper pennies

in the sunlight, had been recovered from a Methodist church in Maine whose parishioners were in the midst of an expansion project and offered to donate theirs at no cost. The Congregational Church needed forty-eight. Forty-eight arrived and fit the space exactly.

And there were other gifts as well.

George Benson donated a good portion of the air conditioning and heating work. Chester Platt never charged for time his crews spent on Saturdays. Even Dorsetville's newest resident, Valerie Kilbourne, a graphic artist who lived across the street with her twin daughters, had lent a hand. Due to her artistic talents, the downstairs Sunday school classrooms now sported a brightly colored mural representing a biblical time line.

Also stationed across the street was the Sister Regina Francis Retirement Home where under the watchful eye of Mother Superior and her nuns, residents had cut, sewed and embroidered the new altar linen. Even Father Keene, St. Cecilia's former pastor, had helped with the hemming, a skill his saintly mother had taught him as a child in Ireland.

Barry Hornibrook, who owned the hotel and conference center, donated new hymnals. Harriet Bedford, owner of the town's nursery, donated the plantings.

Rotary Club members spent several weekends painting the interior of the church, and the Kiwanis, not to be outdone, had laid the floors.

In fact, by the time the church had been completed, just about everyone in Dorsetville had played some part in its restoration which was why so many rose from their beds this morning to offer up a special prayer of thanksgiving.

Weather is always a grave concern for New Englanders.

Regardless of the amount of fancy meteorological equipment owned by professional weathermen, forecasts were never accurate. Instead folks looked to more reliable resources, like the state of Mrs. Margaret Norris's arthritis; its absence dictated a clear, dry day in store for the rededication ceremonies. The weathermen had predicted rain. They had been wrong.

And since the weather had cooperated, folks were up early, bustling around town, scurrying to get in a few extra errands before the festivities began. Voices rose and fell all along Main Street as neighbors exchanged pleasantries.

"Have you lain in your lettuce yet?"

"Just the other day. Another row of peas as well. Haven't put in the impatiens though. Went against my good sense last year and planted before Memorial Day, and sure enough, a late frost arrived and leveled every one of them."

"Did you hear George Benson was sponsoring the Little League again this year?"

"Good old George. That reminds me. It's been awhile since I fed him supper. I think I'll call him to change the washers on my kitchen sink. Heard he was just at your house."

"Yep. We had him adjust the thermostats. Wife served pot roast. Sent him home with the leftovers."

George Benson was Dorsetville's local air conditioning and heating specialist. He was loud and opinionated, which some said was the reason his wife, Gertrude, had left him for a vacuum salesman a few years back. But regardless of his shortcomings, and there were many, he was one of Dorsetville's own and needed looking after.

The men's groups were careful to include him in their

poker games; Barry Hornibrook always called when he went fishing even though George scared most of the fish away; and the women made certain that he was properly fed, a relatively easy task since he planned many of his service calls around mealtimes.

George was also the town's fire marshal, scheduled this morning to meet with the Congregational Church's parish council and explain why he still had not issued the church's fire and safety permit.

ONE

$\mathcal{F}$ather James had been awakened this morning by the clamor outside. Just past the park entrance next door, which divided the town green, preparations were underway for the Congregational Church rededication ceremonies. This afternoon dozens of state officials and most everyone in Dorsetville would gather to witness the rededication of this historic building.

The priest opened one eye and stared out the window. The sun was just rising above the mountain ridge that surrounded the town like an embrace. Shards of pink light pierced the predawn darkness. It was going to be a glorious day, he thought, sliding out from under a pile of handmade quilts.

From somewhere outside came a loud *thud* followed by several rapid Spanish phrases fired off like machine gun bullets. He made his way over to the window and looked down below. A delivery truck was parked on the Congregational side of the town green. Its side panels read "Filbert's Party Rentals." He leaned forward to get a better view. Folding tables and chairs were being delivered. Several had fallen off the back of the truck. Two men worked to untangle the melee as a third man stood on the tailgate, wildly waving his arms and spewing phrases Father James was thankful he did not understand. He closed the window.

Since it was nearly time to get up anyway, he figured there was no sense going back to bed. He grabbed his bathrobe from the foot of his bed and headed down the rectory's back staircase toward the kitchen. Before he showered, he needed his jump-start, a cup of rich, black coffee.

In deference to this need, his housekeeper, Mrs. Norris, had set the coffeepot's automatic timer the night before so it would be ready when he first came downstairs. It was programmed to start the brewing cycle in fifteen minutes. And although all electrical gadgets and appliances were a complete mystery to him (his use of the electric teapot had once resulted in the removal of an entire section of kitchen wallpaper), he just couldn't wait. So he said a quick prayer for protection, both for him and the kitchen, and pushed several buttons. Much to his relief, the grinder began to whine as it ground fresh Colombian beans to a fine powder. The early-morning air was instantly filled with an intoxicating aroma.

"Thank you, Lord, for favors big and small," he intoned, then went in search of his favorite mug, the one that his housekeeper teased was "the size of a small planter." Since coffee was his favorite beverage, its size saved him from making repeated trips for refills.

The smell of coffee had set his stomach rumbling so he popped two slices of stone-ground whole wheat bread in the toaster (one of his few concessions to Doc Hammon's order to increase the fiber in his diet), then went in search of the butter. The refrigerator was filled with dishes Mrs. Norris had prepared for today's function. She had attached Post-it notes on each that read: "For today's luncheon. Keep hands off!"

Not much of a chance of him stealing a bite of that or anything else his housekeeper referred to as health food. He carefully lifted the plastic wrap off a bowl and took a sniff. Dear Lord, it smelled like rotting tree bark! He hastily patted the plastic in place and pushed it aside while yearning for the good old days—German potato salad, Boston baked beans, apple crisps, Yankee pot roast—all of which Mrs. Norris now labeled "death to one's arteries." She wasn't at all amused when he pointed out that everyone had to die of something, so why couldn't she let them die in peace?

He found the butter hidden behind a large bottle of carrot juice. He hoped Mrs. Norris didn't plan to spring that on him this morning. Last week it had been prune juice. His stomach had still not recovered.

He filled his supersize mug to the brim, threw in several teaspoons of sugar, slathered his toast with enough butter to clog several main arteries, and headed toward his study.

The early-morning light rendered the chestnut paneling a soft gold, infusing the room with a sense of warmth and serenity. Father James entered happily, feeling his heart leap once again with praise and thanksgiving. It wasn't too long ago that both the rectory and the church next door were in such disrepair that the archdiocese had ordered it closed. But God had intervened by way of the Daughters of Mary of the Immaculate Conception who, under the leadership of Mother Mary Veronica, had convinced the archbishop to restore St. Cecilia's as part of the nuns' plan to open a retirement home for the religious across the street.

He carefully set down his coffee mug, settled in behind his desk, and moved his well-worn Bible closer. There was still work to be done on the speech he was to give at today's ceremonies. The Bible fell open to one of his favorite psalms.

Blessed are those whose strength is in you,
Who have set their hearts on pilgrimage . . .
. . . they go from strength to strength . . .

He was quickly lost in thought, absentmindedly munching on his toast, when the phone rang. He picked it up on the second ring.

"St. Cecilia's Rectory. Father James speaking."

"Still getting up with the roosters, are you, Jimmy?" It was his old mentor, Monsignor Casio, calling from New York City.

"You once told me as a young seminarian that no priest worth his salt sleeps past sunup," Father James reminded him.

"So I did," Monsignor answered.

Father James noticed a tired edge to his voice and grew concerned. His mentor was nearing his seventy-fifth birthday and should have retired several years ago. "Is everything all right?"

"It's been a long, hard night," he said. "One of our parishioner's sons was killed in a gang fight. Gunned down in an alleyway. They found his body in a Dumpster. His was only fourteen years old."

"Dear Lord . . . what a waste of such a young life. I'm so sorry. I'll lift him and his family up at Mass this morning."

"I appreciate that, Jim. He was a good boy, just couldn't stand up to peer pressure. Unfortunately, I see far too many of these scenarios."

"I'm glad I pastor in a small country town," Father James confessed. "We may have our share of problems, but at least folks here still hold life dear."

"Which is one of the reasons I'm calling," Monsignor admitted. "I need a favor."

"Anything that's in my power to do, you know I will," Father James assured him.

"Good. I thought you'd say that." He cleared his throat. "If you have a few minutes, I'd like to tell you the story about a young man I've known since he was a boy."

Father James grabbed his mug and settled in. "I've got the time. Go ahead."

"His name is Stephen Richter, and he's just gotten out of prison."

"What was he in for?" Father James asked.

"Manslaughter, but . . . let me tell you the whole story before I get into that."

"I'm listening."

"I've known Stephen since he was six years old. His family lived in the neighborhood back in my old parish. He was a good kid but came from a troubled background. His father was in and out of jail. His mother used to turn tricks in their living room to keep up her heroin habit. He also has two brothers, but they were just as messed up as the parents.

"I took a liking to him right away. Great smile. Great enthusiasm for life, which you had to admire considering the circumstances he lived in.

"Stephen was a very talented artist from an early age. I still have a couple of drawings he did when he was only eight, nine years old. He had a rare gift that I knew if nurtured would someday get him out of this place. So, one summer, a couple of us priests pooled our money and sent Stephen to an art program that was being sponsored by the Whitney Museum. Well, the kid took to it like a duck to water. You should have seen some of the things he produced. What an imagination! He was especially adept at portraits.

"One of the curators saw his potential and helped him get accepted into the Rhode Island School of Design. Stephen did exceptionally well there. In fact, one of the instructors went out of his way to get him a summer internship in the advertising department of the *Boston Globe*. We all were thrilled for him. It seemed that our prayers and support was paying off.

"Much to Stephen's credit, he never forgot us, not even with his busy schedule. He called every week, filling us in on all the great things that were happening in his life. He even managed to find himself a nice Catholic girlfriend. We couldn't have been more pleased."

"So, what happened to land him in jail?" Father James asked, placing his empty mug on the desk.

"I was just about to get to that," the monsignor said. "It was during his sophomore year that things began to fall apart. First, his father died in a prison fight. Stabbed to death. Then his mother was diagnosed with AIDS. She'd abused her body for so many years that she had no resistance left to fight the disease and in a couple of months was dying.

"Around Christmastime, she decided she wanted to see him. Only God knows why. She had been stoned most of his life. I would have doubted if she even knew she had a son named Stephen. Anyway, she sent his two older brothers up to Rhode Island with instructions to bring him back to New York for the holidays; and like a dutiful son, Stephen agreed to come home.

"On the way back, the brothers held up a liquor store near Greenwich. Stephen, who was asleep in the backseat of the car, never knew a thing until the cops showed up.

"In the interim, the robbery hadn't gone as smoothly as the brothers had planned. The cashier resisted turning over the money and was shot. He died a few days later."

"Dear Lord! Were the brothers caught?"

"One got away scot-free. The other one was eventually caught and charged with murder."

"And Stephen?"

"Charged as an accessory. He served eight years. Just got out last week."

"Poor kid. He sure got the worse end of the stick," Father James said, shaking his head. Sometimes life just didn't seem fair.

"I agree. The brother Amos, who actually pulled the trigger, is still out on the streets making trouble, which is why I'm so concerned. I'm afraid that it's only a matter of time before he pulls Stephen into another mess."

"So, how can I help?" Father James asked without hesitation.

"I was wondering if he could stay with you. He needs to get out of the city."

"Any chance the brother might follow him up here and make trouble?" As much as Father James wished to help this young man, he had Father Dennis and his parishioners' safety to consider.

"No, I can make sure he doesn't find out," Monsignor assured him. "I'll have one of my parishioners, a detective friend, pick Amos up and hold him for a few days. That way Stephen will be free to take off undetected."

"And what does Stephen think about leaving New York to come and live in the country? There aren't many diversions here."

"There weren't many diversions in prison either, but he managed to survive that," Monsignor parried. "Listen, Jim, he's eager to start over again. And if you ask me, he has a far better chance of doing that in a place where nobody knows him, and away from the city streets than staying here. . . . Excuse me, Jim."

A muffled conversation took place on the other end of the phone.

"Sorry, I have to go. That was my housekeeper. The police have caught the murderer of the young boy that I was telling you about. They want me to go with them to tell the boy's parents. But before I hang up, I just want to add that Stephen is an exceptional young man. You shouldn't have any qualms about taking him in. Even with all the stuff that he's been through, he's somehow managed to maintain a sense of hope."

"Sounds like God's grace and your prayers have been actively at work in his life."

"Reminds me of what Basil King once wrote about grace." The monsignor quoted, "'Grace is an inflowing of spiritual power which gives a man strength beyond anything he himself can generate.' It's the only explanation. How else could he have made it through such a tragic life intact?"

"Send him up," Father James said. "He can stay here at the rectory. Father Dennis and I would welcome the company. Meanwhile, I'll ask around. See if I can line him up a job."

"Thanks, Jim. I appreciate your help. I'd just like to see him make it."

"With you as his prayer partner, I'm sure he will."

"Let's hope so. And don't be too picky about finding him a job. He'll be happy to do anything."

"Can you give me about a week to get things prepared here? Send him up say . . . next Tuesday."

"That will be fine. And, Jim . . ."

"Yes, Monsignor?"

"Thanks again. This young man means alot to me."

"And even more to the Lord," Father James reminded him.

"Code is code," George said, loud enough to be heard in the next county.

The Reverend Curtis, standing on George's left side, shifted back, his ears ringing.

"But, George," said Mayor Roger Martin, who was also

the Congregational Church council president. "We've seated two hundred and twenty-five congregants in this church since . . . since . . ."

"Forever," Rochelle Phillips offered.

"Well, at least since I was a boy," Roger continued. "And no town official has ever told us otherwise."

George moved the unlit stub of his week-old cigar to one side with his tongue and wagged a finger underneath Roger's nose. "I don't care what was or wasn't done before I was elected as fire marshal. But *I'm* the town official now, and the seating capacity for this sanctuary remains as I wrote down here on the permit, two hundred and twenty-three. Code is code."

"But we expect at least two hundred and twenty-five to be here today," the reverend said. "What are we suppose to do with the two extra? Ask them to listen from the church steps?"

"Code is code," George repeated stubbornly.

"Now, George. You're not going to make a big fuss over two more bodies, are you?" Rochelle asked, using the same cajoling voice she used when addressing the boys in her Sunday school class.

George pulled the mangled, saliva-coated cigar out of his mouth and pointed in their general direction. In unison, they looked away. "Since when is upholding the state fire codes considered making a fuss? These codes were set up for a reason. In case of a fire there are just so many ways to clear out of a building. The size of this sanctuary, when calculated against the present state codes, mandates a seating capacity not to exceed two hundred and twenty-three people. End of discussion."

"I don't see what difference two more parishioners

will make. Heck, George, it's not like we're inviting strangers."

George remained unmoved.

"So what would happen if we exceeded that number by two members?" Roger asked belligerently. "Would you actually shut us down?"

"If you exceed it, I'll shut you down. It's my sworn duty." He stuck the stub back in his mouth and surveyed the mutinous-looking group with a dark eye.

"We understand," the reverend said, positioning his body between the two men. "George is only doing his job."

"Thank you, Reverend. At least *someone* appreciates my position."

"I also appreciate Roger's position. He's just trying to find a way to allow our church community to continue to worship together."

"Well, he's going to have to keep trying because only two hundred and twenty-three people are worshiping together in here."

Roger's blood pressure began to rise; his face grew flushed as he pointed a finger at George. "Tell me this. If two extra members weren't a seating problem before the fire, why are they now?"

"That was before. This is now," George countered, feeling no other explanation was warranted. "You're just darn lucky that no one got hurt in that fire, or you would have had a swarm of hungry, man-eating lawyers buzzing all over this place and suing your church for all it's worth."

"You can't sue a church," Charlie Littman said with authority, even though he hadn't the vaguest idea if such a thing were possible. It just seemed reasonable that people shouldn't be allowed to sue a church.

"And what law school did you go to, Postman's Prep?" George challenged. Charlie delivered the mail.

"Gentlemen, gentlemen, please," Rochelle intoned. "This isn't getting us anywhere. George is . . . well . . . George. We all know that he's not likely to change his mind so we might as well find a way to deal with this."

George folded his arms together and accepted that as a compliment.

"Besides," she continued, "the whole town will be here in about two hours, not to mention a bunch of state officials. And even if most of them are about to be turned away at the door, I for one don't want to give George a reason to shut us down. So, let's just agree to whatever he says and go on. If not, I have ten pounds of potato salad I made for this afternoon's luncheon sitting in my refrigerator that will have to be eaten by my husband if this is canceled, and his cholesterol is already too high."

"I think that's wise advice," the reverend said prudently, choosing to ignore the others' dark murmurings. "So, we're all agreed, then?"

Everyone begrudgingly gave their consent.

"All right, George, we all agree to abide by the seating capacity that the state law mandates of two hundred and twenty-three people."

"But what are we going to do about this afternoon?" Roger asked.

"What about it?" asked George.

"The whole town is going to try to squeeze in. This is the reverend's first sermon in the new church."

"I suppose we'll have to do a head count as they come in," the reverend offered.

"I'll be there to oversee things," said George, handing the mayor the permit.

"I liked you better before you became a Catholic," Roger said, referring to George's recent conversion. "At least when you were a Methodist, you knew how to compromise."

Father James stepped off the back porch of the rectory with a decisive bounce and a mouth wreathed in a smile. Across the town green, four striped tents had risen, giving the area a festive look, like a Renaissance fair. Father James heard them going up through his study window. He had just finished his conversation with the monsignor. The men's shouts and good-natured barbs had swept in along with the scent of hyacinths.

Two tents were owned by the fire department, the other two by the Knights of Columbus. All four were lent back and forth around the town for a wide variety of events. St. Cecilia's used them each year for its fall Pumpkin Festival, the Salvation Army for its summer revival services, and several large families for reunions or anniversary parties.

Over the years, the fire department and the Knights had developed a rivalry over who could erect the tents the fastest. The competition always started out friendly but sometimes led to trouble.

Last year Tom Pastronostra, who was also a volunteer fireman, had forgotten to secure a center pole in his haste to beat his brother-in-law, Sirius Gaithwait, a Knight, at the town's Fourth of July festival.

Just as the fireworks were about to begin, the pole

gave way and a twenty-foot piece of canvas had fallen on the town's senior population. No one was hurt but the Gray Hornets (as Sheriff Bromley later christened the group) called down a rain of curses as people rushed to disengage walkers and canes from a blanket of heavy canvas. By the time all was set to right, the fireworks were over.

Father James crossed the town park, his head tilted skyward, taking in the silhouette of the new Congregational Church steeple, which seemed to spear the sky. To think, just a short time ago, all that had been left of the historic old church was a pile of ashes. Which reminded him. He must remember to compliment Chester. He and his crew had done a first-class job.

The loss of this beloved landmark had devastated the town and put a strain on the relationship between the Congregationalists and the Catholics, since it was two of Father James's altar boys who had been responsible for the fire.

Ten-year-old twins, Dexter and Rodney Galligan, had been playing with matches inside the sanctuary and inadvertently set the church ablaze. Although the fire had completely destroyed the building, things could have been much worse. Eight-year-old Sarah Peterson had been trapped in the basement. If it hadn't been for Chester Platt's heroism, Sarah would have perished in the blaze. The thought still sent a chill down Father James's spine.

Although the festivities weren't slated to begin for several hours, the lawn around the church was already crowded with people whose voices volleyed back and forth. George Benson lent his unmistakable boom to the clamor, shouting at a group of small boys who came perilously close to overturning the table with covered serving dishes.

"Hey! Watch it or I'll have Sheriff Bromley haul your little behinds down to the jail and lock you away for the rest of the day."

The sound of Sheriff Bromley's name sent the children scurrying. Around town the sheriff was affectionately referred to as the rottweiler.

Emily Curtis, the reverend's wife, was in the food tent, directing a legion of volunteers, including several women from St. Cecilia's. The women looked up and waved as the priest neared. He waved back, then walked over.

Emily wore hot rollers, a frayed apron, and a strained smile. Father James surmised that by now she was regretting her offer to spearhead today's luncheon. Emily had attended a famous Parisian culinary institute before marrying her husband; but the closest she ever got to haute cuisine these days were the trays of hors d'oeurves she made for their annual New Year's Day open house.

It had been a long time since she actually had put her skills to the test, and at this moment her self-confidence was as frayed as the apron she was wearing.

"Good morning, Father James," Emily said in a distracted kind of way, staring at a platter, seemingly lost in thought.

"Taste these," she said, thrusting a morsel of something into his hand.

Father James obediently popped it into his mouth.

"So? What do you think? Does it need more basil? Here, try this one. Is there enough garlic? Asagio? Father

Dennis is stationed at the stove. If they need something more, there's still time to make another batch." She handed him a platter.

Father Dennis had become her cooking student shortly after Mrs. Norris had embarked on her new health food kick. Emily had been delightfully surprised at his natural talents.

Father James brought the platter up to his face and inhaled. Suddenly he was in a piazza, seated at a small outside café with the Tuscan hills gently rising behind him. He slipped another into his mouth and allowed the melody of flavors to dance across his pallet.

"Mind your cholesterol," Arlene Campbell cautioned as she flew by with a woven basket filled with artfully folded napkins in the shapes of swans.

Father James hastened a frown. Why did the entire town feel it was their duty to oversee his diet? In defiance to Arlene's warnings, he sampled several more.

"Well?" Emily queried.

"If heaven serves food only half as good, I will be eternally blessed."

The reverend's wife, who had been holding her breath, exhaled loudly. "Oh, what a relief. Now that that's settled, I can get to work on the desserts." And without a backward glance, she hustled toward the parsonage's kitchen, leaving Father James slightly disappointed at not having been offered a second helping.

There were seasons in life when one felt as if heaven couldn't be far away, Father James thought, slipping through the doors of the newly renovated church. Today was one of those moments.

The air was charged with celebration, people were working together in relative harmony toward a common goal—the restoration of this holy space—helping, encouraging each other, reminding their neighbors and friends that God was good, His mercy endureth forever. A sense of unity permeated the air.

Father James lifted up his voice to give thanks.

Dear Father,

Bless this new sanctuary, Lord. Fill it with your Holy Presence. Allow all those who enter this space to find the hope and faith they came looking for through a new revelation of Your Son, Jesus Christ.

And when those who enter come to pray with heavy hearts, temper their sorrows by reminding them of their many blessings, like the privilege of living in this fine country which allows us to congregate and to worship in the many diverse ways You have pressed upon our hearts.

And may we Christians especially remember that we are one body but many members; and let not Satan tempt any Christian into throwing up doctrinal walls that separate us from the fullness of fellowship You wish us to share.

A breeze filtered in through a partly open window, lifting the corner of the altar cloth and leaving in its wake the soft scents of spring. Father James breathed in deeply, allowing it to uncap forgotten memories of similar happy moments. Days spent on his grandparents' farm. The warmth of the sun on his cheeks as he lay on the hay bailer during a lunchtime break; the down of his grandmother's cheeks as she kissed him good night; the feel of a jackknife as it melted into the soft pine as he whittled shapes and forms that only he could ascertain.

How easy it would be just to close his eyes and explore the forgotten trails that had twisted and turned, winding their way toward this moment. But he had work to do.

He needed to find a quiet spot, to search his soul, to confess all sin—what he had done and what he had failed to do—and to seek God's forgiveness. Only then could he offer himself up as a pure vessel, an instrument of the Holy Spirit and a channel through which God's people could be blessed.

The ceremony was scheduled to begin at two o'clock. By twelve-thirty many of Dorsetville's citizens were already seated, having heard the news that George Benson was limiting the number of people inside the sanctuary.

True to his word, George was stationed on the front steps, resplendent in his official fire marshall's uniform. He stood to the right side of the double doors, a counter in his hand.

"Two hundred and sixteen," George counted off.

The mayor and his wife were standing alongside, shaking hands, passing out programs, and growing anxious.

"Two hundred and twenty."

There was still a line of people stretching the length of the sidewalk.

"Two hundred and twenty-three. Stop there," George bellowed, causing the next two visitors in line to jump as if they had been shot.

"That's all, folks. The rest will have to listen from out here." The crowd murmured its disapproval.

A man elbowed himself toward the front. "Excuse me. I'm Senator Walker." Attached to his arm was a young, curvaceous woman. "If you could just let us through."

George barred the way. "Legally, the building's not designed to hold any more. You'll have to stay out here with the rest of these folks."

The senator blinked several times as if he had misunderstood. "Are you saying that I can't come in?"

"That's what I said."

"I see." The senator flashed one of his best campaign smiles and began again. "What did you say your name was, sir?"

"George Benson. I'm the fire marshal."

"Yes, and doing a first-class job too. You're to be commended." The senator threw an arm around George's shoulders. "But here's the thing, George. You don't mind if I call you George, now do you? I was the one who fought for the federal monies needed to help restore this church, and I'm sure that the town officials and the church trustees are expecting me inside."

"Let me get this straight, Senator," said George, shrugging off his arm. "You—a servant of the people— want me to disregard a state code that you're pledged to uphold so that you and your lady friend can sit inside while your constituents—the people you serve, who are abiding by these laws—sit out here on the lawn. That about right, Senator?"

Several in the crowd below turned to wait for his response. The senator, however, was a foxy politician and knew when he had been outsmarted. Reelection was in a few months. He headed back down the church steps, all smiles and waves, just "one of the people," he declared, as his aides went in search of some folding chairs.

"Did you have to do that?" Roger asked, watching the senator and his companion settle underneath a large maple tree.

"Do what?"

"Couldn't you have at least made one concession? Dear God, man. Walker is a U.S. Senator."

"I don't care if he's the president. Code is code."

"So you told me."

The first strains of organ music wafted through the doors. A general hush came over the congregation. The ceremony was beginning.

Ted, George's young assistant, tapped him on the shoulder. "The new indoor sprinkler system checked out. Everything is up and running."

"Good. Don't want any mishaps with this kind of crowd."

George climbed up the last step and pushed Ted in front of him, then refastened the red velvet rope that had been positioned inside the church doors.

"Where do you think you're going?" Roger asked incredulously. "You just said that we had already reached the maximum capacity."

"That number doesn't include an official fire marshal on duty."

"Ted's not an official."

"He's my assistant."

"Assistant fire marshal? There's no such position."

"Plumbing assistant.

"What has that got to do with anything?" Roger said, his voice rising with each word.

People in the back pew turned around, fingers to lips. "Shush!"

"Ted's here in case of a plumbing emergency."

"Plumbing emergency? George! George Benson, you come back here!"

But George was already headed toward the balcony, where he had previously set two metal folding chairs against an outside wall in direct violation of the code.

$\mathcal{T}$wo

$\mathcal{S}$ome might think that life in a small New England town is rather dull, that days drag by with the speed of a box turtle crossing the interstate. But most folks in Dorsetville had never known a dull moment.

There is always something to be done, regardless of the time of year. In the fall, there are leaves to rake and firewood to store. In the winter, sidewalks to shovel and driveways to plow. But the busiest time of year always seems to be spring, when gardens needed to be tilled, seedlings planted, fences mended, and screens put up in addition to a host of other ongoing chores.

Generally at this time of year, dinner invitations and church suppers are few. Folks are just too exhausted to go out. This is especially true the week the women decide it's time for spring cleaning.

Dorsetville men always have been mystified by this ritual, never fully understanding why women would spend a full week tearing a house apart only to put it back together again. More perplexing, however, is the timing of this yearly event, which no man has ever been able to accurately predict. If they had, they would have gone fishing.

It seemed that one minute they were having a nice, friendly chat with a neighbor over the backyard fence and the next, their wives were shouting at them from the porch . . .

"I think it's time we put up the screens."

This was the indication that spring cleaning had arrived along with a week of cold suppers and store-bought desserts and enough extra work to rub off the knees of a new pair of jeans. But as any species must learn to adapt in order to survive, the men in town had found a most effective way of countering this rite of spring. They developed "the list."

"Honey, if you want me to fix the back screen door, I'll have to run into town." At this point, the men would hold a piece of paper aloft and point. "See here, I need a tube of caulking; a couple of ten-penny nails and some white paint for that back fence. Then I figured, I might as well run over to Kmart. They have a sale on heavy-duty garbage bags. I need those to clean out the back garage."

And so it was on this fine Saturday morning that Dorsetville's men were seen walking to and fro along

Main Street, occasionally stopping for a chat or a game of checkers outside several storefronts while their lists remained tucked away somewhere in their shirt pockets.

By the time Timothy McGree and Ben Metcalf arrived downtown to begin taping footage for the local cable show, every parking space had been filled with an assortment of SUVs and pickup trucks.

"You'll have to double park in front of the hardware store," Ben told Sam Rosenberg, unbuckling his seat belt.

Sam anxiously looked around. "What about Deputy Hill?"

Deputy Frank Hill had once ticketed a blind lady for jaywalking. He never gave anyone a break, and double parking along Main Street was illegal.

Timothy swung around. "Don't see him anywhere."

"I don't know," Sam said. "Maybe we'd better just keep circling around until something opens up."

"That's not going to happen anytime soon," Ben predicted.

"Spring cleaning," Timothy reminded Sam.

What could Sam do? His friends had a deadline. Carl Pipson, the station manager, wanted the footage back within the hour. If he parked at the bottom of Main Street and they tried to haul the equipment all the way up the hill, it could easily eat up twenty minutes and cause one of them a coronary. But if he double parked he could be ticketed, and with money so tight it was an expense he could ill afford. He still hadn't picked up the new prescription Doc Hammon had given him; he was waiting for his social security check to arrive.

Ben interrupted his thoughts. "Just give me a couple of minutes. Won't take long. Timothy and I can get this stuff out and on the sidewalk before Hill even discovers we're here." And before Sam could protest, the two men hopped out of the car and started piling things onto the ground.

But "just a minute" quickly turned into several more as Timothy wrestled with the seat belt they had locked around the camera. It belonged to the station, an expensive Sony DVCAM, and since Sam often applied the brakes with the same force a rodeo cowboy applies to a bucking bronco, the men figured it would be safer tightly strapped in.

"Hurry, Timothy. Hill just walked down from School Street," Sam said.

"I'm hurrying as fast as I can." The seat belt wasn't budging. In frustration, Timothy grabbed it with two hands and gave it a sound shake.

"Maybe if you took it a little slower. Be a little more gentle," Sam offered. He was worried for his seat belt.

"But you just told me to hurry."

"Here, let me try it again," Ben offered, crawling into the backseat.

Sam pulled a handkerchief from his back pocket and wiped his brow.

"You push down on the buckle while I pull up," Timothy told Ben.

"I can't. Darn arthritis."

"Then move and let me get over on that side."

Sam could taste his breakfast repeating. The deputy had just spied him. He was headed their way.

"Hurry! I've got to move the car now!" How much did a traffic ticket cost nowadays? Sam wondered. Twenty, fifty dollars? Whatever it was, it was more than he could afford.

"We've almost got it. Just give me another minute or two." Ben was hunched half in the car and half out.

Deputy Hill came up to the back of the car, whipped out his ticket book, and proceeded to remove a pen from his shirt pocket.

Sam threw the car in gear. There was no more time left to wait. "I'm moving it," he shouting, thinking that maybe they could borrow a shopping cart from Grand Union to haul the equipment.

"Wait, we've almost got it undone," Timothy yelled.

Sam hit the gas pedal at the precise moment as Timothy released the seat belt. The car lurched forward, back doors flapping wildly like a bird caught in midflight. Both the camera and Timothy were in peril of flying off the backseat and out into the street. Ben knew he could only rescue one and grabbed for the camera as Timothy rolled out of the open car door.

Deputy Hill had been standing behind Sam's car when the old gent gave it gas, causing Timothy to pop out of the backseat like a champagne cork and land on a forty-pound bag of dry cow manure that Mark Stone had just carried out of the hardware store for Charlie Littman.

Hill rushed over. Timothy was staring up at the sky.

"Are you all right, Mr. McGree? Can you hear me?"

Timothy heard him all right, but he just couldn't seem to respond.

Hill raised his hands as if he were directing traffic. A crowd of men were gathering.

"Clear the area. We've got a seriously injured man

here. Don't move, Mr. McGree. You may have internal injuries."

What was he saying? Timothy wondered. The voice sounded distant.

Hill unclipped his walkie-talkie from his belt. "Dispatch, this is Deputy Hill. I have an emergency situation. You'd better send some backup."

Betty Olsen, the town's dispatcher, had been teaching the assessor's daughter how to knit when the call came through. She put down her work without dropping a stitch.

"Deputy Hill, please state the nature of your emergency."

"I have a male victim approximately eighty years old—"

Who is he calling eighty? Timothy tried to sit up.

Hill pushed him back to the ground. "Calm down, Mr. McGree. Help will be here shortly."

In a dull haze, Timothy was faintly aware that his right calf muscles were beginning to constrict. Since he was subject to excruciating muscle spasms, he needed to get up and work out the kink. He tried to sit up again but the deputy pushed him back down.

"Get your hands off me," he said, slapping Hill's wrist.

"Now, Mr. McGree, there is no need to get violent."

Violent? Who was getting violent? He just needed to stand up.

"He's hallucinating," Hill told the crowd. "It happens when there's been a head trauma."

"Deputy? Deputy Hill." Betty's voice sounded through the walkie-talkie. "Did you say Timothy McGree had been injured?"

"That's a roger, dispatch. Looks like we'll need an

ambulance. Better tell them to hurry. I suspect a possible head injury and internal bleeding."

"Good Lord," Betty said. "I'll alert the paramedic and the EMTs."

Sam and Ben had finally caught up after legally parking the car.

"Timothy! How badly are you hurt?" Sam cried. This was all his fault. He should have let the deputy give him a ticket. What was money among friends?

Ben bent down at the waist, staring into the face of his dear friend. "How bad is it, Tim?"

"I'd be a lot better if this darn fool would just leave me alone," Timothy hissed.

Sirens sounded in the distance.

"Help is coming. Everyone get back," Hill ordered. "That means you too, Mr. Metcalf and Mr. Rosenberg. They're going to have to get some heavy equipment through here."

"Oh, this is ridiculous!" Timothy said. "I'm perfectly all right. There's absolutely no reason for all of this fuss."

He started to get up when the mother of all charley horses clamped down on his leg like a vise. He screamed in pain, arched his back, and tried to straighten out his leg.

"Looks like he's having a seizure." Hill grabbed his walkie-talkie and shouted new instructions. "Dispatch. We have a new emergency. The victim is seizuring. Apparently, it's much more serious than I thought. Call Life-Star. We need an airlift to the nearest trauma center."

Ethel Johnson, who had been at the town clerk's office reregistering Honey's dog license, had just written out a check for $13 when she heard the news. She called Harriet Bedford.

"Harriet, this is Ethel. Timothy's had a car accident outside of Stone's Hardware. I don't know if Sam was hurt. You'd better start the prayer chain."

Harriet called Arlene Campbell. "Arlene, this is Harriet. Timothy's been in a horrible car accident. Sam might have been hurt as well. It happened on Main Street. I'm on my way down there. Pray!"

Arlene called Mildred. "Mildred, this is Arlene. There's been a terrible automobile accident. Timothy and Sam are seriously hurt. I don't know if Ben was with them. You'd better call Margaret."

Mildred called Mrs. Norris. "Call Father James. Timothy, Ben, and Sam have been in a terrible car accident. A delivery truck carrying cow manure crashed into Sam's car. Life-Star's been called. They don't know if they can save them. Channel Three News is already on the scene. It doesn't look good."

Mrs. Norris wasted no time in contacting Father James on his cell phone. "Timothy, Sam, and Ben have been in a terrible ten-car pile up. Mildred Dunlop saw the whole thing. You'd better hurry." Her voice began to crack. "We're not sure any of them survived the crash. It looks like they'll need the Last Rites."

"Are you all right, Father James?" Harry Clifford asked, stacking an assortment of mismatched cups and saucers next to the coffeemaker. Nothing in the Country Kettle had matched since it had opened it doors in the early 1900s.

The priest was slumped over his cup of coffee staring out into space and looking much like Timothy McGree when the paramedics had slapped an oxygen mask over his face, torn open his shirt, and prepared to administer an electric shock if necessary.

Father James had been returning from Mercy Hospital when Mrs. Norris called. These three old men held a special place in his heart, and his only thought as he careened around sharp corners and plowed down ribbon-thin country roads was to get there before it was too late. He made the thirty-minute ride in fifteen.

He swung onto Main Street driving at a reckless forty miles an hour. The Jeep's front wheels lifted off the ground as he took the corner. Seconds later he was forced to slam on the brakes. Traffic had come to a dead stop, creating the second-only traffic jam in all of Dorsetville's history.

Father James jumped out of the Jeep with the engine still running, grabbing a small black bag. Inside was a stole, a vial of anointed oil, and a pyx that contained the host. He dashed up the hill, praying all the way.

The crowd extended out into the street and he had to elbow his way through. Once there he was surprised to discover that there had been no massive car pileup, and there was no need for Last Rites. Timothy McGree had simply rolled out of Sam's car and landed, unharmed, out in the street.

Harry poured coffee into an "I ♥ New York" mug and joined Father at the counter.

"So . . . Deputy Hill steps in it again." He laughed. "That poor guy can sure get himself into a peck of trouble, can't he? Wait until the sheriff hears about this one. He's still at that police convention in Texas." He settled his coffee mug on the counter. "But like you're always saying, good often comes out of bad."

"Oh? How so?"

"Sold more orders of breakfast today than I sold all of last week. In fact, all I have left is coffee and some hard rolls."

"No more home fries?" Father James asked. He was extremely fond of Harry's home fries and felt they deserved a food group listing all of their own.

"Not a slice of potato left."

Father James tried to hide his disappointment by changing the subject. "Just a few more weeks of bachelorhood, hey? How are the wedding plans coming along?"

"Okay, I guess."

"You *guess*?"

"Nellie's taking care of that stuff. I find it's safer to stay out of her way and just do as she asks."

Father James smiled into his coffee. Harry was a bear of man and the town's most famous high school quarterback. Nellie stood just five foot two and weighed under a hundred pounds.

"You know, Father, lately I've been thinking about marriage and all."

Father James waited quietly. He had wondered when the doubts would begin.

"Don't get me wrong. I love Nellie something fierce and can't imagine my life without her. It's just that . . ."

"Things are changing," Father James offered.

"Yeah, and I'm not sure I'm up to it."

"Marriage is an adjustment for both parties. You'll work it out."

"I hope so. Suddenly I feel as if I'm no longer in

charge of my life. Take last week, for instance. Barry calls on Tuesday and asks if I want to go fishing. The small-mouth bass are running. Have you seen his new boat, Father? It's a honey. Barry says the insurance company paid him top dollar for the one your altar boys blew up."

Why were the Gallagher twins suddenly being referred to as "his" altar boys? the priest wondered.

"Things were slow around here so I decided to hand the place over to the girls, pick up George and Chester Platt, and head out. Figured we'd have a couple of beers, talk about old times. You know, guy stuff.

"But as I'm packing up my gear, I got to thinking. I wonder if I should give Nellie a call, ask if there's something I could do to help out with the wedding. She's always saying that I need to be more supportive. I figured this would qualify.

"Anyway . . . I call her, thinking she'll say, 'Go on. Have a good time.' Instead, she asks me to drive over to the printer's and pick up those darn wedding invitations again. You heard about the last time, didn't you? No? I never proofread the thing, but Nellie assumed I had . . . mind you, she never said anything about proofreading. I was told just to pick them up, that was it. Two weeks later she goes to send them out and discovers a misprint. Her maiden name was spelled wrong. Now they have to be reprinted and for some unfathomable reason, it's all my fault. So, when she mentions those darn invitations again, I'm not particularly keen on picking them up, but I tell her okay, I'll grab them after I get back from fishing.

" 'Fishing?' she shouts into the phone, loud enough to rupture an eardrum. 'How can you even think about going fishing at a time like this?'

"A time like what? I ask. And she hangs up the phone." Harry sighed. "Maybe that's why I've stayed a bachelor all of these years. Women tend to confuse me."

"Sorry to interrupt, but do you have a minute, Harry?" Lori Peterson called, rushing over from the bakery side. Her face was flushed, and her arms were filled with an assortment of cookbooks bearing such titles as *The Wedding Cake Bible, Prized Wedding Cakes; Wedding Cakes of the Rich and Famous*. She dumped them onto the counter with a *thud*. One slid off and crashed onto the floor on the opposite side.

"I'll get it." Harry was more like a big brother than her boss.

"You look like you've been busy," Father James commented.

"Sit down and have a cup of coffee with Father James, Lori," said Harry. "You look like you're about to fall down."

"I can't, Harry. I have some gingerbread in the oven."

"That wouldn't be your famous Haddam Hall Gingerbread, now would it?" Father James asked hopefully. Since he'd missed out on the home fries, the thought of Lori's gingerbread did much to assuage his disappointment.

She gave him a tired smile. "I promise to drop one over at the rectory on my way home."

"Just don't let Mrs. Norris see it. Anything with sugar is considered contraband at our place. I wouldn't want to run the risk of having it confiscated."

She patted his hand. "I'll put it in the backseat of your Jeep. That way she'll never know."

"I like the way you think, my dear girl," he said, savoring the idea of a piece after his housekeeper had gone home.

Lori closed her eyes and rubbed her chest.

"Are you all right?" Father James asked concerned.

"No, she's not," Harry answered for her. "This wedding cake business is stressing her out."

"No, it's not," Lori protested.

"Oh, no? Well, who was in tears this morning when the supply house forgot to send over the Lindt white chocolate?"

"I was counting on it. I wanted to practice making chocolate leaves," Lori said, reaching in her apron pocket for some Tums.

"Heartburn? Again?" Harry asked.

"Just a little."

"That's the fourth day in a row. You can't live on antacids. I bet you still haven't made an appointment to see Doc Hammon."

"I will as soon as I get a free moment."

Father James looked at her anxiously.

"I'm sure it's nothing," she assured them both. "I'm just a little overtired, that's all."

"And it's no wonder," Harry said. "You're here mornings before five, work all day, then go home and tend to your family. I should have never talked you into partnering with me in the bakery. It's too much for you to handle."

"It is not."

"It is so, and now someone tells me you've accepted the PTA vice presidency for the elementary school."

"It's an empty title. All I have to do is run two bake sales a year."

"You're going to make yourself sick unless you take

some time off," Harry said, fixing her a cup of lemon and ginger tea.

"I will," she said weakly, reaching for the sugar.

"When?" Harry pressed.

"Soon."

"I don't have to remind you that my wedding's in a few weeks and you'll be in charge of things here until I get back from my honeymoon. You should rest up while you have the chance."

"Harry's right," Father James chimed in. "You have been looking a little tired lately."

Lori looked up at the two men and suddenly burst into tears.

"*I can't go*," she said, rising quickly and pulling out a napkin from the dispenser to dab her nose. "Not until I find out if it's to be an amaretto pound cake with royal icing or a white chocolate cake with buttercream. And until that decision has been made, I would appreciate a little more support from you two!"

"But, Lori, we were trying to be supportive," Harry said, crushed.

"That's not what I call being supportive," she snapped. "Now here." She shoved several cookbooks Harry's way. "Give these to Nellie and tell her to call me at home tonight."

With that she stomped back toward the bakery.

The two men were silent for several seconds. Finally Harry reached for a cloth and began to clean the counter. "Like I was saying, Father. Women tend to confuse me."

The phone rang and Harry went to answer it. Father James sipped his coffee while silently agreeing with Harry's assessment of women. He, too, often found them baffling. Take Mrs. Norris, for instance. No amount of argument could dissuade her to go back to her old style of cooking, the one favored by the priests. Once savory pork chops and gravy, whipped potatoes with cream and butter, and tantalizing chocolate three-layer cakes had graced their table and made coming down the icy cold back staircase for a midnight raid worth the while. But since Mrs. Norris's health food kick, it was steamed rice and vegetables, soybeans or tofu, and enough bean sprouts to feed a small barnyard.

Personally, Father James thought Mrs. Norris's recent peevish behavior was directly attributable to consuming too much roughage. Lately it seemed even the tiniest mishap could set her off. Last week Father Dennis left his rubber boots on the kitchen floor beside the back door. You would have thought the man had committed a mortal sin the way she set to caterwauling.

"I just washed the floor. Now look at it! Just look at the muddy imprint those boots have left. Do you think I have nothing better to do than to clean up after the likes of you two?"

She must have carried on about those boots for nearly an hour before diverting her attention to Father Dennis's rumpled bed. Father Dennis had sat on it to tie his shoes.

Then on Monday, Father James had been on the way out to deposit Sunday's collection money when he was called away to the phone and left the large manila envelope on the kitchen table. He had forgotten that Mrs. Norris liked to give the weathered pine table a good scrubbing after breakfast. This memory lapse had set off another tirade. Something about "being foiled at every turn," verbiage he assumed came straight from one of the gothic romance novels she favored.

The priest finished his coffee and got up to leave, his thoughts echoing Harry's. Women confused him too.

While digging in his pants pocket for some change, he happened to glance at the clock on the side wall. *Blast!* In all the confusion, he had completely forgotten about Monsignor Casio's friend, Stephen, who would be arriving in about fifteen minutes in Woodstock.

Father James threw some coins on the counter and hustled out the front door.

Sam had had better days.

Today he had nearly killed one of his best friends, and Deputy Hill had given him a ticket for reckless driving. He was due to appear in court next Wednesday before Judge Peale. He wondered if they put people in jail for reckless driving. He might even lose his license, and then who would take over his route for the Meals on Wheels program?

Oy vey.

Of course, all of this might just be a moot point. If he didn't get the Plymouth's transmission fixed soon, he would have no car to drive. He had barely made it home this afternoon. Several times it had refused to shift out of second gear. His mechanic, Nancy Hawkins, was right. It was just a matter of time before it broke down completely, leaving him stranded.

Sam would have to tell Harriet Bedford that their trip to Newport was canceled. He couldn't chance it. The news was bound to disappoint her. She had talked about nothing else for months. Harriet had been asked to be the main speaker for next month's meeting of the Newport Garden Club.

Harriet, who had started an exotic flower business with her granddaughter Allison a few years ago, had become a sought-after speaker on the garden club circuit. Since the business's inception, it had been featured on the *Victory Garden* and in *Better Homes & Gardens*; and with the launch of their new web page, orders came in from around the country.

Maybe they could rent a car, although he didn't feel comfortable driving anything other than his 1972 gold Plymouth Duster, but how was he going to cover the costs of those expensive repairs?

His social security and small pension were already stretched to their limits, and now Doc Hammon had added another prescription drug to help lower his high blood pressure. Sam had checked out the price with the pharmacist. It would cost $150 a month. It looked like he would have to delve into his savings again.

But, all things considered, Sam felt blessed. He had come to America as a boy of twelve with nothing more than the clothes on his back. Through the kindness of the folks in Dorsetville he had gotten a good education and later found a job at the mills, where he worked and advanced for several decades before retiring. He was blessed with good friends and a fine synagogue and enjoyed a sense of safety that he never took for granted, having survived Nazi-occupied Germany.

But of all Sam's blessings, he especially gave thanks for his little home. It was a small, neat ranch (twelve hundred square feet) that sat at the base of the mountain like a knickknack on a shelf. There was an eat-in kitchen and a living room on the north side and two small bed-rooms and a tiny bathroom on the south. A screened-in summer porch just off the kitchen opened onto his wife Rachel's flower gardens. They had been her special joy. Rachael had died several years ago. Sam still tended her gardens.

In the 1950s Sam had paneled the basement and put in a small sink, stove, and a bathroom with a shower for his mother-in-law. But when her arthritic legs could no longer abide the stairs, and she grew to hate the cold New England winters, she moved to Scottsdale, Arizona, to be with her son.

Later, Rachel used the space as a sewing area. Now it was just a repository for all the things he didn't know what to do with yet didn't have the heart to throw away.

Aside from the current car issue, Sam had always been a contented and happy man.

"Happiness is a choice," he always said, well before that title had been made into a book.

"You have no control over life's events, but you do have control over how you process those events. God gave us the power of free will. We get to choose if we will let things get us down, or if we'll rise above the storms. I choose life and laughter over despondency and tears."

For someone who had lost his entire family in the Holocaust, these were not empty words.

Now, looking at his watch, he chose to be happy, to forget the morning's events. It was almost time to pick up Harriet, his favorite companion. She needed a ride to St. Cecilia's where she was to meet with George Benson. Something to do with the Clifford wedding flowers, al-though Sam couldn't fathom what a plumber had to do with flowers. He just hoped that his car was up to the trip and that nothing else would go wrong that day.

"Don't tell me it can't be done!" Harriet, who never raised her voice, was shouting. "The wedding flowers will be dead in half an hour without the heat turned on. You know how cold it is in here. The sanctuary doesn't begin to loose its chill until July. The flowers need to be arranged the night before. They'll never survive until morning without heat."

George made a face.

Harriet stood her ground. "You turned it off. How complicated can it be to turn it back on?"

"You make it sound as if it's as easy as throwing a switch!" George boomed.

"Well, isn't it?" Harriet challenged.

George pushed back his cap. "No, it isn't! It takes a full day to clean the burner, close off all the heating pipes, bleed the radiators . . . and if you hadn't noticed, there are twenty-six radiators in this sanctuary alone. Then it takes another half-day to set up the air conditioning, clean the filters, and clean out the vents."

"Your point is?"

"In order to switch it back I'll have to do the same process in reverse, then, after the wedding, do it all over again!"

"So?"

"So? So? You think I have nothing better to do with my time? I've got a list of jobs as long of my arm that I haven't even started yet and that are a sight more important than some wedding. Besides, I don't know why those two are getting hitched in the first place. Especially at their age. If you ask me, they should just leave things the way they are. Enjoy the pleasures without the responsibilities, if you know what I mean."

"George Benson! I'm shocked. How can you say such a thing right here in God's house? Don't you have any respect?"

Sam tried to redirect the conversation. "Harriet, what type of flowers are you planning for the altar?"

"If this . . . this . . . so-called Catholic will turn on the heat so my arrangements don't freeze, I plan to use gardenias."

"What do you mean 'so-called Catholic'?" George demanded. "Have you forgotten that *I* was the one the Blessed Virgin Mary appeared to, not one of you resident Catholics? So if you're thinking you're so high and mighty just because you were raised in the church all of your life, I suggest you think again."

Resident Catholics? Sam didn't know there were resident and nonresident Catholics. It went to prove no matter how old you got, there was always something to learn.

Harriet rolled her eyes. "Not that again. *Pleasssse . . .* Everyone except you seems to recognize the fact that it was not a *real* apparition. It was a hologram that Matthew Metcalf and his friend set up."

George had been the first to see the image, and no amount of explanation since could shake him from his belief that Mary's appearance had been real.

"That's what they *say*," George said. "But I know better. That story was concocted by the archdiocese. It's a cover-up."

A cover-up? Sam hadn't heard about that either, so he asked George, "Why wouldn't the church want people to know about the apparition?"

"Oh, Sam . . . now don't you start. There was no apparition."

"I was only asking."

"Well, don't!"

George looked at Sam with pity. "You poor old guy. You two aren't even married and she's ordering you around."

"I am not!" Harriet sucked in her breath. "Sam, are you going to stand there and let him insult me like that?"

Sam threw up his hands. No matter what he said someone was going to be mad at him. "I'll be waiting out in the car."

"Sam Rosenberg, I thought you were a gentlemen," Harriet called after him. "I thought you were the type to defend a woman's honor. But I can see now that I was wrong. Don't bother waiting for me. I'll have Father James drive me home."

Sam kept walking. What could he say other than he had had better days?

Stephen watched the scenery slide by as the Greyhound bus neared the turnoff for Woodstock. After being confined to a six-by-eight-foot prison cell for eight years, he still couldn't get used to the openness, the unlimited sense of space. At times, he still felt anxious, as if he were walking along the edge of a cliff without benefit of handrails. What if he was to slip?

He leaned his head against the headrest and closed his eyes, hoping to shut out the fears that pecked at him like a flock of angry birds. What was wrong with him? He had never been fearful before.

In fact, once he had been fearless, secure in his future and his talent as an artist. For one shining moment he actually had believed that he had escaped his ill-fated heritage, one of alcoholism, drug addictions, and lengthy rap sheets. From an early age, he had known he was different. He was not like his parents or his brothers. His place among them must have been a mistake; a mixup at the hospital. Any day his real parents would come to claim him. Take him home to a place without alcohol and drugs, seedy men emerging from his mother's bedroom, and cops wanting to know where his father was on a certain night. But no one ever came to rescue him. Then, when he was about eight years old, he happened to walk into the Catholic church that sat just around the corner from his family's fourth-floor walk-up, and discovered a precious gem amid a pile of rubble.

Inside was a place of order and quietude, a space of unblemished grandeur, filled with treasures: intricately embroidered altar cloths, rich tapestries, stained glass windows, and a heavily carved crucifix whose suffering savior looked so real that at times he could barely lift his eyes to gaze upon the scarred and beaten form.

Stephen always had felt a special kind of peace whenever he gazed upon a thing of beauty. It was as if these objects provided a portal into another world filled with grace. The church soon became his secret haven, and Father Casio, the pastor, and he became good friends.

Stephen quickly began to look to him as an earthly father. Father Casio encouraged him to get good marks in school, to become a member of the church, and helped him to study his catechism.

On soft summer nights, the priest often rewarded him with an ice cream cone after a game of softball played in the park. And when things got so rough at home that he was forced to sleep in the streets, Father Casio would go fetch him, take him back to the rectory, and try to explain to a frightened boy why God allowed this to happen.

It was through those talks that Stephen came to know a God who did not interfere in the lives of men, but who was always there to console those who were victims of man's poor choices.

"Man sinned and through that sin free choice was given," Father Casio explained. "But men did not understand that they lacked the wisdom that only God possessed to make the right choices. Having given man free will, however, God could not go back on His Word; but because He could not bear to see His children suffer, He sent His son, Jesus, to come and share His wisdom. Through His words, the world might know the peace and faithfulness of the Father's divine love.

"But not all men believe and so sin continues to grow. But upon those who accept Jesus as their savior, God bestows a special grace. He said that although He will not separate us from this world of suffering, He will empower us to get through it no matter how hard the trial." Slowly, understanding illuminated the darkness. Stephen never felt alone again. God's presence remained with him always.

Shortly afterward, he found some oil paints inside a Dumpster and decided to paint a picture for God. He had given him understanding, and Stephen wanted to give a gift back. Something magical happened as his hand moved across the canvas. He painted by instinct with bold colors that gave the painting an incredible sense of movement. He had chosen to paint the sanctuary, a subject that would have been incredibly difficult for a seasoned artist, but Stephen tackled it with a surety of purpose, led by an inner prompting.

It took him several weeks to finish and depicted the church filled with parishioners, their attention riveted on the host being consecrated by the priest. A golden ray of light reflected off the host and fanned out, touching the hearts of several congregants, but not all.

Why were some touched and others not? viewers would ask, as they studied the intricately detailed faces that portrayed a large range of emotion—pain, sorrow, boredom. The detail showed a level of skill far above Stephen's tender years. He showed it to Father Casio.

"You did this all by yourself?" the priest asked, amazed.

Stephen nodded shyly.

Father Casio was awed by its depth of imagery.

"You are very talented," he told the young boy. "You possess a rare gift, and you must pray to discover how God wishes you to share it with the world."

Father Casio set aside a small portion of the rectory's basement for Stephen to use as a makeshift art studio. There the young boy could be found everyday after school and weekends. Stephen worked running errands and shining shoes in order to pay for canvases and paints. He had discovered a whole new world that he was free to create in any way he chose, and he chose to leave behind the sordid, limiting life of his family and create a world filled with beauty, peace, and hope.

As he neared the end of high school, Father Casio instilled a new dream in his heart.

"You must continue to study," he said. "Enroll in an art school that will help you refine your skills, help you expand your talents."

And when Stephen reminded him that he had no money for such a school, the priest simply said, "God will supply," and He did.

Stephen applied to the Rhode Island School of Design and was accepted. Father Casio strong-armed several of his rich friends into acting as patrons. Life was suddenly luminous, filled with hope. The future held endless possibilities.

Then in his sophomore year, the black cloud that had followed his family moved to cover his future in darkness, shutting out the sun. Eight years of his life were now gone. He looked down at his hands, hands that had once held a paintbrush so deftly, with surety of talent. He wondered if they still possessed the magic. He was filled with uncertainties that only increased as he read the exit sign announcing Woodstock.

THREE

*F*ortunately, the New York City bus that carried Stephen Richter was late and had just arrived at the Travel Center when Father James pulled in. He quickly slid out of the Jeep, threw some coins into the parking meter, then dashed across the street to greet him.

It didn't take him long to spy the handsome young man with trim, model good looks—high forehead, sharp cheekbones, aquiline nose—who was dressed in a pair of faded jeans and a sparkling white T-shirt. The priest drew closer and noticed a fashionable stubble covering Stephen's chin, but his blond hair, the color of ripe wheat, was neatly cropped.

Suddenly feeling grossly out of shape, Father James sucked in his gut. "Stephen Richter?"

"You must be Father James," Stephen said with a disarming smile. He extended a hand in greeting.

Father James gripped it firmly. "I guess the 'uniform' was a dead giveaway, huh?"

"It's kind of hard to miss," Stephen parried.

Father laughed. He liked this young man. "Welcome to New England. I hope the ride wasn't too long or boring."

"No, in fact, it was rather pleasant. I'd almost forgotten how awesome this part of the country can be. It's absolutely beautiful around here."

The bus driver began to unload luggage. They walked over.

"Those two are mine," Stephen said, pointing to a large black nylon bag and a tote that held some sketch pads.

"I think you'll find lots of pretty countryside to inspire you," Father James offered. "Monsignor said you were an artist."

Stephen heaved the strap to the large bag over his shoulder. "I used to be . . . but I'm afraid that artwork is going to have to take a backseat to finding a job. I plan on making my own way as soon as I can."

"That's commendable, but there's no time element attached to my offer of hospitality," Father James assured him.

"And I appreciate that, Father. I do. But I'm sure you can understand, it's important to me to become fully self-sufficient again. I need to know that I can still make it on my own."

Father James patted his shoulder. "And you will, young man. Just give yourself and the Lord some time to work it all out."

Stephan smiled shyly as they waited at the curb for a tractor trailer to pass before crossing the street.

"I do have some good news along those lines. I may have already found you a job," Father James told him as they headed toward the Jeep.

"You have?" Stephen asked somewhat incredulously.

"A parishioner of mine, his name is Chester Platt, owns a construction business," Father James explained. "And with the building boom that's going on all around New England right now, he's always looking for good men. When I called him, he said he'd be happy to hire you on if you didn't mind starting as a 'grunt' although I haven't the foggiest idea what a 'grunt' is."

"It's someone who does all the things around a construction site that no one else wants to do, like cleaning up sheetrock and nails or unloading supplies. Things like that," Stephen told him.

"Here's my car." Father James dug into his pants pocket for his keys. "You wouldn't mind that kind of work?"

"Happy to have it."

"Good. I'll drive you over there tomorrow morning." He opened the Jeep's back gate. "And until you can afford a place of your own, you'll be living with me and Father Dennis at the rectory. Nothing fancy, but it's clean."

This he knew for a fact because he and Father Dennis had personally scrubbed it down in an effort to avoid any more of Mrs. Norris's complaints. She was still seething that he had extended an invitation for Stephen to come and live at the rectory without first consulting her.

Stephen hesitated for several seconds before asking the question that was most prominent in his mind. "Does anyone know about me? I mean, about the time I served?"

"Just two," Father James answered. "Father Dennis, my assistant, knows. And Monsignor Casio made arrangements with our local sheriff, Al Bromley, to act as your parole officer while you're in town. I spoke with him just before I left. He asked us to swing over on our way into town."

"They're the only ones?"

"That's all."

"If you don't mind, Father, I'd like to try to keep it that way. People have a tendency to get a little nervous around ex-cons."

For weeks, Nellie Anderson had the strangest feeling that people were whispering behind her back. It seemed that lately every time she walked into the teachers' lounge, conversation stopped and coworkers assumed that guilty look people always got when they were talking about you in your absence.

She attributed some of the whisperings to the "secret" bridal shower that was being planned, even though she had most emphatically stated that she didn't need a thing. She and Harry were already drowning in a sea of household goods as they tried to integrate two homes. At last count they had four irons; sixteen sets of full-size sheets; an extra kitchen table with six chairs; two twin beds; three toasters—two that toasted two slices, the other four; an assortment of garden tools and snow shovels; and enough extra dishes, serving bowls, and silverware to keep the Country Kettle supplied for years.

Harry had recently surveyed the growing pile of castoffs with quiet despair. "We'll just have to box everything up, store it in your garage, and donate it to the church's tag sale this fall."

Nellie looked around and sighed. "That relegates my car to the driveway. There's not enough room for all of that *and* my car."

Combining two separate lives was proving to be something of a challenge, but not half as challenging as trying to figure out what people were whispering about. It couldn't be all about the bridal shower, could it?

Take last Sunday, for instance. After Mass, Margaret Norris and Ethel Johnson were standing at the foot of the church steps and seemed to be involved in a serious debate. But when they glanced up and saw Nellie and Harry emerge from the front doors, they had grown as quiet as a pair of cloistered nuns.

Then yesterday in Dinova's, Nellie distinctly heard her name being mentioned by Betty Olsen, who had been speaking to Gus Dinova. Betty hadn't noticed Nellie enter the grocery store and grew as red as a cherry tomato when Nellie tapped her on the shoulder to say hello.

Something was afoot, that was for sure. Nellie just wished she knew what it was.

Maybe folks felt that she and Harry were making a big mistake and were too timid to say something to their face? After all, both had been single for the better portion of their adult lives. Maybe people thought that they were too set in their ways to make a marriage work? They could be right. She and Harry had already had a tiff over his inattention to details concerning the wedding invitations. How could he *not* have noticed the misspelling of her maiden name? She always paid close attention to details.

Thoughts of love and marriage had stopped years ago for Nellie. But then one day she awoke to birdsong outside her bedroom window and a sense of euphoric happiness. Since little had changed in the way she conducted her life—she still got up at six o'clock every morning to go to early Mass; taught school during the week and religious education classes on Saturdays; shopped at the same stores; rented the same videos; even ate the same breakfast of cooked oatmeal and raisins everyday—the roots of this sudden bliss could only be traced to Harry's entrance into her life.

She had rolled over in bed and closed her eyes, searching for her previous state of being: placid, steady, and without ardor. Safe. But like a dreamer awakened, she could not recapture it; it had disappeared like a vapor, replaced with feelings of love, the very newness and depths of which had shocked and surprised her. She tried to erase them from her thoughts but quickly found that it would have been easier to erase the memories of the town that she had called home since birth or the faces of the children she had taught down through the years.

Meanwhile, she worked to keep these emotions in check. She and Harry were just friends. Nothing more. But in the dark recesses of her soul, she yearned for more. She longed for romance, commitment, marriage.

But what was God's will in all of this? At first, it was a

question she was hesitant to ask. What if His will did not align with these new hopes and dreams? Then she remembered the wonderful passage in Ephesians that proclaimed that God wanted the very best for her: "exceedingly abundantly above all that we ask or think according to the power that works in us." Now, in earnest, she could pray for guidance.

Several months later, God answered. Harry proposed.

She remembered that day in vivid detail. The sky was a flawless blue. The smell of sweet, freshly mowed grass rode the currents of a gentle wind. The sun, pure and warm, had made Harry's black hair shine like a polished piece of coal as he knelt to formally ask for her hand.

As Harry had slipped his mother's antique ring on her finger, the words of the psalmist had played a melody on her heart: *Commit your ways unto the Lord. Trust in Him and He shall bring it to pass.*

And so He had.

She had been so assured of God's will for their lives at that moment, but now that assurance had begun to waver under the silent disapproval of so many of their friends. Wedding invitations had been mailed out three weeks ago, yet not one RSVP had been received.

The concerns for her upcoming wedding, the lack of response from friends, and the nervousness she felt at becoming Harry's wife circled round and round her mind like a restless swarm of bees this afternoon. Occasionally a stray worry would swoop down and she'd feel its sting.

What if no one came to their wedding?

She tried to silence such fears as she lined the drawers to her father's old pine dresser with scented paper. It was soon to be Harry's. She hoped he liked the scent of musk since it was either that or lavender, the only choices left at T.J. Maxx, and Harry didn't seem the lavender type.

The project would have gone along a lot smoother if she could just remember where she had left her paper scissors. She was using a pair of children's plastic ones, which was like cutting through a rain forest with a pair of nail clippers. Where had she last laid them?

She seemed to be misplacing a lot of things lately only to rediscover them in the most ridiculous places. Yesterday she had found two books of stamps in the freezer. Apparently she had slipped them inside a plastic bag along with a pot roast on the way home from the store, and had forgotten to take them out.

A ray of sunlight caught the corner of the dresser and turned the dark, lifeless wood into a golden amber. Memories of her father flooded back.

He had been a gentle, quiet man with a steadfast faith in God, a faith that never wavered. Not when the crops failed or the mortgage payment came due at the same time the tractor broke down. Not even when he slipped a disk while bailing hay and was bedridden for several months.

"God's in the bad times as well as the good," he always said. "Either way He's there walking right alone with us, so there's no need to fear."

She often wished she had her father's faith, one that did not question life's trials, one that was not based on reasoning or emotions but solely on God's promises.

Harry also possessed that kind of steadfast faith along with the spirit of gentleness and compassion. These were the things that had drawn him to her.

Nellie once overheard Father Keene comment, "Harry doesn't preach Christian principles, he simply walks the talk."

Thoughts of these two special men whom God had so graciously allowed into her life seemed to stir a forgotten tune: *"And I will lift you up on angel's wings . . ."*

It had been her father's favorite hymn. He sang it often, especially when confronted with one of life's many obstacles. Only snatches of the verse came to mind, which she sang, humming in between. And as she followed its gentle refrain, like a winding country road, she found a new lightness to her spirit. Joy returned.

Maybe she should call Harry. Ask him to do some snooping around. It seemed half the town passed through his restaurant each day. He should be able to find out why no one had RSVP'd.

She closed the dresser drawer and gathered her supplies. This project could wait.

"Meow."

"Theodore?"

"Meow."

She opened a bottom drawer.

The tabby cat popped out, his fluffy tail twitching madly with indignation. Then in one fluid movement, he sailed out onto the carpet.

"Oh, Theodore, I'm so sorry."

Theodore marched out of the room without so much as a backward glance.

"Harry, I need six hamburgers, two cheeseburgers with all the fixings, and a corned beef on rye to go. The corned beef is for the sheriff, so pile on the onions," Wendy Davis said, clipping the order to the top of the range hood.

"He's back?" Harry asked.

"Got back a few minutes ago." She pointed to the table by the front window. The sheriff was talking with ⸻ on the town crew. "Doesn't look like he knows the ⸺ Hill ⸺ et."

"⸺ Let's hope no one blurts it out. His temper could be hell on the furniture."

Harry threw some beef patties on the grill, along with several slices of corned beef. Grease spit and splattered as Wendy went to answer the phone. She caught it on the second ring.

"Country Kettle. Yeah, he's here. It's Nellie," she told him, handing him the receiver. "Says it's important. You want me to take over while you two lovebirds talk?"

He handed her the spatula, ignoring the rib. "Thanks. I'll just be a minute."

"Hi, Harry," said the sheriff, throwing a leg over a stool. "That corned beef going to take long?"

"Wendy has it covered," Harry told him. "I've got to take a phone call. Wendy, give a holler if you need me."

"How long will my sandwich take?" the sheriff asked her.

"As long as it needs to," Wendy said, flattening the hamburgers with the spatula. More grease oozed out. The grill sizzled.

"Maybe I'll send Hill to pick it up later. I want to get to my office and start right in on the paperwork. Amazing what accumulates in just two weeks' time."

"Be ready in about fifteen minutes," she told him.

"Will do," the sheriff said, heading for the front door.

She'd sure like to be a fly on the wall when the sheriff found out about his deputy's newest screw-up. Hill's antics kept her friends back home in Queens in stitches. This newest one would have them rolling on the floor.

"Gladys," she yelled. "Your pastrami and egg sandwich is up. And put a move on it, will ya?"

Harry walked back to the grill, scratching his head. Nellie had just told him that no one had responded to their wedding invitations, and he was at a loss to understand why. Heck, their wedding had been the talk of the town for months. Everyone said they'd be there with bells on.

Something wasn't right. A troubling thought began to surface. He wondered. Naaah, they couldn't have.

A few days later, the St. Cecilia's crowd, as Harry referred to the group of seniors who showed up at least once a day for coffee and gossip, was gathered at the center table all sporting birthday hats.

"So, Fred, how does it feel to be seventy-two?" Timothy asked, seated alongside the Henderson sisters whose Evening in Paris perfume filed the air like a heavy fog.

"I'm seventy-two?" Fred asked, appearing genuinely surprised. He turned toward Arlene. "I thought you said it was my sixtieth birthday."

"Oh, Fred, you're such an old jokester." Arlene gave a nervous little laugh and patted his knee, hoping no one would notice the cover-up. Fred was growing more and more confused. It worried her. Her father-in-law had begun his mental decline around Fred's age.

"Well, whether a man be sixty or eighty makes no matter as long as he stays young at heart," Father Keene said with his soft Irish lilt, raising his cup of tea in a toast. "To Fred. May God grant you many more years, for the earth has angels all too few and heaven is overflowing."

"I'll second that," Harry said, pulling out a chair and joining the festivities.

He caught Wendy's eye and winked, the signal that it was time to bring out the cake. Lori appeared, bearing a large sheet cake aglow with sparklers. Wendy and Gladys followed with cake plates and a pot of freshly brewed decaffeinated coffee as everyone joined in singing "Happy Birthday."

Lori placed the cake in front of Fred, put out the sparklers, and got ready to slice. "How large a piece do you want?"

Fred looked at Lori as if she were a stranger.

"Fred?"

"A small piece will be just fine," Arlene hastened to say. "This cake is beautiful. Didn't Lori do a wonderful job, Fred?"

Fred sat staring at an extinguished sparkler.

The bell over the front door tingled as Deputy Hill walked in with his usual swagger.

Sheriff Bromley still hadn't discovered the invoice for the Life-Star airlift for Timothy McGree, and no one in town was brave enough to tell him. Meanwhile, the guys over at Kelly's bar had started a betting pool as to when that might happen. Saturday morning was the favorite among the gamblers. The sheriff played golf with some police friends over in Manchester on Saturdays. They figured one of them was bound to tell him.

"Hey, a party. Whose birthday?" asked Deputy Hill, wandering over.

"Fred's," Sam offered.

Harry pulled out a chair. "Come join us. There's plenty of cake." He couldn't help feeling sorry for the guy. Hardly anyone in town was talking to him.

"Don't mind if I do," Hill said, sliding in between Timothy and Sam. Timothy inched his chair away. He was still harboring a grudge

"Harry, you want a piece?" Lori asked, licking frosting from the tips of her fingers.

"You bet," he said. "Hmmm. Lori, this is great! Has Nellie tried this recipe? Tell her it's my wedding cake choice." Which reminded him. He put down his fork.

"Speaking of weddings . . . Are any of you planning to come to ours? No one's responded to our invitations."

Those gathered around the table looked at him mutely.

"We were just wondering how things stand, that's all," he added.

"But, Harry, none of us has received an invitation," Harriet said. "In fact, we've all been wondering about it for weeks."

"You haven't?"

"No," Ethel said. "In fact, we were beginning to think we'd done something wrong."

"The whole town is wondering," June Henderson added.

"Yes, it's like having theater tickets and not knowing where the play is being performed," her sister, Ruth, stated. She often spoke in parables only she could understand.

"But how can that be?" Harry asked. "Ben, I gave you the invitations to mail a couple of weeks ago. You said you'd take care of them. Remember? It was the day the high school coach brought the entire football team in for lunch. I couldn't get away."

Ben looked at Timothy who looked at Sam.

"Why am I getting a sinking feeling?"

"We were going to . . ." Ben began.

"But?"

"We got a call on the cell phone from Carl, asking us to hurry over to Woodstock and tape the governor. He was giving some big speech."

"And what happened to the invitations?"

"We gave them to Deputy Hill to mail," Ben said, unable to meet Harry's eyes.

Harry moaned.

All eyes turned on Hill, who was quietly sneaking another piece of cake and looked up. "What? You told me there was plenty."

"The wedding invitations? We asked you to mail them," Timothy reminded him.

"What wedding invitations?"

"I think we're in serious trouble," Sam predicted.

Hill gazed up toward the ceiling. His eyes began to move back and forth as if the memory were stored somewhere between the crack in the plaster over the grill and the hanging plants by the side windows. "You mean that bunch of small envelopes, right?"

"Right. What did you do with them?" Harry asked

Hill took a sip of coffee while everyone waited. "I was planning to mail them but something came up. Now let's see. What was it? Oh, yeah . . . the sheriff's dog caught a skunk behind the police station. Dispatch called me on my walkie-talkie and told me to get right over there. Sheriff wanted me to take Harley over to the Country Clippers for a shampoo. And let me tell you— the ride over there . . . well . . . the smell nearly blinded me. Did you know that stuff about tomato juice getting rid of skunk odor is a lot of bunk? Kim over at County Clippers, she told me—"

"HILL!" everyone shouted.

"WHAT HAPPENED TO THE INVITATIONS?" Harry bellowed. Other customers seated in the restaurant turned to stare.

"Oh, the invitations. I put them on the passenger seat of my truck for safekeeping."

"Are they still there?" Harry asked hopefully.

"No."

"Then where are they?"

"There was this accident . . ."

Harry put his head in his hands.

"You see, it was like this," Hill continued. "I put them on the floor when I went to pick up Harley. I have to put him in the cab when he rides in my truck. Last time I put him in the back bed, he saw a cat and it took me nearly a half a day to find him. That dog has a way of getting away from me sometimes.

"So I tell Harley to jump in and he does and knocks over a can of forty-weight oil I had sitting on the floor. I'd opened it the night before but forgot to put it in. I was running late that morning. Had it wedged up against the side wall with a pair of boots. Of course, Harley moved the boots when he got in and spilled the can of oil all over the box of envelopes. You should have seen them. Couldn't even make out the addresses." He stirred some sugar into his coffee. "So I figured since no one could read them, I might as well pitch them."

"You threw out Nellie's wedding invitations!" The women shrieked. "How could you?"

Harry moaned. He wasn't even married and already he felt as if he were headed toward a divorce.

"What did I miss?" asked Mrs. Norris, plunking her black patent leather pocketbook on the table. "Sorry I'm late. My eye exam over at Sears took longer than I thought."

"Deputy Hill threw out Nellie's wedding invitations," Ethel said.

"I didn't know they were wedding invitations." Deputy Hill said in his defense. "I thought they were some kind of advertisement for the restaurant."

"And *they*, of course, were safe to throw away?" Timothy sniped. His low opinion of Deputy Hill had just dropped another notch.

"You're a dead man, Deputy," Mrs. Norris said, sinking down into a chair. "I'd say it's just a matter of who finds you first, the sheriff or Nellie Anderson. Which reminds me . . . I just bumped into Betty over at the gas station. She said the sheriff found the Life-Star invoice. I think it's safe to guess he's looking for you about now."

"Darn. I just lost twenty bucks," Sam griped. His bet had been placed on Saturday.

Al Bromley worked his way through two weeks of paperwork and wondered why everyone seemed to be avoiding him at the station. Not that he was complaining. Without interruptions he had been able to clear away the first layer of papers, catalogs, and office memos. Now he was waiting for Betty to bring him in a new garbage liner. He'd already filled the last one to the brim.

Might as well leaf through all those pamphlets he'd collected at the convention, he thought, and began to pitch the discards in a pile by Harley's feet.

"Keeping the Streets Safe from Prostitutes." Nope, he wouldn't need that one. "The Power of a Neighborhood Watch against Drug Trafficking." He pitched that one too. "What You Should Know When Firing an Employee." This he'd keep. He slid it into Hill's personnel folder.

Betty's voice drifted down the hall. A call had come in from dispatch. He probably should get up and get his own trash bag.

A folder from the accounting office downstairs caught his eye. He opened it. Inside was a $2,400 invoice for a Life-Star airlift. Marianne Whitehouse, the town's treasurer, had clipped on a note.

Al,

  For your information . . . This expense is being charged against your budget since it was generated from your department.

What the heck? He studied the invoice more closely. Who had authorized an airlift to the Yale trauma center?

The sheriff, who had steadfastly ignored the intercom system since its installation in 1982, yelled. "Betty! Put down that phone and get in here!"

Betty came running. "You called me?"

"Who else around here is named Betty? What's this?" he asked, waving the bill.

She took a step back into the hall. "That?"

"Yes, this!"

"I was hoping you'd find it on someone else's shift."

"Betty . . . I'm losing patience!"

"Deputy Hill ordered it."

FOUR

*F*ather James glanced out his office window, which looked out onto woods and was conducive to contemplation. Slowly his thoughts begin to drift. Aimlessly, like a feather on the wind, they floated lightly over this week's homily, Mrs. Norris's perpetual bad mood, the need to order more sacramental wine, before finally landing on Fred Campbell's birthday party currently under way at the Country Kettle.

He sighed. He hated to miss it, especially since he feared that this might be one of the last birthdays Fred would be able to enjoy. To most everyone, except Arlene, it was growing more and more apparent that Fred was suffering from some type of dementia. Poor Arlene, Father James thought. She tried so hard to cover for her husband's lapses, acting as if nothing were wrong.

Movement by the cluster of hydrangeas caught his attention, and he drew the curtain aside to get a better look. It was Stephen, who had returned to spend his lunch hour sketching. Father James was pleased to note that the young man had begun to spend a great deal of time with a sketchbook in hand. Stephen had even allowed him to glance through some of his drawings. Monsignor was right. He was a gifted artist and a hard worker. His last conversation with Chester had confirmed that.

"He's a little quiet," Chester had said. "Doesn't like to mix in with the other men. Keeps mostly to himself. But I can't fault him for that. He does what's required of him and more. I even hear that he's got himself a little side business. A couple of my customers hired him to do some house painting."

Father James relayed the information to Monsignor Casio during their weekly phone call. He also reported that Stephen was attending church regularly and even had confided that someday he would like to minister to prison inmates.

Father watched Stephen settle back against a tree, wondering how this young man had managed to endure all he had suffered with his faith intact and without a trace of bitterness. It seemed a miracle. Most people in Stephen's position would have spent the rest of their lives with a chip on their shoulder, damning God for all that had gone wrong.

What made one man hold on with hope and the other give up in despair? he wondered.

Monsignor Casio said it was the gift of God's grace,

and Father James concurred. But he also knew that in order to receive it, one could not harbor feelings of bitterness or unforgiveness. Stephen was exceptional in that department. In truth, Father James wasn't certain that if he had been in Stephen's position, he could have found forgiveness after being so badly wronged.

The hall clock chimed. He pried himself away from the window and looked at his watch: 1 P.M. He longed to join the festivities for Fred but knew that the messages covering his desk would not be answered by themselves and with his busy schedule this week, it was the only time he would have free to return calls.

He shuffled through the stack of pink slips. At least twelve people had left messages earlier in the week, and another four had been added to the pile this morning. There was also a rather terse note from Mrs. Norris: "Please tell people that I am not the church secretary."

As he had feared, Mrs. Norris had grown even testier since Stephen's arrival, especially since he refused to offer any information about the young man's past. To be fair, he could understand her hurt feelings. He had always confided in her before, but not this time. He had promised to keep Stephen's past a secret.

He heard the hall clock chime half past the hour. He had better get going on these calls. He took a deep breath, grabbed the first slip, and began to dial.

"Father James? I'm so glad you called. There's something that's been troubling me for several months now, and I finally thought I should voice my concerns.

"It's about the mothers of young children who give their kids bags of Cheetos and potato chips during Mass as if they were at a sports event instead of a church service. Why, last week, I even saw a mother hand out a bottle of Snapple.

"Don't you think you should say something about this, Father? It doesn't seem right."

"I will prayerfully lift this up to the Lord," he told her, hung up, and dialed the next number.

"Father James? It's about time you called me back. I left a message over a week ago.

"My husband, Herbert, and I feel you must put a dress code into effect for Mass. Why? Have you seen the way those teenage girls dress? Father Fanny would never have allowed it. Why, he must be turning over in his grave.

"Imagine, exposing one's navel in front of the Lord who is present right there in the Host.

"Now, I'm sure that there must be a dress code for Mass listed somewhere in the Bible. You need to look it up. Make copies and insert them in the next bulletin."

"I will prayerfully lift this up to the Lord," he told her, hung up, and dialed the next number.

"Father, as you know, I'm not one to complain, but feel I have to speak up in my daughter's behalf.

"Twice the poor darling has been passed over as the altar server on holy days, yet I notice that those Gallagher twins are always scheduled. Have you considered what a wrong example this sets for the rest of our youth? I mean . . . especially with the twins' criminal record and all."

"I will prayerfully lift this up to the Lord," he told her, hung up, and dialed the next number.

"Father James, thank God you called before it was too late. Yes, it is an emergency. The soul of one of your parishioners is in great peril.

"Who? Why, it's Nellie Anderson. Now, far be it from me to carry tales, but in this instance, I think, as a priest, you should know what's going on in your own parish even though I'm pretty certain you'll take her side. After all, she's a bigtime author now, and must give lots of money to the church. I'm sure you don't want to tick her off. I heard her newest children's book sold five hundred thousand copies. Some folks don't understand why she is still teaching. Whereas I'm just a lowly teacher's aide. My paltry ten percent doesn't add up to much.

"Widow's mite? Who's widowed?

"Anyway . . . as I was saying . . . Nellie is inviting only the town's elite to her wedding and has completely snubbed us common folk. Now, isn't that a sin, Father? Doesn't she stand in danger of Purgatory?

"What elite? I . . . er . . . You're missing the point, Father.

"Martha LaClaire is going. She teaches fourth grade. The amateur photographer. Nellie asked her to take their wedding photos, and now that's all she talks about. You should hear her in the teacher's lounge: 'Nellie wants me to include this shot . . . Nellie suggests that . . .'

"None of us teacher substitutes has received an invitation.

"You haven't received one either? Dear Lord, it's worse than I thought."

"I will include this matter in my prayers," he said,

and refrained from adding that she, not Nellie, would be his focus.

When Mrs. Norris's car pulled up into the driveway, Father James walked into the kitchen to greet her. Stephen had asked earlier if he could use the attic room as an art studio, and Father James thought it was a splendid idea. But before he would give his final approval, he thought it best to run it past Mrs. Norris.

He entered the kitchen just as the back door swung open and his housekeeper came clamoring through with a load of groceries.

"Here, let me give you a hand with that," he said, scurrying to catch the contents of a paper bag that had just torn in half. The health food store she frequented was heavily into recycling, but unfortunately, most of their paper bags needed to be retired.

Mrs. Norris put her purse on a kitchen chair while Father James tried to keep things from rolling off the counter.

"Catch the kumquat," she yelled as it started to slip toward the floor.

"Kum . . . *what?*" He caught the large, round fruit in midair and placed it safely at the back on the counter. He stood uncertainly, watching her put the groceries away.

"Do you need something, Father?" she asked.

"I . . . er . . ." Why was he having trouble finding the right words? It wasn't as if he needed approval.

"Yes?"

"I've been thinking about the attic."

She eyed him suspiciously. "What about the attic?"

"I've . . . been thinking that it's a shame to have all that space up there and not having it used."

"And what has brought this on?"

"No reason," he lied. Darn! He'd have to deal with that later. "I was just thinking that it might make for a nice art studio for Stephen. Did I mention that he was an artist?"

She grabbed a large head of cabbage and headed toward the refrigerator in a huff. "No, as a matter of fact, you didn't. In fact, you haven't said anything about him since he came here to live. For all I know he's an ax murderer."

Father James refused to be baited. He tried steering things on a safer course. "Stephen said he'd clear it out."

"Do you have any idea how much junk is stored up there? Why, it would take him a month of Sundays just to find the floorboards."

"Yes, I know it's a little cluttered . . ."

"Cluttered my foot! There's enough stuff up there to close a landfill."

He took a deep breath and tried to clear the sound of exasperation from his voice. "Whatever, Mrs. Norris. The fact is . . . Stephen has asked to use it as a studio and I see no reason why he can't use that space if he cleans it out."

"Fine. It's *your* rectory," she said in a huff en route to the pantry with an armload of canned lima beans.

He hated it when she used the term "your rectory" to imply that he was some kind of despot. He wasn't, was he?

"What do you plan to do with all that stuff that's up there?" she asked.

He watched her place the cans on the top pantry

shelf and tried not to think what she might be planning to do with those. "I thought we could store it out in the garage."

She stared at him as though he had grown a second head. "And when was the last time you found room to park your car inside the garage?"

Oh, yeah. He had meant to have it cleaned out when he had first arrived at St. Cecilia's but had never got around to it. Father Keene had been something of a packrat.

"Then we'll have a tag sale," he blurted out. Yes, that was it. They would throw a tag sale and use the proceeds to refurbish the church organ. Allen Dambrowski, the choir leader, had been hinting for months that it needed a complete overhaul. He smiled inwardly. Sometimes he was just brilliant.

"And who do you plan to get to run this tag sale, or do you plan to do it yourself?" she asked.

With his schedule, he clearly could not run it, but surely someone could be persuaded.

"And don't you dare look at me," she warned, as she passed him on the way back to the refrigerator.

"I wasn't even considering you," he said a little too abruptly.

"Oh, is that so? Why? Don't you think I'm capable of running it?"

Fortunately, the back door swung open before he could utter a reply that would have had him on his knees repenting until next Christmas. Father Dennis strolled in carrying a tray of freshly baked cinnamon buns. He had obviously been visiting with Mrs. Curtis.

"Hi, everyone. Look what I made for the scouts'

meeting tonight. Don't they smell heavenly?" he said, wading into the room.

"Father Dennis could run it," Father James said.

"Run what?" Father Dennis asked cautiously.

Their housekeeper went back to her groceries. "Father James wants to clean out the attic of all that old stuff so Stephen can use it as an art studio and then he wants to run a tag sale, regardless of how disruptive his plans might be for the rest of us."

Father James lower jaw dropped. How did he become the bad guy? "Mrs. Norris, that's not what I said. I just *suggested*—"

She plowed ahead as if he were absent from the room. "I don't know what he expects of me. Doesn't he know that I'm getting much too old to take all this on? Why, I already have much too much to take care of as it is."

"I'm sorry," Father James said. "Maybe the tag sale was a bad idea. Stephen can clear it out and we'll deal with the stuff later."

"And who's going to keep that room clean when it's all done? I hope you don't expect me to lug that heavy Electrolux up an additional set of stairs," she griped, pulling something large and leafy green out from a bag with an inordinate amount of force. "I'm no spring chicken anymore."

"No, of course you're not," Father James began. She threw him a nasty look. This wasn't going at all well.

"Maybe I didn't phrase that quite right." He began again. "Of course, you don't look a day over . . . over . . ."

He wasn't quite sure what might pacify her. Should it be fifty? No, she would sense that he was lying. Sixty? But she wasn't much older than that. It hardly seemed like a compliment. He settled for "You certainly don't look your age. And, besides, no one expects you to keep that space clean. Stephen will take care of it, or maybe we could get someone in to help with the cleaning."

"Oh, so now you think I need help to do my job, do you?" she said, sucking in her breath.

Father James ran his hand through his thinning hair. How did the Lord do it? How did He keep His temper in check when dealing with the likes of Mrs. Norris day in and day out throughout the millennia? It was a wonder He hadn't turned mankind to cinders.

"My offer was not a comment on your job performance. It was only an offer to help, since you said that you already have much too much to do.

Father Dennis, who made it a point of staying clear of all discussions with Mrs. Norris, offered one of his rare opinions. "I can take over all the cooking. I'd be happy to do it."

Mrs. Norris turned on him like a rabid dog. "I bet you would. And you'd have Father James's cholesterol raised through the roof within a week. I work very hard at keeping you both on a healthy diet, not that I get any credit or one word of appreciation from either of you. In fact, all I get is complaints, day in and day out. I don't know why I even bother."

"Now, Mrs. Norris. Father Dennis was only trying—"

"I know what Father Dennis was trying to do," she said, tucking a stray hair into the bun at the nape of her neck. "You've both made it very clear how you feel about my cooking."

"Not *all* of your cooking," the young priest amended. "Only your health food regime—"

"See! See how unappreciated I am. I slave and work

myself to the bone trying to keep you both fit so you can do God's work and what are my thanks?"

"Mrs. Norris, you've got it all wrong. We greatly appreciate your efforts on our behalf, don't we, Father Dennis?"

Father Dennis opened his mouth to speak. *Hiccup.*

Great! Once Father Dennis started hiccupping, it could go on for days.

Mrs. Norris turned on the faucet and began to fill the sink. "I'll save you both the trouble of lying. Truth is, I've been thinking about retiring for some time and this just seals my decision. Since I'm no longer appreciated by either of you, I hereby give you my two weeks' notice."

She squirted some liquid detergent onto a sponge and began to wash a plate with enough force to rub off the pattern.

FIVE

✦

Father James was so befuddled by Mrs. Norris's sudden resignation that he completely forgot his appointment with Valerie Kilbourne until she knocked on the rectory's front door.

"Am I early?" she asked, noting his confusion.

"Early? No, no, you're right on time. Come in. We can sit in my study," Father James said, stepping aside and leading her into his office.

"Take a seat." He motioned to an overstuffed chair.

She settled in and immediately began to

study the office walls that were filled with crayoned pictures. "I like your sense of design."

"Aren't they wonderful?" he said. "Our parish is greatly blessed with many talented young artists, who, fortunately for me, save us having to hang wallpaper."

She laughed. "I particularly like that one." She indicated a wedding picture, fashioned with the boundless sense of joyful abandonment that only a child could create.

"That was done by my dear friend Sarah Peterson. She's very talented for her age," he said, just like a proud parent. "But then Sarah's quite an extraordinary child in many respects."

"I agree. In fact she's the reason I'm here," Valerie admitted.

"Oh?"

"My girls and Sarah have become good friends. She's like a big sister. For the last few months, the girls have been attending Mass with Sarah and her parents, and recently they've even gotten me to attend. I have to confess that it's been many years since I have been to Mass."

And a little child shall lead them, he mused.

"Things were pretty hard for us before we came here," she admitted. "I worked every chance I got, even Sundays."

"Didn't your parents help?" Father asked.

"No," she said sadly. "They . . . distanced themselves from me after the girls were born."

"I'm sorry to hear that," he said. "It must have been hard on you being all alone."

"It was," she conceded. "Besides that, our old neighborhood was a tough place to live in. I constantly worried about my children's safety. Even the schools weren't safe."

"And since coming here?" he asked.

She smiled, "It's been great. Take last night, for instance. I woke up around midnight and remembered that I had forgotten to lock the front door. Instead of being in a panic, I just rolled over and went back to sleep. I've never felt so safe. I love living here. And the people . . . they're just great. A week hasn't passed since moving here when someone hasn't invited us to their home for dinner."

"They're the salt of the earth," he agreed. "And how are your daughters adjusting? Are they happy too?"

"They love it. There's a park across the street, and they've met so many nice kids like Sarah." She paused. "Father, I've never felt like part of a community before and I want to change that. Besides volunteering for things in town, I want to feel a more integral part of this church. I've made so many friends here at St. Cecilia's."

"I think that's a wonderful goal," he told her.

She studied the carpet. "I'm ashamed of the fact that my girls were not brought up in the Church, but if it's not too late, I'd like to enroll them in a communion class."

"We'd love to have them," he told her. "The classes don't begin until this fall, so there's still plenty of time. Sister Claire runs our CCD program. I know that she will be delighted to have your daughters join them."

Valerie's eyes slid back onto the carpet. "There's only one problem."

"Only one?" he joked, and was rewarded with a smile. "Then that's an easy fix."

"Seriously . . . you see, Father, I-I never married the girl's father. I mean, the girls are—"

Father saw her discomfort and was filled with compassion. "Are the children of God," he finished. "Nothing else needs to be said."

"So it's all right? My girls can still receive their first Holy Communion?"

He took hold of her hands. "Your daughters are the children of God whether they were born in or outside of wedlock. The Church warmly welcomes them into the fullness of the sacraments. And may I add that, as a parish, we would be most honored to include you and your girls in our family."

Tears sprang to her eyes. "I was afraid . . ."

He moved a box of Kleenex next to her chair.

"Oh, Father, I've done so many stupid things."

"My dear, I've been at this post for many years, and I've still to meet someone who hasn't."

"But how can God forgive me?"

"It's His job." He smiled gently.

"I haven't been to confession in about eight years, and know I should, but I've got some things I have to sort out first," she said.

"When you're ready, God will be here. He's not going anywhere."

While Valerie blew her nose, he reached for a manila folder and pulled out two application forms. "Now, let's get those girls of yours enrolled. When you've finished filling these in, drop them off here and I'll walk them over to Sister Claire."

"I can't begin to tell you how thankful I am for your help," she began, then glanced at his desk clock. "Oh, dear. Look at the time." She sprang to her feet. "I'm sorry, but I have to get going. Nellie is watching the twins, and I don't want to take advantage of her kindness."

Father walked her out into the hall. "Tell Nellie I said hello and that she's in my prayers. Only two more weeks until the wedding."

"Harry was one of the first people I met when I came to town. He's a great guy and Nellie is a wonderful person. I'm sure they're going to make a lovely couple."

"I'm betting on it," he said, opening the front door. "Now don't be a stranger. Come and talk anytime you'd like."

"Thank you, Father. You've made this much easier than I thought."

Stephen had been standing on the upstairs landing with a bundle of old magazines he had just cleared out from the attic when he heard her voice. Valerie? It was a little deeper, more mature, yet there was no mistaking it. He felt his heart begin to pound like a jackhammer.

Staying safely out of view, he peered cautiously around the stairway as she walked past with Father James and headed toward the front door. His mind flooded with emotions. He wanted to shout out her name, race down the stairs, and gather her into his arms. Beg her for forgiveness. Find absolution. Instead, he drew back and waited for the sound of the door closing behind her. How could they have come together at the same time in this small New England town after all these years?

He laid the bundle of magazines on the hall floor and raced to the window that looked out onto the street. "Valerie," he whispered, tracing her silhouette on the windowpane with his fingertip.

Seconds later, she had slipped into her car and driven away.

It was just a short ride to the school, yet it gave Valerie several minutes to savor the feeling of contentment over her new surroundings, quite removed from her previous residence, a scruffy industrial town where all-night bars with exotic girls proliferated and police sirens were so common that for the most part they were ignored.

The town had never been her first choice, but she had run out of choices when she realized that apartments in safer towns would charge double the rent. And so Valerie and her daughters had settled in a small two-room apartment on the top floor of a three-family house in a neighborhood filled with flashing neon signs and litter. The families downstairs didn't speak English and didn't care to make friends, which was fine with her. Late-night visitors and hastily conducted transactions on the front porch or outside stairwells told her they weren't the kind of people she wanted to know on a personal level.

They lived there for six years and during that time watched the neighborhood grow steadily worse. Drive-by shootings became more frequent. Two thirteen-year-old boys were gunned down and killed within the space of a week. Police began to decrease their patrols, fearful for their own safety.

Valerie increased the locks on her door and kept a baseball bat ready in the corner as she wondered how much longer she and her daughters could last without one of them coming to harm. Her salary barely kept them in necessities. A move to a safer, therefore more expensive apartment, was out of the question. Then someone set fire to the lot behind their house, and the decision was made for her. It was time to move before something tragic happened. Where would they find another place they could afford?

Just when she was about to give up in despair, a letter arrived with a return address from an attorney in a neighboring state. Her first instinct was to burn it. Pretend she never received it. Letters from attorneys were seldom good.

Fortunately, she overrode her fears and was surprised to find that she had been left a small inheritance from an aunt she had long ago forgotten.

Then fate stepped in again. A former client who now lived in a northern part of the state called to ask her to design some new business stationery. Valerie made a date, and on a crisp autumn day, she packed up the girls and a picnic lunch and headed out of town, grateful to be rid of the bleak gray outlines of abandoned buildings and rundown houses. Thirty minutes outside the city limits, they rolled down their windows and breathed in the fresh country air.

"Mom, look!" the girls had shouted from the backseat, as they passed a herd of cows grazing on a gentle slope of land. "Can we stop and pet them?"

"I don't think cows like being petted." Valerie laughed, slowing down to take in the sylvan meadows and lush, rolling mountains. With each mile, she felt the tension she had lived under for so many years begin to melt away. What must it be like actually to live in a place like this? she wondered.

Her client was thrilled with the layout, and within the hour, they headed over to the local print shop to have a talk with the printer about executing her designs.

The owner, Mr. Oddo, studied her work with intense interest.

"You're very talented," he said. "Any chance you're looking for a job? We just lost our graphic artist. Her husband accepted a job in Arizona."

"I don't know. What are you offering?" she asked boldly, having no intention whatsoever of accepting a position.

He offered her an hourly rate, double what she was currently receiving, plus a fifteen percent commission on any new work she brought into the shop. Unfortunately, since he was a small businessman, he couldn't offer her health insurance.

She told the owner it was tempting, but where would she live? She had two daughters to consider, and from Woodstock's prosperous looks, she doubted if rents around there were affordable.

"I have a cousin who is a Realtor over in Dorsetville. It's not far from here," the owner said. "His name is John Moran. Why don't I give him a call?"

Valerie had never done an impulsive thing in her life (except, of course, for the night the twins were conceived), but that day she threw caution to the wind and accepted his offer contingent upon her finding a home.

She and the girls met with John that afternoon and immediately began house hunting.

"Your budget is kind of tight," he told her, "but if you don't mind an older house that needs some fixing up, I'm sure we can find you something."

She told him that since she was an artist, she'd welcome the chance to bring an old home back to life."

"In that case . . ."

John turned onto a side street that ran up a steep hill

and rounded the town green, on which stood two churches. One was a lovely white clapboard church, the other was a stone edifice of indiscernible architectural heritage. And between the two churches was the entrance to the town park.

Farther down the street, opposite the town green were several older homes, the largest of which now bore a sign reading "Sister Regina Francis Retirement Home for the Religious." A rather stout nun dressed in a blue habit was bent over at the waist, clearing fallen leaves from a storm drain, while a short, wizened older priest stood holding a black plastic bag ready to catch the debris. He waved as they passed by.

John pulled into a driveway bearing a for-sale sign, and she felt a flutter of excitement. It was a charming Victorian with a wide, wraparound porch, leaded front windows, on a half acre of land. The house was in need of some serious TLC, but that didn't matter. She already loved it and could envision herself sipping lemonade on the front porch, filled with white wicker and hanging plants, watching her girls skip across the road to the play in the park.

As soon as John opened the car doors, the twins spilled out onto the lawn and raced around toward the back of the house.

"Don't go too far," she cautioned.

"I know it needs some work," John explained, closing the car door. "But it fits your budget, and basically the house is sound. I had one of our local contractors, Chester Platt, check it out when I listed it."

He inserted an old skeleton key into the front door lock. It gave a heavy metallic *click*.

"After you," he said, pushing the door open.

Valerie stepped inside and caught her breath. Although the house was in need of a good cleaning, nothing could distract from its fine craftsmanship. The ceilings were encircled with heavy moldings, doorways arched with intricate trims, and the outer rim of the wooden floors had been set in marquetry.

As an art major, she had briefly studied house design and knew that Victorian entryways were designed as statements of social status, and this one spoke highly of its occupants. The walls were paneled in rich mahogany that had turned a deep ruby with age. A spiral staircase with an open upstairs landing gracefully followed the curves of the room and was set off by a magnificent stained glass window that flooded the room in a kaleidoscope of colored light.

"You've found yourself a buyer," she said, running her hands over the wooden banister.

"But you haven't seen the rest of the house," John said.

"I don't need to."

John knew the owners and made arrangements for Valerie and the girls to move in right away. He even got the owners to take back the mortgage.

Valerie drove back to their old place and began packing. Within a few days, Dorsetville had three new residents.

Valerie found her daughters busy working on posters for the spring tea, which, she realized, she had completely forgotten about. What had she promised to bring? Fairy cakes or finger sandwiches? Her work had kept her so busy lately that it forced everything else right out of her mind. Not that she minded being so busy. In fact, it was the first time in her career she was actually making some decent money. She had just signed on two new accounts, and Mr. Oddo, true to his word, lopped fifteen percent off each contract as her commission. If things kept up like this, she might even be able to buy the girls those new bicycles for Christmas that they had seen at Wal-Mart.

But even with her heavy workload, she had not forgotten Nellie's surprise bridal shower this Saturday, although she still needed to buy a gift. Maybe she'd take the girls out to dinner tonight over at the mall. That way she could kill two birds with one stone.

"Linda, Leah, your mother is here," Nellie announced.

The twins flew to her like little chicks, clucking about what they had drawn and pointing to posters filled with crayoned teacups.

"Miss Anderson said we can put these up in the hall," Leah explained.

"Mine is going by the front office," Linda added proudly.

"They're just wonderful," Valerie said, careful to give equal praise to both. "You've done a great job. Now, why don't you go back to your classroom and gather up your things and then I'll take you to Chucky Cheese for dinner."

"Can we have an ice cream too?" Leah asked.

A Dairy Queen sat opposite the restaurant. Leah was always bargaining.

"We'll see how well you do with your dinner first. Now scoot. I have to get a load of wash in off the line and folded before we leave."

"I bet I can beat you there and back," Linda taunted her twin.

"Bet you can't!"

The girls took off like a shot.

"No running in the halls," Nellie called after them.

"How were they?" Valerie asked, laughing as her daughters tried to slow down to a power walk.

"Delightful, although Leah had begun to grow bored with coloring," Nellie said.

"She doesn't have the patience her sister does," Valerie admitted.

"I think it might be something more," Nellie said, gathering strips of colored paper. "She seems to be having trouble seeing up close. When was the last time she had her eyes checked?"

"Both girls had their prescriptions changed about six months ago," Valerie said, biting her lower lip. She hoped nothing was wrong. It had been the second change in less than ten months. Leah's eyesight seemed to be deteriorating faster. Fortunately, the girls had an appointment with Doc Hammon early next week for their yearly physical. Maybe he could give her some advice.

"Looks like you've been busy," Valerie said, changing the subject. The large table was filled with various art projects, ranging from placemats made from construction paper and paper doilies to place cards.

"Our art teacher is out with a broken leg and since there isn't time to get a replacement before the spring tea, the principal asked us teachers to pitch in." Nellie placed the paper scraps in a large plastic bin. "I just wish all of this wasn't coming at the same time as I try to make plans for my wedding."

"Oh, by the way, Father James says he's praying for you."

"I could use his prayers," Nellie conceded.

"Something wrong?"

Nellie collapsed into a chair. "About an hour ago, I learned that my wedding invitations were never mailed."

"What?" Valerie asked, joining her.

"It's a rather long and convoluted story. Let's just say that I've learned never to hand a man anything of importance." She sighed. "The wedding is in just a few weeks. We planned it to coincide with the children's spring recess. I don't know what I'm going to do."

"How can I help?"

"Besides roasting my intended on a stick?" she teased. "I don't know if there is anything you can do. There's no time to reorder more wedding invitations. Even if I could get them right away, they would still have to be mailed and people given enough time to respond. We're having the reception at the Old Mills and Hotel complex. Barry Hornibrook would need the meal selections by late next week."

It sure wasn't much time, Valerie mused, but she refused to think that it was hopeless. Her mind began to work in overdrive. What could they do? Then she remembered the crayoned wedding picture in Father James's study. The details followed quickly.

"Nellie, don't you worry about a thing. I think I just figured out a way to solve your dilemma."

Six

I've just come to say my good-byes," Mrs. Norris said. "I've booked a two-week cruise to the Bahamas, and I'm leaving right after Nellie's bridal shower this afternoon."

Father James was finding it hard to believe that she was really retiring. She might have worn his patience thin, but she was as much a part of St. Cecilia's as the building itself. Life around the rectory just wasn't going to be the same without her.

"We're going to miss you," he said in earnest, suddenly feeling all choked up.

"I suspect you'll get over it," she said, more briskly than she had intended, and turned away, not trusting her emotions. She wandered over to the maple hutch beside the kitchen table and lovingly ran her hand over the wood. How many times had she polished it over the years? she wondered.

"Father Dennis and I have a little something for you." Father James said, offering her a neatly wrapped gift box.

"You needn't have done this," she said, thinking how pleased she was that he had, and carefully unwrapping the box. Inside was the Lenox statue of the Madonna and Child that had sat on the dining room sideboard all the years she had served as a housekeeper.

"You always said how much you loved it," Father James said.

"I will cherish it," she said, fighting back the tears, then she rushed over and kissed him on the cheek. It was the first time in all of her life that she had ever kissed a cleric.

Unexpected tears filled his eyes and he gave her a hug. "We're going to miss you."

"Now that's enough of that," she said, trying to regain her composure. "It's not like I'm going away. I live right next door."

"A comforting thought, especially if we need to find something," he joked.

"Well, I can tell you this," she said, quickly reverting back to her old self. "If you and Father Dennis don't clean up after yourselves, you won't be able to find a blessed thing around here within a week. Tell Stephen to do the same. And don't go leaving your coats hanging on the stair post like you normally do. Doesn't look good for parishioners to visit with your personal items in plan view for all to see."

Personal items? he wondered. What did she think he and Father Dennis were going to do in her absence, hang their underwear from the banister?

"Or tracking mud all through the house with those thick-soled shoes of yours." She shook a finger at him. "Mark my words, if you're not careful, this place will go to rack and ruin in a heartbeat."

"Lori? This is Valerie. I need a favor or, rather, Nellie does. It's about her missing wedding invitations. Oh, you've heard.

"She's asked me to help and I think I've come up with a plan, but I'll need the assistance of Dorsetville Elementary School's new PTA vice president. Can I come over? Great! I'll bring the girls and some munchies."

Lori gathered the teacups after Valerie's visit and began to stack them in the sink. It had been an exciting and very productive afternoon. She was still marveling at Valerie's plan to salvage Nellie's wedding invitations. It was brilliant.

First, Valerie had borrowed the crayoned wedding scene that had hung in Father James's office and designed a new wedding invitation around it, then she'd had them printed at work. It was simple yet incredibly clever. All the recipients were bound to be charmed.

Next, they began to round up PTA moms as volunteers, using the roster Lori had received along with her new position as Dorsetville Elementary School PTA vice president. Everyone they called was eager to help, and within a short time they had enlisted over a dozen women who promised to deploy responsible children to hand-deliver the invitations and run a tally of main course choices (steak or salmon). All was to be returned to Nellie by the end of the week, plenty of time for Barry Hornibrook's chef to prepare the reception dinner.

It had been a fun, rewarding afternoon, and for the first time in weeks, Lori actually began to feel herself unwind.

She glanced up at the kitchen clock over the sink. It was almost six o'clock. Bob would be home soon and expect dinner. She made quick work of the dishes then headed into the living room to confront the chaos left in the wake of three children left unsupervised for a few hours.

As she suspected, the room looked like it had been under siege. Coloring books were scattered about. A box of crayons spilled out onto the floor. Pieces of half-eaten cookies and ring marks from glasses of Kool-Aid marred the coffee table; and a couple of dozen *Veggie Tales* and *Rugrats* video covers lay separate from their contents. It would take her awhile to figure out which belonged to what. En route to turn off the VCR, she stepped on a piece of Silly Putty that took up several woolen strands of carpet when she tried to pry it loose.

Upstairs, she could hear Sarah happily singing to herself. No doubt her daughter's room wasn't in much better shape than this, but at least she had had some fun. Sarah loved to play with younger children and would have made a wonderful sister.

It saddened Lori to think of her daughter as an only child. But according to the doctors at the hospital, Bob

had been left sterile due to the radiation and chemotherapy used to combat his cancer. Lori worked hard at
covering up her disappointment. She would have loved a
large family, but as Bob's mother always said, "When
God closes a door, He opens a window." Adoption was
still an option. Friends of theirs had adopted a little girl
from China. She was as cute as a button.

But before earnestly pursuing any course, Lori and
Bob had decided to take a *real* vacation. Not the tent-in-
the-woods type that had been standard issue for their
family for years, but one that involved a hotel with room
service, meals cooked by someone else's hands, and the
leisure to do nothing.

The bakery was making a nice little profit each week,
and Bob had just gotten a raise. He was now Chester
Platt's chief estimator. The couple was so accustomed to
scrimping and doing without that it seemed somehow
strange having a savings account that was growing. And
although savings were important (Bob's illness had taught
them the necessity of having a financial cushion), lately
Lori worried that they might have forgotten how to enjoy life.

They were tentatively planning to take a week's vacation right after Harry and Nellie returned from their
honeymoon. Lori was the acting manager while he was
away and couldn't leave until then.

Bob had already cleared it with Chester. Over the last
year, he had worked some heavy-duty overtime, nights
and weekends. The building trade was booming, and he
had become one of Chester's most treasured employees.
Chester was happy to oblige.

"Your husband has saved the company thousands of
dollars. He's a savvy estimator. He knows what to cut

and where to look for cost overruns," Chester had told her at a recent church picnic. "If the business keeps growing like this, I'll have to make him a partner."

Knowing Chester, Lori wouldn't be surprised if he did just that.

Suddenly she felt as if someone had pulled the plug. Every ounce of energy had drained away. She slid down onto the couch, leaned back against the pillows, and closed her eyes.

Why was she so tired lately? Normally, she had energy to spare and could easily survive on only four hours' sleep a night. Now she couldn't get enough of it and often slept through her alarm.

She really did have to make an appointment with Doc Hammon, especially if they planned to go on vacation. She wanted to enjoy it. Maybe he could give her some new vitamins or a B12 shot.

She hauled herself off the couch and headed toward the kitchen phone. Maybe Shirley, Doc's receptionist, could squeeze her in for an appointment.

Nellie's cheeks hurt from the frozen smile she had worn for the last two hours, as she sat facing a mountain of shower gifts that for some strange reason seemed to grow instead of diminish.

She sat wedged in a chair bedecked with streamers and balloons, trying to produced the appropriate *ooohs* and *aaaahs* as she unwrapped an eclectic assortment of gifts. So far she had received a bird-chirping kitchen clock; a three-foot-tall stuffed waiter-slash-doll carrying an empty hors d'oeuvres plate; a plethora of oven mitts shaped like cute little animals; plaques bearing saying like

"If you can't stand the heat, then stay out of my kitchen," and a sexy negligee that had made her blush from her head to her toes when the women forced her to hold it up for inspection.

Rochelle Phillips, the self-designated camera person, shooed everyone out of the way. "Nellie, hold up Arlene's tea cozy."

Rochelle's brother, Rubin, was the editor at the *Dorsetville Gazette* and had promised to include the photos in this week's center section along with those taken at the Goshen Fair tractor pull. She wanted to make certain he had a wide range of choices.

Nellie held up the cozy, flashed a weary smile, and started to unwrap the next gift. She was exhausted from trying to project equal amounts of joy over each. How many platitudes could one conjure up?

"Thank you, Mildred. Why, it's . . . it's . . ." What exactly was it that she holding in her hand? It almost appeared to be a small lamp that had been chopped in two. The lampshade was especially ugly, a leopard pattern edged in Maribou feathers.

"Isn't it the most darling night-light you've ever seen?" Mildred Dunlop cooed.

"Yes, of course, a night-light," Nellie said.

"Won't it look absolutely adorable in your downstairs bathroom?" Mildred asked.

Nellie nodded and kept on smiling.

"I heard what happened to your invitations, dear," said Rochelle, waiting for her camera to rewind.

"But like I always say," Ethel chimed, "good often comes from bad. The new invitations are just adorable! And what a clever idea to have your students hand deliver them."

"I can't take credit for that," Nellie told them. "It was all Valerie's idea."

Everyone turned to look at Valerie, who was seated on the recliner by the fireplace, speaking with John Moran's wife.

"Leave it to a man to mess things up," Mrs. Norris said, passing a platter of cheese puffs. "You sure you want to get married after that? There's still time to back out, you know."

"Harry is a good man who made a stupid mistake," Nellie said. "I wouldn't trade him for the world."

"Awww," the room reverberated.

Mildred popped a pretzel into her mouth, shoved it to one side with her tongue, and said, "I hope you're ready for all the other mistakes he's going to make."

"Yeah, they sure do make a bundle, don't they?" Wendy Davis added. Her husband's affairs had nearly wrecked their marriage. They had moved to Dorsetville a few years back in the hopes that things might mend, information she chose not to share.

"Harriet? Any more of that piña colada mix?" It was Wendy's third since arriving and had slowed her normally rapid-fire New York accent to a crawl. For the first time, many of the women in the room could actually understand what she was saying.

"Harold and I've been married for about five years. It's his third marriage. My second," she said, pausing briefly to take a sip from her glass, which left a white line of foam along her upper lip.

"You know how they always say . . . marriage is better the second time around? Well, they're right. By your second marriage you know that you're not going to change your husband, so you don't even bother trying. If he's a slob before you married him, he'll be a slob until the day he dies. What you see is what you get."

"Don't let them tease you," Lori said, carefully setting her glass of peach iced tea on a coaster. "Bob and I are happily married and I've yet to uncover any of his bad habits, unless you can call giving Sarah an extra cookie after supper a major flaw."

Nellie smiled in appreciation of her defense of matrimony.

"No offensh, honey," Wendy said, slightly slurring her words. "But you're still young. How long have you been married? Give him time. He'll disappoint you."

"Now, don't you listen to any of this, Nellie," Arlene Campell cautioned. "I think men make fine husbands."

"It's not like God gave us another choice," Wendy countered.

"Fred and I have had a wonderful marriage," Arlene assured her.

"I shuppose your Fred is perfect?"

"No, not perfect," she said, uncrossing her legs to better balance a plate of potato salad.

"Noannoyinghabits?" Wendy chugged down another drink. "Any more of these, Harriet?"

"Well . . . there is one thing."

"Aha!"

"Fred does have a habit of wolfing down his food. It sometimes seems that I've just sat down at the dinner table and he's done."

"My husband's the same way," Rochelle said, searching her purse for a new roll of film. "I really hate going out to eat. Either I have to say absolutely nothing and concentrate on my food, which takes all the fun out of dining out, or I find myself still eating my entrée while he's ordering dessert."

"You know what used to drive me the craziest about my husband?" Mrs. Norris injected, while gathering the empty plates. "The way he used to go off and buy a new family car without ever asking me what I would like. It was as if he were the only one who was going to drive it. That's why after he died. . . . God rest his soul . . . the first thing I did when I got that insurance check was to go out and buy myself a new automobile."

"My husband used to do the same thing." Ethel Johnson remembered. "Harold once bought a new Ford with a stick shift. Remember that, Harriet? It was back in the mid-sixties. He said that standard shifts were better on gas and needed fewer repairs. But I didn't know how to drive a stick shift so he had to teach me. It was a disaster. All he did was yell, and all I did was cry."

"What about the way men never wash around their necks no matter how many times you ask? If I had a nickel for every minute spent scrubbing those rings out of Jason's shirt collars, I'd be a rich woman," Marge Peale, the judge's wife, chimed in.

"That's nothing next to the smelly socks they drop right alongside the bed every night," Doris Littman added.

"And don't expect Harry to come home and keep you company," Fran warned. She was married to Gus Dinova. "A few months after the honeymoon, Harry will head straight for the remote and the recliner."

"Let'shaveatoast," Wendy boomed, swaying to her feet. "To Nellie. Maysheenjoyalongandhappymarriage . . . *and-ddd* . . . mayshebeasblessedasallthemarriedladieshereinthis-room."

$\mathcal{S}$EVEN

$\mathcal{I}$t had taken Stephen nearly two solid weeks to clear the attic of stacks of old news‑papers and magazines, trunks filled with stained or disused altar cloths, motheaten choir robes, and an assortment of broken bits and pieces of old furnishings. He wel‑comed any physical labor, however; some‑how it helped to level the emotional seesaw he was riding ever since spying Valerie.

He looked around the attic room and for a brief second was nearly overcome with despair. What made him think that he could still paint or that the magic he had once possessed could be resurrected with the wave of a brush? Although his recent sketches had proven that he still possessed strong compositional skills, transferring those line drawings onto canvas—using color to give the illusion of depth, vibrancy, and tenor—called for something much more. It demanded confidence and a sense of boldness. At this moment, he lacked both. If he had possessed either attribute, he would have confronted Valerie and told her the truth behind his disappearance, confident that she would believe him and offer forgiveness.

He watched the light that streamed in from the four dormer windows. It seemed alive with dancing particles of dust that had been left in the wake of his broom.

But what if she wasn't the same girl he had once so passionately loved and been forced to leave behind? What if she cursed him for leaving because he had lacked the courage to put their love to the test?

They had met at the Rhode Island School of Design their freshman year, and quickly became inseparable. Neither had family relationships or friendships they wished to retain, so they spent most weekends together, exploring the college town and the surrounding countryside. Sundays they often hopped a bus to Boston and idled away hours at the museums. Passionate discussions always followed. Stephen preferred the melancholy sepia light of the Dutch masters while Valerie leaned toward the carefree, soft pastels of the Impressionists. The hours they spent together took wings, and all too soon it was time to return back to campus.

Then one day he suddenly realized that they had begun to speak in terms of "we."

"When we graduate, I'll support you while you work on your portraits until your career takes off," she had said as if his success as an artist was a given.

"Then we will get a smart apartment in the city and a country home in the country," he had said, and at that moment he believed all things were possible as long as they remained a "we." The future stretched out before them in a dizzying, unlimited golden stream.

Then life had taken a radical turn.

A week before Christmas, Stephen's brothers showed up at his dorm. Their mother was dying and wanted to see him one last time. He tried to protest. Said that since she had never needed him before, he didn't see what difference his presence would make now. But they had beaten him down with words hammered in guilt. She was his mother. It was Christmas. He would never get another chance to make amends. Finally, he had acquiesced.

His brothers said that they were in a hurry and there was no time to track down Valerie to tell her he was leaving. Call her when you get home, they said, as they led him toward a brand-new Cadillac DeVille that he feared was either stolen or purchased with drug money. Several hours later, he was being roughly awakened from a deep sleep in the backseat of the car by two police officers and charged as an accessory to murder.

He never made that call to Valerie. Not even to say good-bye. Instead, he elected to disappear without a trace. It was for the best. She deserved better than to be connected with a man serving time.

But having seen her again, he wondered if this decision had been a huge mistake. He wasn't the criminal they said he was. He was innocent. Why should he spend the rest of his life living someone else's lie?

Monsignor Casio always said that there were no such things as coincidences in life, but, rather, these seemingly chance happenings were God acting anonymously on our behalf. What if God had set this whole thing up? Planned for him and Valerie to meet again? It was the only thing that made sense since the chances of them both arriving in this little New England town at this particular time seemed statistically impossible.

"Dear Lord," Stephen murmured, "what I am supposed to do?"

On the heels of that query, he heard an inner voice say, *Confront her. Tell her the whole story. Seek her forgiveness.*

If only He could be certain that this was God's voice . . . that this was His plan . . . Stephen would have boldly approached her. The fact was, however, he was not certain. Just the opposite. He was filled with doubts and fears.

What if she didn't believe him? What if she could find no forgiveness in her heart? What if he could never find the courage to ask?

"I don't know how much longer I can nurse this transmission along," Nancy told Sam, slamming down the Plymouth's hood. She took a rag that had once been her husband's T-shirt out of her back pocket and wiped her hands. "You're going to have to replace it, and if I were you, I wouldn't hold off too long."

"I know you're right," Sam said, following Nancy into the office of the auto shop. "It's just that things are a little tight right now. I just found out that my pension funds were invested with one of those companies that went belly-up. I got a letter this morning."

"Oh, Sam, that's terrible. Did you lose it all?"

"Just about."

"People who do things like that should be shot," she said with vehemence.

"Maybe not shot, but they should at least have to live like the people they've defrauded. I saw in this morning's newspaper that the courts have allowed them to keep their fancy mansions."

"Dirty dogs," she swore, walking around the counter. "I want you to know that if I did the transmission work here instead of having to send it down to Waterbury, I would have thrown in my labor for free and just charged for the parts."

"You're a good lady," Sam said.

Nancy, unaccustomed to compliments, became brusque. "How about asking your friends to pitch in? After all, you're their main form of transportation."

"No, they've got their own expenses," he said, shaking his head. "Ben's Medicaid doesn't cover the full cost of his heart medicine. His son helps him out. And Timothy has to survive on just his social security check."

"That might explain why he dresses the way he does," Nancy mused.

"Timothy dresses the way he does because he's Timothy," Sam explained.

"Well, don't you worry. One way or the other, we'll find a way to fix your car. Remember what Father James always says."

Sam smiled. "Big needs are the seeds for big miracles."

"I'll ring Mr. Pipson, once he gets off the phone and tell him you're here," Gracie Abbott, the receptionist at WKUZ, told Valerie. "You're the artist who just moved to Dorsetville, aren't you?"

Valerie said yes to both queries.

"Imagine that. Me, meeting a real, live artist. . . ."

As opposed to a "dead" one? Valerie silently mused.

"This job is soooo interesting," Gracie continued, keeping a close eye on her boss's line. "I never know who I'm going to meet. Last week I met the president of the craft center over in Brookfield. Jack . . . ? Um, I don't remember his last name, but he was so very nice. Invited me and my family to the center for a personal tour. Imagine that!"

Gracie still hadn't come to grips with her good fortune. Never in her wildest dreams did she ever imagine that she might someday land a job like this, especially since her skills were in serious need of updating. When she had left the workforce several decades ago to have her first child, receptionists were still using typewriters and taking notes in shorthand. Consequently, computers mystified her, and she had proven just as hopeless at sending faxes. (The fax sent this morning to New York City was now being received in Liverpool, England.) But, fortunately for Gracie, the station wasn't looking for a receptionist skilled in modern equipment. Instead, it wanted someone who was an effusive greeter, genuinely liked people, and was filled with enthusiasm. Few could top Gracie Abbott in any of these areas.

"Oh, good. He's finally off the phone. Mr. Pipson? Valerie Kilbourne is here with the artwork for the new station logo, and you should see the cute little skirt and sweater set she's wearing. She looks absolutely darling in it," she sang into the phone. "Yes, sir. I'll tell her."

She replaced the receiver. "He apologizes. He's running a little behind."

"Will he be very long?" Valerie asked. "I have a doctor's appointment for my girls at four o'clock."

"No, I don't think he'll be more than ten . . . fifteen minutes tops. Can I get you a nice cup of coffee? It's hazelnut. I like to use a new flavor every day. Helps liven things up around here."

"No, thanks. I'm fine. I'll just sit here and read *Oprah* while I wait."

The phone rang.

"Excuse me, Valerie. You don't mind me calling you Valerie, do you? After all, Dorsetville is such a friendly little town.

"Good morning, this is your favorite television station, WKUZ. How may I help you? You just heard that we're starting a new cooking show. Then you heard correct. Mr. Pipson used to work as a station manager in Chicago. Did you know that? He's just filled with new show ideas. In fact, he's revamping the station's entire program lineup. Why, WKUZ is going to be the most popular local television station in the state, you just watch and see.

"Oh . . . you're a chef, you say, and you want to apply as host for the cooking show? I'm so sorry, but that position has already been filled. Mr. Pipson has hired Father Dennis. Yes, he's a priest. They're calling the new show *The Fat Friar*. Isn't that the cutest thing you've ever heard?"

Mrs. Norris had been retired for less than a week when the rectory began to look like a frat house. The kitchen was the worst. Countertops were buried underneath a motley assortment of empty cans and cereal boxes. Dirty dishes filled the sink, and every jet on the stove housed a food-encrusted pot or pan. The pattern on the linoleum floor, which had been installed less than a year ago, was completely obscured, hidden under a yellowish sticky film that snatched at Father James's slippers as he made his way to the coffeepot in the morning.

The rest of the house hadn't fared any better. Furniture was shrouded under a white coat of dust, and the wooden floors were littered with grass cutting that George Benson had tracked into the kitchen and somehow managed to spread through the house like a plague. Fortunately Stephen had offered to keep the bathrooms clean.

Added to that, Father James was wearing the same boxer shorts he had worn yesterday. No one had thought to run a wash. He was also down to his last pair of socks.

But being the optimist that he was, Father James hoped that at least the kitchen would have been cleaned by Father Dennis, as promised, by the time he returned from his hospital calls. But now, standing in the middle of the room, his optimism crashed like a cheap computer program. Things were pretty much the same as he had left them earlier this morning. In fact, in the glare of the midday sun, they seemed infinitely worse.

A dark red splatter was now clearly visible behind the stove, which must have come from the wine sauce Father Dennis had made the other night to go with the beef tenderloin, an entrée he was planning to use on his new cooking show. No doubt it was the show that had kept his young assistant from cleaning the kitchen. Lately it seemed as if every spare moment was spent with Emily Curtis, devising new menus.

Well, there was nothing left for him to do but to roll up his sleeves and dig in while praying that a new housekeeper would materialize quickly so things might get back to normal. Unfortunately, the search was proving to be a bit more difficult than he had anticipated. Even with the help from friends, the supply of applicants was dwindling.

Mildred Dunlop had sent over her niece.

"She could really use the money," she said.

The niece had arrived with two toddlers who managed to slide down the banister and straight into a glass bookcase. Fortunately, the bookcase was the only casualty.

"Hope you don't mind if I bring my boys along when I work," she said, while admonishing her boys to stay clear of the glass. "Can't afford to pay child care with the kind of wages you're offering."

Charlie Littman had sent over his Aunt Julia, who turned out to be a very large, buxom woman who needed to pause frequently to catch her breath and stated, in between gasps, that she would not clean anything above street level.

Two weeks ago, he had met Barry Hornibrook over at the Country Kettle. Barry said he knew of a college professor looking for a part-time job for one of his students. Hopes rising, he told Barry to send him right over, thinking it would be a wonderful meld. The rectory would be cleaned and orderly once again while they assisted a college student with tuition.

The student turned out to be a nineteen-year-old

boy with spiked, Creamsicle-colored hair who nodded his head like a plastic dog in a rear car window as Father James gave him a tour of the rectory.

Toward the end, Father asked, "Tell me why you think working as a housekeeper might be something you would like to do."

"I'm looking for a job that wouldn't, like, interfere with my social life and this seems kind of radical. Dig it, dude? I hope you don't mind if I invite some friends over to keep me company while I work."

When Harriet called to say she had the perfect housekeeper, Father James's spirits soared. He had great faith in Harriet's judgment.

"She's the mother of one of my customers. Her name is Helen Johnson, recently retired. Moved here to be close to her daughter and grandchildren. But she's getting a little bored, hanging around by herself while her daughter is at work and her grandchildren at school, so she's looking for something to do.

"Now, here's the good part, Father. She the former housekeeper of a small parish in upstate New York. I've already spoken to her and she's very interested in the job."

Father James could have kissed Harriet. Instead, he called Mrs. Johnson at her daughter's home and made an appointment for the very next day.

He had planned to get back to the rectory and straighten things up a bit before she arrived, but he was unexpectedly delayed by a meeting with the bishop. He had tried calling Father Dennis but his cell phone was turned off. He called the television station direct and was informed by a bubbly woman named Gracie that he was in the midst of taping a show and couldn't be disturbed.

When Father James finally pulled up in front of the rectory—fifteen minutes late—he found Mrs. Johnson patiently waiting in her car. He liked her already.

These feelings were enhanced as she walked over and introduced herself. She was a lovely woman with soft, silver hair and a shy smile. His hopes rocketed as they walked up the path to the front door and he turned the key.

"Now, I hope you're not too put off by what you see. None of us three men have proven to be any good at keeping house."

She smiled sweetly and assured him that she understood, then bravely stepped over the threshold and screamed.

Harley, the sheriff's 110-pound German shepherd, was standing in the center of the front hallway, surrounded by reams of garbage that he had dragged in from the kitchen. Apparently Father Dennis, in his haste to get to a television taping, hadn't closed the back door properly and the dog had wandered in. It was the third time this week that Harley had broken free from Deputy Hill.

The dog studied them closely and began to growl around a very large ham bone locked between his powerful jaws. As far as Harley was concerned, this was his home now, and it was his job to protect it. Suddenly he took chase. Father James and Mrs. Johnson barely made it unscathed out the front door.

"I'm so sorry, Mrs. Johnson. He's not ours. He's the—" He started to explain but Mrs. Johnson was already halfway down the driveway speeding toward her car.

———

"So, we have a new celebrity in our midst," Mother Superior said, settling in a chair on the patio adjacent to her office. She and Father James met once a week for a cup of tea and a chat. Since the weather had been cool and dry, she had decided to serve tea outdoors.

"The sisters tell me that the *The Fat Friar* has become our residents' favorite show. They especially liked the episode last week when he set the stove on fire."

"Yes, I heard about that," Father James said. "He does have a tendency to get carried away when working with wine."

She laughed. "Well, one thing's for certain. Things are never dull for long in Dorsetville. One lump of sugar or two?"

"Four."

"Have you heard about the mailbox snatchings all over town?" She handed him a cup.

"The sheriff mentioned it the other day when I dropped by. He seems to think it's a bunch of kids from across the river." Father James settled his cup and saucer on the glass patio table and eyed the dessert tray laden with pastries. The chocolate-dipped shortbreads looked especially appealing.

"Now, if we had pulled a stunt like that when we were kids, our parents would have taken a switch to us."

"Corporal punishment has gone out of style," he reminded her, taking two.

"Perhaps it should come back. A good swat on the posterior never hurt anyone. Look how we turned out. Their mischief costs innocent people money. I understand that they've taken the Campbells' mailbox twice. Disgraceful!"

She lowered her teacup and said quietly, "Have you

heard that Fred has been diagnosed with Alzheimer's? Harriet called just before you arrived. She had driven the Campbells home from the doctors."

"No, I hadn't. Poor couple," he said, deeply saddened by the news. "Did your sister say how Arlene was handling the news?"

The nun's eyes filled with pity. "Poor dear, she insists that the doctors are mistaken, and Harriet says she refuses to go for a second opinion. And if this wasn't enough, these poor people have to deal with acts of vandalism. I told Arlene that I would send Sister Claire to stay with them for a while. If anyone could deter these hoodlums, I know she could."

Father James laughed. "And did Arlene take you up on your offer?"

"I'm afraid not." She sighed. "Instead, they've asked to borrow Ethel's golden retriever. Arlene thinks Honey's presence will act as a stronger deterrent."

Harley would be a better choice, he thought, remembering his recent confrontation. The dog hadn't allowed him back into the rectory until the sheriff had arrived.

"I'll add the Campbells to my prayer list. Speaking of prayer lists . . . how is your 'rent a nun' program doing?"

Mother Superior shook her head with amusement. "I'm at a loss to understand why this works. In fact, when Sister Claire first approached me with the idea of allowing the public to 'rent' a nun as a prayer partner, I thought it would never fly. But apparently the ways of God are beyond my small power to comprehend. We get so many requests that we now have a waiting list. If we didn't the poor nuns would never get off their knees. More tea, Father?"

"Yes, thank you." That last bit of cookie had stuck in his throat. "Have you collected enough to finish your top-floor renovations?"

"That *and* some," she said. "In fact, we're thinking about buying the property next door and expanding. We're checking town codes to make certain zoning would be approved and, just to be on the safe side, I've invited Rochelle Phillips over for lunch next week." Rochelle was the town's zoning committee chairperson.

"Oh . . . I almost forgot. I met Stephen Richter the other day. He was helping upstairs with the renovations. Chester tells me he's a wonderful employee." She studied the priest over the rim of her teacup. "I hear he's staying with you and Father Dennis at the rectory."

"For a while."

"Nice young man. Will he be staying long?"

"That depends upon God."

"I see," she said, making no further inquiries. True to his word, Father James offered no insights.

Lori entered the doctor's office just minutes after Valerie had left with her daughters on route to an eye specialist at the Yale Medical Center in New Haven.

"Doc will be with you in just a few minutes," Shirley, the receptionist, told her. "He's in an exam room with the Gallagher twins. Got into the poison sumac again. How their mother manages to survive those two with her sanity intact is a mystery."

"I don't mind waiting," she said, and that was the truth. She could use a few minutes' rest. Things at the bakery were growing more and more hectic as word spread about Lori's fine pastries and pies. Several times she had been surprised to hear customers say that they had driven all the way over from Manchester. And last week Barry had asked her to provide all the desserts for a convention being held at his hotel. If things kept up at this pace, she would have to hire a full-time person to help run the counter so she could stay in the back and just bake.

But her hopes of resting were quickly dashed. She had just picked up a copy of *Better Homes and Gardens* when Shirley called her name.

"I'd say you're about three months pregnant, going into your fourth," Doc Hammon told Lori across his cluttered desk.

"B-but . . . how?" Lori stammered.

"I would think the usual way," he joked.

"No, I mean the oncologist said that Bob could never father a child."

"Apparently he was wrong. Granted, it's very unusual for a cancer patient who underwent the kind of extensive treatments that Bob had, but I've been a doctor for a good long time, and I've seen my share of the impossible happen." His thoughts ran back to Chester Platt, whose lung cancer had mysteriously disappeared.

"It's really a miracle, isn't it?" Lori said, her face aglow.

"All pregnancies are miracles," he concurred.

"Can I still work at the bakery? Harry will be gone on his honeymoon. I offered to take over things until he got back."

"Don't see any reason why not," Doc said. "Just don't lift anything heavy and if you get tired, take a break."

Bob had spent most of the morning reworking the figures for the Sister Regina Francis Retirement Home proposal. Mother Superior envisioned purchasing the adjacent home and building a three-story addition that would connect both facilities. This would give the home an additional twenty-seven rooms and a day care facility. His job was to determine if it was financially feasible.

He had just finished calculating the figures gathered from the list of subcontractors—electricians, plumbers, excavators—when he happened to look out the window and see Lori pulling up in her Dodge Caravan.

"Hi, honey," he called as she sailed into the office. "How did your appointment with Doc Hammon go?"

She grabbed him by the shoulders and planted a kiss on his lips that he felt right down to his toes.

"What was that for?" he asked, a little puzzled.

"That is because I love you."

"And I love you," he said, laughing.

"And because we're going to have a baby."

*E*IGHT

*G*eorge opened his mailbox for the first time in several days and pulled out a pile of mail—a circular from Grand Union announcing a sale on sweet corn, a bill from the electric company, copies of the *Dorsetville Gazette* and the Woodstock paper (George ran weekly advertisements in both), and enough catalogs to fell a forest. His estranged wife, Gertrude, seemed to be on every mailing list. He should have told the post office to return them "addressee unknown," but he had never gotten around to it.

George swung the wheel sharply to the left as he got ready to enter the two-car garage. The maneuver reminded him of the day Gertrude's Dodge Omni skidded on a patch of ice and careened into one of the garage doors. She refused to attempt to park it in the garage again that entire winter and complained bitterly that it was another reason for her hatred of country living.

But the home's location suited George's misanthropic streak just fine, a tendency that had only grown with age. Hidden from the road, he felt free to go about his business unencumbered by passerbys asking for directions or the townsfolk stopping by just to chat. He talked to enough folks on the job. He didn't need to do it on his time off.

George parked the van and headed toward the house. The wood-frame screen door that connected the breezeway to the garage creaked loudly. The thing had squeaked since last winter, but he still hadn't gotten around to oiling it. He kept the oil can in the van but never felt like treading all the way back to the garage to get it.

An old rattan chair, whose rush seat had been replaced by a piece of plywood, sat to the right of the kitchen door. He sat and unlaced his work boots, not in deference to the dirt or mud he might track into the house, but through years of conditioning. Gertrude always had insisted that he leave his dirty shoes outside.

Inside, George was greeted by a sinkful of breakfast dishes, containing a stained coffee mug, a plate with dried eggs, and a greasy frying pan. He pushed down the rubber stopper, shot a blue stream of liquid detergent into the mess, and ran the hot water. While the sink filled with suds, he went to the pantry and pulled down a box of bran flakes. Doc Hammon was after him to add more fiber to his diet. The stuff tasted like dried plaster, but was tolerable when he washed it down with a Bud Light. He didn't bother to grab a bowl; he ate it right out of the box.

He finished his makeshift dinner, cleared a space on the table, and began to sort through the mail. He pitched most of the catalogs with only a cursory glance until he unearthed an envelope wedged between Talbot's and Perkins Roses. The return address read Bradford Jacobs, Attorney at Law, Plattsville, Vermont. Someone had told him that they had seen Gertrude shopping in Plattsville. He had a gut feeling that this had something to do with her but was in no hurry to find out. First, he needed another beer.

Since the fridge was stationed next to the kitchen table, he didn't have to get up. George had moved it there right after Gertrude had taken off. In fact, for weeks after her departure, George had moved furniture back and forth across the wooden floors like giant erasers, trying to eradicate all memories of their life together.

The couch, positioned under the front bay window, where he and Gertrude had sat every evening to watch game shows, was moved directly in front of the television. Their bed, stationed between two windows, a repository of quiet passion that had dwindled over time, had been repositioned closer to the doorway and the hall bathroom.

But no matter how much he rearranged things, he would never remove the shame he felt at having his wife leave him for another man. It was a low blow for any man's ego.

The guy's name had been Albert. He was a vacuum salesman who had come to Dorsetville one fine spring day a few years ago to ply the backcountry roads in hopes of sales. But someone should have told him that Dorsetville folks liked to keep their business in town and would never have bought anything from a stranger, especially not a vacuum. Mark Stone stocked two models of Hoovers—an upright and a canister—at his hardware store. Couldn't go wrong with a Hoover, and folks were very fond of Mark.

So they listened politely to Albert's sales pitch, even invited him for some iced tea and molasses cookies, but no one bought a vacuum except Gertrude Benson.

Later, everyone agreed that Albert hadn't seemed the type of fellow who went around stealing someone else's wife. But on the last day of his visit, an unseasonably hot spring day with thunder sounding in the distance, Albert stole Gertrude away.

When George came home that evening he found a note pinned on the back door.

I've left. Don't try to find me. It's over.

George refused to leave the house until Father Keene, St. Cecilia's pastor back then, called one day in desperation. The water heater in the rectory was on the fritz and Mrs. Norris was threatening to quit. Could he come right over?

George said he wasn't making any service calls that week, but Father Keene would brook no nonsense. Mrs. Norris was on his tail, he said, and he didn't intend on spending another sleepless night with her voice ringing in his ears. He told George that if he didn't get his fanny over to the rectory that instant, he was calling Sheriff Bromley to fetch him in the squad car. George knew he meant it, so he packed up his tools and drove the back roads into town.

He was getting ready to leave when Mrs. Norris took him aside and gave him a sound talking to. "Now, you listen to me, George Benson. You've lost a wife, not a hand or a foot. You'll mend. Besides, you knew from the beginning that Gertrude never liked living in the country. She was a city person from the get-go and more's your shame because you knew it before you married her.

"So, instead of you going around feeling sorry for yourself, you need to get on with your life. No one thinks any less of you because your wife left with that salesman . . . although what she saw in a man with ears as large as cantaloupes and a heavy dependence on nasal spray eludes me. But be that as it may, fact is, we're all praying that she finally finds some happiness and, being a good Christian, you should too."

As much as he hated to hear it, Mrs. Norris was right. Gertrude had never been happy in Dorsetville. In fact, she had been miserable since the day he had brought her there to live as his bride.

They had met right after George received his discharge from the service. He had done his two-year stint in Vietnam and somehow had managed to come back in one piece without any strong addictions to either booze or drugs.

Gertrude was a folk singer at one of the bars by the base. She had a great voice, he remembered, although she never sang much after they were married. Sounded a little like Joan Baez. A record offer had even come after they were engaged. But George said no future wife of his was traipsing around the country. Gertrude, young and in love, hadn't argued.

They got married and moved back to Dorsetville because George couldn't imagine living anyplace else. He joined his father's heating business and loved working with his old man, always full of stories, always had a joke. George still missed him.

But while George kept busy with the family business, Gertrude was left alone to find her own way. She had been brought up along the Jersey shore. Plenty of nightlife. Plenty of stores and women friends who thought shopping *was* a job description.

To her credit, Gertrude did try to adjust to life in the country. She took up gardening. Joined the Garden Club but stayed a member for only a year. Learned how to quilt but said she found nothing in common with the other quilters. Finally, she stayed mostly at home, filled with a restlessness, a hunger George never quite knew how to satisfy.

Children might have helped, but Gertrude had been diagnosed as sterile. Doc Hammon said it was a result of scarlet fever she had had as a child. They talked about adopting, but it never amounted to anything. He sensed she wasn't really interested.

George would have liked to have kids of his own, something he carefully kept secret from Gertrude. Instead, he coached Little League until his knees gave out. And when his father died and left him a sizable stock portfolio, George anonymously helped to set up a school scholarship program. Every year since, the dividends were used to pay a student's way through college.

———

George hunched over the Formica-and-chrome kitchen table, took a slug of beer, and tore open the envelope. Gertrude had filed for a divorce. His marriage was officially over.

For the first time since Gertrude had left, George felt a heavy sadness. Not because he missed her or wanted her back, he just hated being alone. There was no one to watch *Jeopardy* with, or play a hand of gin rummy, or listen to him read from the newspaper and complain about the way the world was going to hell in a handbag.

He pushed aside the divorce papers—he'd think about that later—and went back to the mail, idly opening the *Dorsetville Gazette* and thumbing his way through the first few pages. Might as well check on his ad. Sometimes they made a slight mistake in the wording, which meant a refund.

Several pages in, George paused by the personals.

> *WF, 54 misses quiet evenings. Looking for company, not romance and someone who likes to play gin rummy.*

She didn't seem half bad.

> *SWF, mid-forties, seeks an occasional dinner partner. Tab's on me.*

He wouldn't mind having a woman pay for his dinner. Maybe he should place one of these ads. He hadn't dated since that time a few years ago when he'd let Barry talk him into a blind date with his second cousin's best friend. The woman was as ugly as sin and as big as a double-wide trailer.

But this wouldn't exactly be like a blind date, he thought, finishing off the last of his beer. You got to exchange letters first, then photos. At least this way, a guy didn't have to feel as if he were buying a pig in a poke.

He read a few more. Maybe he could find a woman who liked to cook or do laundry. Nah—laundry was too personal. No need to put any ideas in their heads.

He had to admit, he liked the *general* idea of a personal ad. For one thing, he could retain his anonymity. No names were exchanged, not until he was sure that the woman might be someone he'd like to meet.

This called for another beer. It was his third, but what the heck? It might inspire him to write an ad of his own, a thought that occupied him for several minutes as he leaned back in his chair and studied the ceiling.

First, it had to be plain, straightforward, and to the point. Nothing fancy. He didn't want women thinking that he was one of those kinds of guys who wore ruffled shirts and read poetry or anything. Second, he would definitely stay clear of words like "romantic," "loving," or "commitment".

By the time he had drained the Bud, he had settled on the perfect ad.

DWM fifties and fit. Still has his own hair and teeth. Looking for a mature, independent woman. Must like Elvis Presley movies.

Doc had ordered an amniocentesis for Lori. Just precautionary, he had told her. Nothing to worry about.

But as her scheduled two o'clock appointment neared, she was filled with a strange sense of foreboding. At the last moment, she phoned Harriet and asked if she might want to come along for moral support.

"Be happy to, dear," the older woman said. "I've got plenty of help here at the nursery, so I won't be missed. And besides, it will give me a chance to catch up on my knitting."

Lori pinned a note on the refrigerator for Bob before heading out. It simply said that Sarah was staying with Valerie and that she and Harriet had gone to the mall in search of a dress for Nellie's wedding. She reasoned there was no sense in telling Bob the truth. Why worry him needlessly? Doc Hammon had said that the test was just precautionary, right?

She and Harriet arrived at Mercy Hospital's outpatient clinic fifteen minutes before her scheduled appointment. Lori registered with the receptionist, then the women went in search of seats. They found two directly beneath the mounted television set.

Harriet settled in, placing her knitting bag on the floor as Lori reached for a dog-eared magazine. Above their heads the characters of *Days of Our Lives* played out the newest love triangle.

Suddenly a cold shiver ran down Lori's spine. She shuddered.

"Would you like me to go out to the car and get you a sweater?" Harriet asked.

"No, I'm not cold. Just frightened," she confessed.

Harriet gave her a motherly hug. "I know three other women who have had this test done. They said there is little discomfort."

"It's not the test I'm worried about. It's the results."

———

Father James had just enough time in between weekly Mass at the Sister Regina Francis Retirement Home and a promise to help Father Dennis load everything into his car for a taping of the *The Fat Friar* cooking show to place an ad in the *Dorsetville Gazette* for a new housekeeper. He was hoping the search would go quickly. He had run out of friends' recommendations and clean socks.

Father James was in a rush as he walked down Main Street, his mind clicking away at the myriad items needing his attention and wondering which ones he might let slip by.

He needed to deliver this week's bulletin to the printers, but not before a careful edit. Father Dennis had written it on the fly again. Last time Father James had let it slide without proper scrutiny and it had managed to offend both young mothers, with.

> *For those of you who have children and don't know it, we have a crying room downstairs.*

and Alan Dambrowski, the choir master, with

> *The Senior Choir invites any member of the parish who enjoys sinning to join the choir.*

Father James was still making mental notes when he threw open the door to the *Dorsetville Gazette* and headed toward the classified section.

"I'd like to place an ad," Father James told the young girl behind the desk. She looked vaguely familiar.

"Sure, Father James. I'll just get a form."

She was about sixteen years old, with chestnut hair and brown eyes. Where had he seen her before?

"What would you like to say?" she asked, pen poised. She had worked at the newspaper after school since the beginning of her sophomore year and loved helping customers.

"Let's see. . . ." He should have written something down. He was never good under pressure.

Trying to be helpful, the girl asked, "What would you like to advertise for?"

"A housekeeper."

"What exactly does a housekeeper do?"

"Good question. Er . . . I'm afraid I don't remember your name."

"Stephanie."

Stephanie, of course! He recognized her now. She was Matthew Metcalf's friend. The girl he had used to create the hologram of the Blessed Virgin Mary.

"Well, Stephanie, a housekeeper is someone who comes in around six-thirty in the morning, straightens things up, starts the breakfast, and does the wash. Later she cleans the rectory, does the marketing, changes the sheets, does the ironing, cooks lunch, answers the phone, takes messages, and tries to track us down if there's an emergency. She reminds us of things like doctors and dentist appointments. Last, she cooks dinner before leaving around six o'clock."

Stephanie chewed the pencil's eraser, deep in thought. Finally she concluded, "It sounds an awful lot like a mom."

George had waited in his van until Father James left the newspaper office, then headed inside.

"I'd like to place this ad," he told the girl behind the counter.

"I'm just finishing one for Father James. I'll be with you in just a minute.' "

"What's he advertising for?"

"A housekeeper."

"About time." George had dropped by the rectory the other day. The place was a real pigsty.

Stephanie made a few more marks, then placed the ad inside a tray marked "Classified Ads." "There, that's done," she said. "Now, how can I help you today, sir?"

He shoved a piece of paper across the laminated counter.

"What section would you like this to appear in, sir?"

Checking first to make certain that no one was listening, George leaned over and whispered, "Personals."

NINE

*S*aturday morning the temperature hovered in the low eighties and the soft scent of wild roses with their butter-cream petals wafted in the air, mingling with the gentle fragrance of peonies, phlox, and irises. Newly mown lawns added to this potpourri, which collectively created the special perfume known only to those who are fortunate enough to call New England their home.

The sun had barely risen above the mountain range that surrounded the valley like a warm embrace when people were awakened by a chorus of chirping birds and thoughts of the day's nuptials.

Ben Metcalf was up at six o'clock and ready by seven for Matthew to drive him over to Timothy's. Nellie had hired him, Timothy, and Matthew to tape the wedding. It was their first paid gig, and Ben was anxious to see that it ran smoothly. So, while Timothy scrambled eggs, the three reviewed the various shots that were needed for the Cliffords' wedding video.

"We'll start taping inside the church, right?" Timothy asked Matthew. "Pass me a couple of those plates from up top that cabinet, will you, Ben?"

"Right, Mr. McGree. And while I'm acting as an usher, Granddad will tape the ceremony. I set up the tripod at the back of the church. We'll get a few shots afterward of the Cliffords' outside the church, then race over to the reception."

"I hope all of this works out," Timothy said, setting the plates on the table. "Father James already has asked about us taping the confirmation ceremonies. A lot of the parents would like to buy copies. We figured a fifty-fifty split after our expenses was fair." He looked over at Matthew. "I owe you an apology."

"What for, Mr. McGee?" Matthew asked, reaching for the jam.

"When you first came up with the idea about forming a video production company, I thought you were crackers." Timothy settled into a chair. "But we've already got ourselves a couple of jobs. Looks like this might actually turn into a nice little side business."

"Matt, pass me the butter," his grandfather said. "And it will give me a little poker money."

"I'm saving for my own car," Matthew said.

"I think we should help Sam with his car repairs before any of us go off spending any money," Timothy offered.

All three agreed. Sam's transmission was sounding pretty awful lately.

Lori had awakened at 4 A.M. and couldn't get back to sleep. Thoughts of what the lab test might reveal filled her with a strange foreboding.

She lay quietly next to Bob listening to the steady rhythm of his breathing, so blissfully unaware of her worries. She gently kissed his shoulder, feeling his warmth against her cheek. She loved him without reservation, a love that deepened the longer they were married; and, she had come so close to losing him last year. Just the fleeting memory of those moments still made her throat constrict with panic and her heart hammer in fearful dread. She was riddled with similar fears when she thought about her unborn child.

She turned toward the window and glanced as the first rays of soft early-morning light began to peek through the draperies. This was no time for sober thoughts or dark shadows, she admonished herself. This was Harry's wedding day—the man who had become a surrogate brother, a confidant, a cherished friend. It was a day of celebration filled with new hopes and promises, and she would not allow her personal anxieties to cast a pall.

She slid out of bed, threw on a pair of old sweats, and headed toward the bakery. She still had to put the finishing touches on the wedding cake.

The sky had turned a pale pink by the time she slipped the key into the shop's back door. Grabbing an apron from off a peg, she popped in Norah Jones's CD into the player and set to work.

From upstairs in his apartment, Harry heard Lori enter the bakery. Apparently he wasn't the only one who was up early. He thought about going downstairs, starting a pot of coffee. Maybe they could have a little chat while she worked. He knew that it was bad luck for the bridegroom to see a bride in her dress before the wedding. He wondered. Did that carry over to the wedding cake?

Norah Jones's sandy voice wafted up through the floorboards and he dismissed the plan. It was probably best to stay out of Lori's way. He wouldn't want to be responsible for any more wedding-related mishaps. He was still taking the heat over the invitations.

Maybe he should take a walk. Exercise was good for the nerves, and he had plenty of time before he had to be at the church. He grabbed his Red Sox baseball cap and headed out. If he hung around here any longer, he would go mad.

Main Street was deserted. The shops were quiet, including his own. He smiled as he passed the hand-printed sign the girls had made that hung on the front door. CLOSED FOR THE WEDDING. It was the first time the Country Kettle had been closed on a Saturday since his parents started the business several decades ago.

He continued on, watching his reflection in the darkened storefront windows. The town was quiet; most people were still home in bed. Even the street was empty of traffic. He felt as if he had the town all to himself. Normally he would have cherished the quiet, reflective moments to reminisce about the many years he had lived in Dorsetville and how little it had changed; but not today. Today he needed company, a diversion, something to take his mind off the wedding.

He headed across the street, hoping that he would find that Mark Stone had come in early. Mark did that sometimes when he had a delivery coming in. But the hardware store was dark. Still hoping, Harry walked around back, but the parking lot was empty. Mark was probably still home sleeping.

He thought about heading back to his apartment, maybe getting another hour of shut-eye. How long had it been since he had slept in on a Saturday morning? He couldn't remember. But what if he overslept? Missed his own wedding? He decided instead to head down toward the river, feeling like a man about to embark on a course at sea without benefit of a compass. What did he know about love or marriage, anyway? He had been a bachelor all of his adult life. What made him think that he could successfully navigate the role of a husband?

He was filled with questions and concerns from the simple to the complex.

What if his snoring kept Nellie awake? His camping friends joked for years about it.

"Sleeping with Harry is like sleeping under a 747."

What if she cooked meals he hated? What if she wanted to buy things on credit? He didn't believe in charge cards. He felt it was better to save up and buy things with cash. What if she wanted to talk when he wanted to read? Or started planning their vacations? Who was to be in charge of their finances? What about joint savings?

For Pete's sake, he was getting married in a few hours. Why hadn't he thought of settling any of this before now?

Sam helped Harriet with the church flowers until eight-thirty, then went to pick up Ben and Timothy at the television station where Matthew had dropped them off earlier. Matthew said he couldn't hang around. He needed some serious shower time. Besides being an usher, he also had asked Stephanie to accompany him as his date. The pressure was on.

As Sam pulled into the station's parking lot, his car rattled and lurched, sounding like someone had loosed a bag of marbles underneath the floorboards.

"Just a little longer," Sam cajoled. "At least until the end of the wedding. Don't give up on me now."

He left the car running to go inside and help his friends pack up the video equipment. Then he drove all the way to the church in second gear.

"Where did you put them?" Sister Theresa asked, rummaging through Father Keene's sock draw.

Father Keene's new black dress socks, bought especially to be worn with his rented tux, were missing.

"If I knew that, would I be asking you to help me find them?" he asked dryly.

Couldn't the woman see he was as nervous as a pig at a pig roast? He'd never given a bride away before. Was he supposed to walk on her right, or was it on her left? You'd think a man of the cloth would know. Hadn't he performed hundreds of weddings in his time? If only he had paid a little more attention.

Sister Theresa was down on all fours and sweeping underneath this bed with a metal yardstick, which netted one tennis ball, a package of Dr. Scholl's Corn Cushions and an old apple core, but no socks.

"Well, I'm at a loss," she said, kneeling by the side of his bed. "Wait a minute. What's that hanging out of your Bible?"

She pulled out the pair of missing black socks.

"I'll be deviled," Father Keene exclaimed.

On the other side of town, the bride was having trouble with the clasp on the antique pearl necklace Harry had given her last evening. It was his grandmother's; she had worn it on her wedding day.

"I feel like I'm going to faint," she told Valerie, who had come to help her get ready. The twins were with the Petersons.

"Here, let me help."

Nellie stood in front of a full-length mirror in her upstairs bedroom. In a few hours, this room would be "their" bedroom. The thought still made her blush.

"You're going to be just fine," Valerie said, smiling at Nellie's reflection.

"If my legs don't give out halfway down the aisle."

Valerie laughed. "You'll be just find. Now, there, I've got it. Turn around and let me see."

"Is everything hooked? Buttoned? Zipped? How's my slip? Is it showing? I bought a shorter one. It would only take me a minute to change," Nellie asked. Why was she talking so fast?

"You don't need to change anything," Valerie assured her. "You look lovely. Perfect. In fact, you're the most beautiful bride I've ever seen."

Nellie threw her arms around her neck and gave her a hug. "Bless you. That's just what I needed to hear."

Father James was running behind and feared he would be hopelessly late in fetching the bride. He should have picked up Father Keene ten minutes ago. Why had he agreed to act as a limousine service?

It seemed the entire morning had been one crisis after

the other. He had been jolted out of bed at six o'clock by the thought that he had forgotten to fill the Jeep up with gas the night before. It was running on fumes.

He had planned to do it on the way back from visiting parishioners at the hospital; but then another parishioner had learned that her father had died several states away, and he had to rush over to offer his condolences. By the time he had left, he was bone weary and all thoughts of the wedding had flown right out of his head.

Then he had discovered they were out of coffee. No one had thought to go marketing, and he was hopeless without his morning jump-start of caffeine. He searched several cabinets like a smoker on the verge of a nicotine fit. Nothing. In fact, the cabinets were nearly bare.

He decided to combine the gas run with a coffee run, but then remembered that the County Kettle would be closed. After all, it was Harry's wedding day.

At this juncture, he was beginning to slide into a full-fledged state of panic when he remembered the gas station on Route 7 also had a Dunkin Donuts shop inside. Feeling hope return, he clamored up the back stairway to wake Father Dennis, who was scheduled to preside over today's morning Mass.

"Father Dennis?" He knocked lightly on the bedroom door.

"Go away."

Go away?

"I think I'm dying." Father Dennis moaned.

Father James peeked inside. Father Dennis was lying in bed swathed in a bevy of quilts, looking as white as the sheets that were beneath him. "You look terrible."

"I've got a fever and the chills. It must be that virus that's been going round."

"Can I get you anything?" he asked, stepping inside. "A cup of tea? An aspirin?"

Father Dennis waved him away. "You'd better not come any closer. You don't want to catch this bug."

"Just stay in bed. I'll say Mass this morning." He would have to skip the homily. He still needed to get gas before the wedding.

"I'm so sorry, Father James. I know today's Harry's wedding and there's the vigil Mass at five."

"I'll get Father Keene to preside."

"Then you might want to keep a close eye on him during the reception," Father Dennis cautioned. "You know what happened last time at the O'Caseys' wedding."

How could he forget? Father Keene had offered up numerous blessings, each accompanied with a shot of whiskey. By the end of the reception, the O'Caseys were the most blessed couple Father James had ever seen and Father Keene could hardly stand.

"I'll put Sister Claire in charge. You just stay in bed and get better. Can I get you a cup of chicken soup or a nice scrambled egg? I could melt some cheese on top if you like. I think we still have some cheddar. Of course, if you prefer münster, I saw some in the refrigerator yesterday."

Unfortunately, Father James's offer seemed to have the opposite effect that he had intended. His young cleric's face blanched white; he threw back the bedcovers and bolted to the bathroom.

Father James waited until things settled down behind the closed door then lightly knocked. "Are you all right? You sure I can't get you anything?"

The toilet flushed followed by Father Dennis's weakened voice. "Not unless you have something that will permanently put me out of my misery."

There was a knock on his door. Stephen looked up from his sketchbook, a piece of charcoal poised in midair.

"Come in."

"You're not planning to attend the wedding?" Father James asked.

Stephen was dressed in jeans.

"Tell Nellie it was awfully nice of her to invite me, but to be honest, I'm still not comfortable with crowds." Stephen carefully avoided the priest's eyes. He was never much good at lying. Truth was, he feared Valerie might be there. He still hadn't had the courage to confront her.

"We'll miss you but that's understandable," Father James replied. "Then, may I ask a favor?"

"Sure."

"Would you keep an eye and ear out for Father Dennis? He's as sick as a dog."

"No problem. I planned just to hang out here today."

"Thanks, I appreciate your help." Father James started to leave then turned back. "And when you check on him, you might not want to mention anything having to do with food."

Everyone said it was the best wedding the town had ever seen and one that was destined to become the standard upon which all others would be judged until all those who had attended the affair (which by George Benson's estimation was nearly the entire town) went on to meet their maker.

Harriet had outdone herself with the floral arrangements, transforming St. Cecilia's cold stone interior into a cool sylvan glade, a lush medieval forest, elegant in its simplicity. Votive candles that flickered like fairy lights were tucked cleverly among window arrangements of Jerusalem ferns and lilies of the valley, and the altar was awash with gardenias and calla lilies whose soft fragrance rose like incense.

Halfway through the ceremony, the Reverend Curtis was heard whispering to his wife, "I think I'll sneak back before the reception and take some photos." The reverend was president of the Dorsetville Garden Club.

The Henderson sisters said they had never seen Father Keene looking so dapper in his rented tux. Even Timothy was respectably decked out, if one didn't count the circa 1960s psychedelic tie and the yellow socks.

But, of course, it was the bride who stole the show in her silk suit the color of Devonshire cream and a smile that could have lit up Manhattan.

And Father James's homily, many said, was the most impressive one to date, ending with "As Harry and Nellie exchange their vows and enter into the covenant of marriage, a wonderful mystery will take place. At that moment, they cease to be two souls traveling separate spiritual paths. At that moment, they become one before God."

There wasn't a dry eye in the church.

The large ballroom of the Old Mills Hotel and Conference Center was bedecked with lace tablecloths, sparkling crystal, and Harriet's stunning centerpieces. A row of arched windows framed in rich brocades and a balcony that cantilevered over the water provided an uninterrupted view of the river and the college campus across the way.

Toasts and blessings were made throughout the afternoon while Father Keene sat looking wretched under the watchful eye of Sister Claire *and* Mother Superior. Young folks showed the older folks the newest dance steps. Older folks taught the young folks how to rumba, and Nellie and Harry laughed and kissed and generally felt an enormous amount of relief. For better or for worse, they were now officially married.

"And now I'd like to call all the eligible ladies to head up here to the dance floor. The bride is about to throw the bridal bouquet," announced Tom Chute, a local DJ, who was acting as master of ceremonies.

A wave of excitement washed across the room to the accompaniment of giggles and chair legs scraping against the wooden floor, then a flurry of rustling skirts.

"Don't be shy, ladies. Move up a little closer and take your positions right behind the new Mrs. Clifford. Remember the custom. The one who catches the bridal bouquet is the next one to be married."

Sheriff Bromley watched the women rush forward as they made their way in between tables and chairs. He wondered how many women who caught a bouquet actually got married.

"Didn't you like your cake, sir?" a waitresses asked him.

The cake sat untouched, as had the rest of his dinner. "I just wasn't hungry."

"Can I get you something else?"

"Some more water would be good," he said. It was as hot as blazes in there. Someone should tell Barry to pump up the air conditioning.

Hill's distinctive laugh made him turn. His deputy was seated a few tables away. From the looks of things, he was the only one laughing. The others seated around the table shifted uncomfortably in their chairs, looking as miserable as the sheriff did every time Hill walked into the room. Bromley felt for them.

Suddenly his stomach started to rumble and a sudden geyser of bile rose like hot lava up through his throat. Oh, jeeeeeeze. . . . He pushed away from the table and flew across the room, his hand clamped tightly across his mouth. He heard his stomach rumble again. Tasted the salmon he had eaten recently and gagged.

He made it into the hallway outside and frantically looked around. Where the heck was the men's room? Things had started to move. There was no time left. He headed toward a large potted plant.

"We knew you would catch the bouquet, Mommy," Linda and Leah chimed triumphantly as their mother returned to the table.

"I think it was rigged," Valerie joked, laying the flowers aside. "I swear Nellie threw it right at me."

The twins sidled up close and looked hopefully into her eyes.

"Now you will be the next lady to get married," Leah said confidently.

"And then we will have a daddy," Linda added.

———

The party was winding down. People were packing up, getting ready to leave for home. The newlyweds had already left for the airport. They were honeymooning in Bermuda.

Valerie ushered her daughters through the parking lot, the girls jabbering away like magpies.

"I like weddings better than birthday parties," Leah said.

"I like them better than Christmas," Linda chimed in.

"Can we go to another wedding?" Leah asked.

"I want to be the flower girl next time," Linda said.

"Can we play at Sarah's?" Leah asked.

They had finally reached their car.

"Not tonight, dear," Valerie said, fishing at the bottom of her purse for her car keys. "You've seen enough of each other for one day."

"Then can we go for ice cream?" Linda asked.

"No, you've had enough desserts."

"We only had a little cake," Leah said.

Valerie playfully pinched her nose. "Remember what happened to Pinocchio when he lied."

"Ah, Mom. . . ."

"I saw you both take a full plate of chocolate-covered strawberries *and* two pieces of wedding cake each."

"We were getting them for someone else," Leah explained. *"Reaaaally."*

"Valerie, you got a minute?" Doc Hammon interrupted. "Hi, girls. Did you have a nice time at the wedding?"

"Our mom caught the bouquet," Leah informed him, the issue at hand forgotten.

"She's getting married next," Linda said with finality.

"Yes, as soon as I find a frog to kiss. Now why don't you two get into the car. I'll be there in a minute."

Doc waited until the girls were safely ensconced in the backseat, out of earshot.

"I spoke with the physicians at Yale. The girls' test results are in. Are you available on Monday to come into my office?" he asked. "I'd like to discuss what they have found."

By the tone of his voice, the results couldn't have been good. Her mouth went dry. "Is it serious?"

He edged closer and lowered his voice so that those passing wouldn't overhear. "They've discovered several small adhesions on the girls' retinas."

"What does that mean?"

He slowly shook his head. "It means that their retinas are starting to detach."

"And if they do?"

He paused before saying softly, "Without intervention, they'll go blind."

She leaned heavily against the car as if it could help to absorb some of the shock.

"Good night, Doc," Chester Platt shouted, crossing the parking lot. "A great wedding, wasn't it?"

"Sure was," Doc shouted back. "Look, this isn't the place to go into all of the details. Come in on Monday and I'll fill you in on everything then."

"My girls are going to lose their eyesight," she whispered in a daze.

"Not if I can help it," he stated emphatically.

"Will they need an operation?"

"Yes."

"But—but I don't have any health insurance. How

will I pay for this?" Fear began to wind its way around her heart.

"Now you listen to me, Valerie," Doc Hammon said in his best fatherly fashion. "You're not alone anymore. You're part of this community, and together we . . . and the Good Lord . . . will work things out. I promise."

TEN

*ather James studied the vacuum cleaner bag like an opponent at a boxing match. There had to be a way to lick this thing. How hard could it be to fit this cardboard tab over the plastic hole? He slid it in one way, but it got stuck. Getting it unstuck cost him the bag. He tossed it and tried again. This time instead of pulling the cardboard tab up, he tried sliding it facedown. This left the bag hanging outside the canister when he closed the lid.

As a last resort, he taped the bag to the plastic hole with duct tape.

"Old-fashioned ingenuity," he said, feeling pretty smart. He was in the hallway when it exploded, an atomic blast of dust, dirt, sand, and indiscernible debris. It settled everywhere, including on the portrait of the archbishop at the bottom of the stairs, aging him considerably.

Father James slumped down on the floor to wrestle with the remnants of the bag, unmindful of his black trousers, which were now covered in dog hair and lint. Ethel and Honey had recently paid a visit.

He cursed heavily under his breath, then immediately repented. He seemed to be in a constant state of repentance since Mrs. Norris's resignation.

He repented for his lack of patience when the pot of oatmeal burned. He had been distracted by an article in the *Dorsetville Gazette* about the mailbox snatchings.

He repented for yelling at Father Dennis for tracking dirt all over the kitchen floor, which he had just finished mopping. Mostly he repented at not being more appreciative of Mrs. Norris for all of the years she had been their housekeeper.

He looked at his nemesis with even greater disdain. Maybe he should just pitch the blasted thing out the back door and be done with it! There was something to be said for using a broom.

The doorbell rang.

"I'm coming. Just a minute." He went to answer the door. "Someone should invent a vacuum that doesn't require the patience of Job and the wisdom of Solomon to operate."

The doorbell rang again.

"I'm *coming!*" Who the blazes was so impatient?

He opened the door with an inordinate amount of force. *"Yes?"*

A middle-aged woman stood on the other side of the threshold, holding a copy of the *Dorsetville Gazette* in her hand and sporting a hairstyle he had once seen on a Lhasa apso.

"You still looking for a housekeeper?" she asked without preamble, not at all put off by his bad temper.

"Housekeeper? Yes . . . I am."

"Then I'm here to apply," she said.

His mood shifted under a new wind of sail. "You are? Why, that's wonderful. My name is Father James. I'm the pastor here at St. Cecilia's," he explained, smiling like the village idiot. "Won't you please come in?"

She peered through the opening and, for a second, looked as if she might change her mind. But Father James was not about to let her get away. He swooped outside, took hold of her arm, and escorted her in, chattering away.

"You'll have to forgive the mess," he said, stepping over the vacuum cleaner.

He closed the front door, sealing her inside, and suddenly noticed that it was awfully dark. He had forgotten to put up the shades. He gave the nearest one a slight tug and it fell out of the window.

"I'll have to get someone in to repair that," he said rather lamely. "I'm afraid that I didn't catch your name."

"Viola Tunis," she said, taking a look around. "Like the violin."

Wasn't a violin a violin and a viola a different instrument? But not wanting to contradict her, or in any way give offense, he didn't press. Instead, he followed her gaze and to his horror found Viola staring at a pile of underwear he had left by the stairs. He had planned to run a wash as soon as he had finished the vacuuming.

"We're a little behind with our housework," he explained, scooping up the clothing and shoving it into the hall closet.

"Don't look so bad to me," she said.

"It doesn't?"

"Our trailer gets a lot worse than this when Odis, that's my husband, has one of his beer parties. Whe-weeeee." She whistled through two missing front teeth. "You should see the mess when he and his buddies are through."

For some unfathomable reason, this statement gave him great reason to hope.

"Would you like to come in and sit down? I think we might be able to find an uncluttered chair someplace."

"Naw. Odis is waiting in the car."

He heard a phone ring. Please Lord, let someone else answer that, he thought. He was not letting this one get away.

"Father James?" Stephen called, peering through the kitchen door. "It's Wendy. She say's it's important. And Harriet called when you were vacuuming. Something to do with this week's flowers for the church."

"I'll be right there."

"Maybe I'd better come back when you're not so busy," Viola said, heading back toward the front door.

Father James nearly tripped over the vacuum cleaner in his haste to head her off. "No, please don't go. As you can see, we're rather in desperate need of a house-keeper."

"Ain't that the truth?" Viola never minced words. "But I can't keep Odis waiting too long. He's not long on patience. Even less so when he's not had his afternoon snooze."

"I can certainly understand a man's need of his sleep. But there's only one thing I need to know."

She eyed him suspiciously, her being a Baptist and all. "What's that?"

"Do you know how to change a vacuum cleaner bag?"

"Sure. Any fool can change a vacuum bag."

"In that case, you've got the job," he said, not the least bit offended.

Father James needed a few seconds for his eyes to readjust to the restaurant's indoor lighting after walking down from the rectory in the glare of the afternoon sun. The Country Kettle was nearly empty except for Cowboy Joe, who was seated at a side table, reading the racing scores.

Wendy waved the priest over to the front counter as soon as he stepped in the door.

"Boy, am I glad you're here," she said, pouring coffee into a mug shaped like a beer barrel. She pushed it his way as he slid onto a stool.

"Stephen said it sounded urgent. I thought I'd better come right down. What's the matter?"

"It's Lori. She had a doctor's appointment this afternoon. Just got back about an hour ago. You should have seen her face. She looked like death warmed over. I thought she might faint, so I walked over and asked her if anything was wrong, but she didn't answer. Instead, she broke into tears then ran in the back and locked herself inside the office. She's been in there crying her eyes out ever since. Won't answer the door."

"I wonder what could be wrong?" he mused, spooning sugar into the mug. Several granules fell onto the counter. Wendy, always efficient, immediately wiped them away with a cloth.

Cowboy Joe walked over to pay his tab.

"I'll be right with you, Joe," she said, inching her way toward the cash register. "I don't know but I'm betting it ain't good."

Father James knocked lightly. "Lori? It's me. Father James."

"Go away, Father. I just want to be alone."

He waited, debating whether to respect her request or to keep on trying. He said a silent prayer and knocked again.

"Wendy said that you seemed upset. I just thought you might like to talk." He waited for several seconds then, with enormous relief, heard the door unlock. He walked in.

Lori was standing by a partially opened window with a crumpled piece of tissue in her hand.

"Lori," he said softly. She had been crying hard; her eyes were red and puffy. "What is it? What's happened?"

"Oh, Father—" She couldn't seem to go on.

Father James pulled over a chair and helped ease her into it then knelt alongside. "Tell me, Lori, what's wrong?"

She leaned forward, placing her head in her hands. "It's our baby."

This was the first he had heard of it. "You and Bob are going to have a baby? How wonderful."

She looked up at him with pain-stricken eyes. "But it's not wonderful. I just found out that our baby is going to be severely handicapped."

"Oh, Lori, I don't know what to say."

She swiped at her tears. "Doc Hammon had me take some tests a few days ago. He said it was just precautionary, but I *knew* something horrible was about to happen. I remembered how Doc had said those same words to Bob, 'just precautionary,' when he sent him to have some tests, and then we found out he had cancer. And I was right." She could barely speak. "The tests showed that my baby's spine is not developing. Our baby will never be able to walk or sit up, or feed—" She couldn't go on.

"I wish there was something that I could do."

"Do you, really?"

"Of course."

"Then tell me why God is doing this to me."

It was a question he had heard dozens of times before, voiced in a dozen different ways. The answer, however, was the same. "God isn't doing this to you. Things happen—"

Lori jumped up from the chair with such force that she knocked him over. "Don't! Don't make excuses for Him. He's God. He could have prevented this. Hasn't our family suffered enough?" she railed. "First Bob's cancer. Next we nearly lost Sarah last year in the fire. And *now* He expects me to raise a handicapped child? I've had enough! Enough heartache. Enough trials. I'm tired. Worn out. My very soul hurts."

Father James didn't try to get up. He simply stayed on the floor. As much as he wished to console her, to remind her of all the times that God had proven Himself a compassionate and loving God, as when He had responded in the most extraordinary way when she had called out for hope to believe that Bob would be healed, he knew they were words of consolation that she couldn't accept. Not yet. First she must exorcise all the anger, the rage and frustration so many of God's children feel when trials come unbidden.

Fresh tears coursed down her cheeks. "I don't understand. Why would He give us such joy only to take it away? We never thought we could have another child. We were resolved to that, but then He taunted us with hope. Doc said this pregnancy was a miracle. Some miracle," she added bitterly.

She paused in her tirade to look at him with complete despondency. "I can't endure a lifetime of seeing my child suffer. I can't. What mother could? How can I make it through this?"

Father James slowly got to his feet, reached down deep into his pants' pocket, and pulled out his mother's rosary. It was his most treasured possession. Since her death, he had never been without it. But now he placed the beads into Lori's hand.

"Perhaps our Blessed Mother will help," he said. "She never left her Son that day at Calvary. I don't believe she will leave you either in your suffering."

Chester Platt gave the crew a break around midmorning. Stephen was glad to take it. His muscles ached, especially the upper portion of his arms, which had gotten the better part of this morning's workout. The crew was still in the midst of renovating the retirement home.

Stephen liked the work even if every square inch of his body ached. He liked the freedom of movement after being confined for so many years. And both the crew and the nuns were pleasant, a nice change from his prison companions, although he was careful to keep his distance. When you got too chummy, people started asking questions.

So while his coworkers sat on the lawn by the back porch drinking coffee and eating their second breakfast of the day, Stephen wandered off to the far end of the property to do some sketching. A small group of children who had gathered by the back stone wall might make for an interesting study. He reached inside his shirt pocket for a pencil, settled up against the trunk of a maple tree, and within minutes was lost in that familiar world where artists dwell, a world of line and shapes and form.

The girls were gathered around a picnic table filled with construction paper, crayons, and assorted craft supplies. There was a jar of macaroni, a bag of cotton balls, and several skeins of wool.

He recognized Sarah Peterson right way. For the past few days, Stephen had spent time after work painting their second-floor nursery, just one of the many side jobs he had found around town. The Petersons had seemed pleased with his work, especially the mural he had added of Winnie-the-Pooh for which he refused any extra pay.

Gathered around Sarah was a set of golden-haired twin girls whose heads were bent over their projects. They both wore thick glasses that continually slid down to the tips of their noses.

Stephen smiled, wondering what they were so busy creating. The answer to that question was something, that he as an artist, would wish to convey to the viewer. A new energy surged deep within as he quickly outlined their shapes, depending heavily on curves to suggest a sense of movement and exuberance.

While he worked, the girls' voices drifted across the lawn.

"Leah, that's not the way Sister Claire told you to do it," Sarah chided. "Here, let me show you. You're supposed to color in the lamb's eyes and nose *before* you glue on the cotton balls for his body."

One of the twins caught Stephen's eyes and hunched her shoulders as if to say, *How was I to know?* which made him laugh out loud. She smiled in return.

"Who's that over there?" Leah asked Sarah.

"Oh, that's Stephen. Hi, Stephen! He works for Mr. Platt, like my daddy."

Leah had tired of the project and pushed her paper away. Linda was the one who liked to draw. She'd rather be helping Sister Bernadette in the garden. But bossy Sarah was afraid that she would get all dirty. Who put her in charge, anyway?

Leah slipped off the small wooden bench, her eyeglasses sliding down the bridge of her nose. She pushed them back.

"I'm going over to say hello," she announced.

"Stay on the property," Sarah ordered. "And don't go near Sister Bernadette. She and Father Keene are spreading cow manure."

"I won't." She sighed. Sarah was getting to be a nag.

Leah walked over and introduced herself. "Hello, my name is Leah. Sarah said your name is Stephen."

"That's right."

"Sarah said you painted her house."

"I painted a room."

She edged a little closer. "What are you doing now?"

"Drawing."

"Can I see it?"

"Sure." He turned the pad her way.

She studied it with the intensity of an art critic. "It's very good. It looks just like us."

He bowed his head. "I thank you for your kind words, young miss. Would you like to keep it?"

"No, thank you," she said, stepping back. Then, not wanting to be impolite, she added, "It's very nice, but we have lots of drawings."

He laughed good-naturedly, thoroughly enjoying the child's candor. "In that case, I will save it to enjoy myself."

"Leah! Come back here and finish," Sarah called. "Sister Claire wants us to wash up for lunch."

"I'm coming," Leah said, heaving a sigh. "She's really starting to get on my nerves."

Stephen chuckled as he watched her walk away, thinking that if he ever were to have a family, he would like to have a little girl just like that.

$\mathcal{E}$LEVEN

"$\mathcal{I}$s that the vacuum I hear inside?" Charlie asked as he handed Father James a stack of letters and magazines. "Haven't heard that sound for a while. Not since you let Mrs. Norris go."

"I did not *let her go*. She retired," Father James corrected. How many times did he have to say that?

He was seated on the back porch, working on his homily, safely out of the way of Viola's cleaning frenzy. He had to admit, she was thorough. Since her arrival, every closet, cupboard, and corner of the rectory had been scrubbed and polished. Today she was cleaning his study, which was why he was working outside on the porch. But he wasn't about to complain. It was nice having clean socks again.

He sifted through the mail, trying to ignore Charlie who was peering through the kitchen window, hoping to get a peek inside. There was a letter for Stephen from Monsignor Casio. A fuel bill. An advertisement for a Jiffy Lube and four letters addressed to *The Fat Friar* smelling heavily of perfume. What the dickens?

Charlie saw him frown. "Fan letters," he said, dropping the forty-pound mailbag onto the porch with a thud and massaging his left shoulder.

"Fan letters?" the priest asked incredulously. Who would write a fan letter to a priest?

"It's that new show of his, *The Fat Friar*," Charlie explained, sliding into a wicker chair. "Father Dennis has become quite the celebrity. Why, last week he got a letter all the way from Elmira, New York."

Now Father James had heard everything.

The back screen banged shut. The men looked up as Viola marched over, her arms filled with freshly laundered sheets.

"I'm headed upstairs to change Father Dennis's sheets. You want yours changed too?"

"Didn't you just change all the sheets a few days ago?" he asked.

"Yeah, but Father Dennis has been drinking hot chocolate in bed again. Knocked over the cup and there went the clean sheets. Sure wish he'd confine his night snacking to the kitchen."

"I'll see that he mends his ways," he told her in earnest. He didn't want to lose another housekeeper. "Have you met our mailman, Charlie Littman?"

"Yeah, I know him," she said, giving Charlie a look that would have turned the Everglades to glaciers.

"Viola," Charlie acknowledged.

"It's Mrs. Tunis to you," she corrected, then deliberately turned her back on him to address Father James. "I need to leave early today. I promised Odis that I'd make him a batch of chili for his Tuesday-night poker buddies."

"But today's Monday," Father reminded her.

"My chili takes a day to ripen."

He felt it best not to explore the "ripening" of Viola's chili. "Feel free to leave whenever you need to," he said.

"Good. I'll finish making up the beds and then I'll be off." She gave Charlie another cold stare, then left, murmuring under her breath. "Don't know what I ever saw in that man."

"Well, I'd better be going." Charlie hefted the mailbag back onto his shoulder. "Looks like rain."

Father James looked up into a perfectly cloudless sky. "It's too nice for rain."

"That's when it always comes," Charlie said, heading across the back lawn. "It always comes when you're expecting sunshine."

"See you tomorrow."

Father James returned to his homily with a thankful heart that Charlie was not one of his parishioners.

WKUZ's new show lineup was a bigger hit than station manager Carl Pipson could ever have imagined.

Mildred Dunlap's game show, *Crazy About Crosswords*, had soared in the ratings. It seemed that every parent, grandparent, great cousin, and anyone else the family could wrestle into rooting for their child was tuned in.

The *Clothesline Quilters'* show was also doing quite well, taking in new viewers every week with its eclectic mix of quilting and town gossip.

Each segment began as the women took their places around an old-fashioned quilting frame; then for the next few minutes one of the ladies would discuss the pattern they were working on, or a new technique learned at one of the quilting fairs that proliferated throughout New England.

But soon talks of fabrics and quilters turned to stories about local people, legends, and gossip.

Ethel Johnson once told the story of how she had nearly been lost in the fifties' blizzard. This reminded Harriet Bedford of how Father Keene had been lost in a similar snowstorm. This in turn got Arlene Campbell remembering her mother's recipe for frostbite.

They talked about children, husbands, in-laws, what were the best low-fat recipes, and what they would get lifted, tucked, or implanted if money was not an issue.

They spoke about the bad times and the good—all agreeing that good always outweighed the bad—and they shared their common faith in the power of prayer.

Although the program had aired for only six weeks, it had already attracted a loyal audience. Carl's wife had recently overheard two women at the beauty salon discussing the show with admonitions to their hairdressers to hurry. "We don't want to miss the quilters."

But if the quilting show was a hit, *The Fat Friar* cooking show was a mega-hit. Viewers were enthralled by the Catholic priest dressed in clerical garb and a chef's apron, who dispensed corny jokes and tired platitudes along with cooking advice. Ratings soared.

Timothy was seated alongside Matthew at the control board. They were minutes away from air time.

"Tell my granddad that we're counting down in five," Matthew said.

Timothy relayed the message. Out on the studio floor, Ben gave the thumbs-up, indicating he had heard.

"We're getting ready to go live," Ben told Father Dennis. "Five minutes until air time."

"Where's the finished bouillabaisse, Emily?" Father Dennis asked.

"Oh, dear. I forgot to take it off the hot plate in the control room. Timothy! Matthew! Will one of you please bring me that large pot I left warming next to the coffeemaker? Be careful not to spill it."

"Three minutes," Ben counted.

Father Dennis looked to his left and panicked. "Sam, where are my cue cards? They're supposed to be there right next to the camera. I can't perform without my cards!"

"They're missing," Sam replied simply. "Someone must have taken them." Sam was in charge of set design. It was a fancy way of saying he got to move things around.

"Missing? *How can they be missing?*"

"You're going to have to wing it." Matthew's voice boomed from the overhead speaker. "We're about to go live. Granddad, start the countdown."

"Wing it? I can't wing it!"

Ben counted off, "Ten, nine, eight . . ."

Timothy handed the bouillabaisse pot to Emily, who quickly slid it under the counter, then crawled out of camera range.

Father Dennis looked straight into the camera and swallowed hard.

The red light above Ben's camera came on. He gave the sign they were live.

The nervous priest smiled into the lens.

"Welcome to *The Fat Friar* show. I'm Father Dennis here to remind you that the Lord said we were not to live by bread alone. Which is why I'm here to show you today how to make the most delicious, the most scrumptious, the most I-don't-want-to-go-to-heaven-if-I-can't-bring-this-recipe-along—"

He stared blankly into the camera. What was it they were cooking today?

Sam began a frantic search for the cue cards.

By the time Sam pulled onto his road and rounded the last curve toward home, he was feeling as tired as a body could feel.

It had been a full day. Up early to pick up Timothy and Ben and deliver them to Mass before heading over to the synagogue for his own morning prayers. Then back to the Country Kettle to wait for his friends; the restaurant seemed a little empty since Harry had left on his honeymoon. Not that Lori hadn't done a first-class job of keeping it running efficiently. The food was just as good. Orders came out on time. Everyone was pleasant—well, most everyone. Wendy could be a little brash at times. Today she had told Timothy to speak up or lend her his hearing aid.

Sam figured it must be a lot of extra work for Lori, who also ran the bakery and had a young family to look after. Maybe that was why she looked a little drawn lately.

Afterward, he had delivered Ben and Timothy to the television station, took Harriet home, and began his Meals on Wheels route. He was looking forward to a nap.

Sam began to steer the Plymouth up a steep incline when a chipmunk dashed out ahead. He slowed down, watching it sail across the street before he started up again. The transmission took a few seconds before it engaged, but he was thankful that at least that awful clanging noise had stopped.

As he neared the Ferrers' place, he slowed down once again to admire the neat clapboard colonial that had stood on this spot since 1769. It had a wood-shingled roof and granite base built from blocks that had been mined from the surrounding mountains. Legend said that Benedict Arnold and his men had once camped here in the back fields.

Surrounding the house was a skirt of pachysandra and a massive trumpet vine with brilliant orange flowers that wound its way around an ancient oak.

He never passed this spot without feeling a sense of hope. Throughout centuries filled with wars and blizzards and droughts and financial ups and downs, this house had remained intact. It was a good lesson, he always thought, reminding him that that which was built on a solid foundation would always stand the rigors of time.

He was about to pass the front gate when he noticed

the Ferrers' mailbox was missing, torn right off the pine stump where it had sat for all the years he'd lived in town. He felt a sick feeling in the pit of his stomach. He always had thought that his town was immune from this type of vandalism. It saddened him to think it was not.

That was the third mailbox to be vandalized this week. Maybe he should take his down and pick up his mail in town until they caught the kids who were doing this. Sam certainly couldn't afford another expense, and mailboxes were pricey to replace. He heard Arlene say so the other day at breakfast. She also had said that she and Fred wouldn't be joining them after Mass any longer. And although she didn't explain why, everyone knew. Fred's mind was sinking faster into a black abyss, making it harder for Arlene to handle her husband's needs outside the confines of their own home.

At the top of the rise, the road leveled out before beginning its descent. From there it was a short distance to Sam's home. He loved this stretch of road. A small field on the right was filled with wildflowers. Wild phlox were in bloom, and their lilting fragrance filled the air. Farther along, towering trees canopied the road and ran all the way to his front gate. He slowed. A family of deer recently had taken up residence nearby and twice had run out in front of his car.

He was almost home, just a hundred yards from his front gate, when the transmission finally gave out. He pressed the gas pedal down to the floor, but the gears would not engage. With a sinking feeling, Sam knew this was the end. He let the Plymouth coast the rest of the way and steered it onto the grass just outside his front gate.

With a heavy heart, he turned off the engine, then

went inside the house to make two phone calls—one to the Meals on Wheels director; they would need to find another volunteer; and the other to Nancy at Tri Town Auto, asking for a tow truck.

While the twins were with Sarah and her dad getting ice cream, Valerie was seated at the kitchen table, bent over a yellow legal pad, desperately trying to stretch a budget that was already stretched to the max.

A right-hand column of figures listed what she spent on monthly mortgage payments, food, gas, and utilities. There was also a line item for the small amount she religiously put away each month toward the girls' college fund. The left-hand column showed a monthly income that seldom came to more than her expenses.

She leaned her head on her hand and studied the figures. There must be a way to reduce their monthly costs. Maybe she could color her hair herself. The product ads on television made it seem easy. She would have abandoned hair coloring completely if it weren't for the gray strands which had appeared along with her twenty-fifth birthday. It seemed she was taking after her mother, who had gone completely gray by thirty.

And what if she canceled the garbage collection? She and the girls could take their trash to the dump on Saturdays. That would save $13 every quarter.

She threw down the pencil. Whom was she trying to kid? A savings of $52 a year was not going to make up the $120,000 she needed for the girls' operations.

She felt like pounding a wall. She hated being so poor; hated the constant struggle, the untenable choices—dentist or new car battery? New winter coats or water heater?

She hated the fears that woke her in the middle of the night. What if she were to get sick or break an arm and couldn't work? How long could they survive—a month? Two? But more than anything, she hated not being able to provide for her daughters' surgery. What was she going to do? Doc Hammon said that the longer the surgery was delayed, the more permanent the damage to the girls' sight.

Of course, if she had been able to afford health insurance, she wouldn't be in this fix, but then how was she supposed to come up with $675 extra a month? Not on what she made.

She suddenly felt old, tired, worn out from worry. Her thoughts naturally drifted back to Stephen. What would life have been like if they had gotten married? The girls would have had a father, and she a husband to help shoulder the burdens.

She had tried to find him again right after the twins had been born but had come to another dead end. Where had he gone? Why had he disappeared without as much as a good-bye? They had been so happy, so much in love. It had never made any sense.

All right, this wasn't getting her anywhere, she thought. Back to the problem at hand. Where *am* I going to get the $60,000 for each operation?

Doc Hammon was still hopeful they might find a free clinic equipped to handle her daughter's condition. Last week he had thought they had finally found one. A colleague of Doc's recommended a clinic in New York City that specialized in eye diseases. For a brief moment, Valerie was filled with hope.

But when they called, the clinic director informed

them that they only accepted New York City residents as patients. Doc had pleaded their case, but it had fallen on deaf ears.

She bent over the columns once again, determined to find a solution. She would not give up. She would not allow her daughters to go blind. Not as long as there was breath in her. One way or the other, her girls were going to get the medical treatment they needed, even if it meant selling a kidney.

"Al . . . pick up the phone. It's Betty at dispatch," Barbara Bromley yelled from the bottom of the stairs. She waited until she heard him pick up, then returned to the kitchen to finish making his tea.

The poor guy. In all the years they had been married, she had never seen him quite so sick. Unfortunately, he was not alone. It seemed that half the town was laid up with this bug.

She placed the cup of tea on a tray along with some saltines then headed upstairs. As she entered their bedroom, she heard Al tell Betty that he was coming in.

"You can't be serious," she said, watching him head toward the closet.

"Johnson's wife just called the station. Tom's sick with this bug. That leaves Hill. Alone. I have to go in."

"Harley, you get down off that bed," she told the German shepherd, who hopped down and hid underneath the bed before she could banish him outside. "Al Bromley, you're too sick to go into work. Get back in that bed."

"What? And leave Hill alone?"

"Hill is perfectly capable of taking care of things for a few days. Besides, what could happen? This is Dorsetville."

"With Hill? Anything can happen, and it usually does," Al said, doubling over with a stomach cramp.

"What did I tell you?" his wife said. "You're not well enough to go into work. Is Betty still on the phone?"

"I don't know. Jeez . . . when is this thing going to be over?"

She grabbed the receiver lying on the bedside table. "Betty, you're still there? Yeah, he's sick as a dog. Your husband too? I think everyone has it. I hear they've closed most of the offices in town hall? All except your department? Oh . . . I don't know. I'll ask him."

She placed her hand over the receiver. "Where are your keys to the cruiser?"

"Why?" he asked, trying to straighten up.

"Betty says Hill needs them. Al? Al . . . are you all right? Are you going to make it into the bathroom? Betty, he'll have to get back to you on that."

"Betty, this is Arlene Campbell. How are you, dear? We're just fine. No, we haven't had that nasty virus, but we've been staying home. No, not even the Country Kettle." Arlene quickly changed the subject. "The reason I'm calling is that I saw a strange car filled with teenagers driving up and down the road. Yes, that's what I thought. We certainly can't afford to lose another mailbox. Can you send someone over? Oh . . . only Deputy Hill? No one else, you sure? It's just that the last time he was here, he ran over my bed of impatiens."

———

Deputy Hill threw on the sirens, spun out of the parking lot behind the town hall, and charged out onto Main Street. It's Hill to the rescue, he thought, grabbing the handset for the police radio.

"This is Deputy Hill, reporting to base. Do you read me?"

"Yes, I *read you*, Deputy," Betty said with a sigh of exasperation. "Why are you reporting in? You just left."

"Just following proper police procedures. Letting you know that I'm in hot pursuit of the perpetrators."

"Deputy, you'd better not pursue anything too hotly. If you so much as put a scratch on that cruiser, the sheriff is going to be all over you like a bad case of hives."

"That's a 10–4. Over and out."

Women, he thought. You had to love them, always acting like a mother hen, worrying about her chicks.

He turned off Main Street and headed toward the Campbells' place, feeling the adrenaline climb along with the speedometer. The sheriff needed him to keep law and order while he was out sick, and Hill was not about to let him down. The faster he got there, the faster he would have the perpetrators in custody, he reasoned as he accelerated. Then the sheriff finally could relax. These mailbox snatchings had plagued his boss for weeks. It was Hill's duty to solve these crimes and let the sheriff get back to more important matters, like writing the employee reviews. Hill was hoping to get a raise.

He headed right past the Campbells' place. He'd stop later and take a report. It was more important to check out the area first. See if those kids were still around.

Two miles down the road, he hit pay dirt. A blue RAV like the one Arlene had described was just up ahead. Inside were four teenage boys. He edged the cruiser closer and tried to read the license plate numbers, but the plate was heavily smudged with mud. That ruled out having Betty run a check back at dispatch.

Deciding to pull them over, he threw on the lights then waited for them to slow down. From his vantage point, he had a clear view inside the car and could see a heated discussion taking place. Seconds later, the driver shouted something to his friends and floored it. The RAV's wheels began to spin, sending up a brown plume of dust. They were off.

Hill flicked on the sirens and grabbed for the police radio. "Betty, this is car 101. The perpetrators have been spotted and I'm in pursuit."

"Maybe I'd better call for backup," said Betty, sounding anxious. "I could give Sheriff Simmons over in Woodstock a call. He always had a couple of extra men on duty."

"No need. I can handle this."

"Maybe I should call anyway."

"They're headed toward the Ferrers' place. I'm right on their tail. As soon as I have them in custody, I'll call in. Meanwhile, this is car 101, out."

"Hill, the sheriff isn't going to like this."

Hill turned down the volume and concentrated on the chase.

The RAV's small chassis gave the vehicle a decided advantage along these backcountry roads and hairpin curves; by comparison, the police cruiser—several feet longer and twice as wide—lumbered along, forcing Hill to slow down at every turn.

He switched on the bullhorn and his voice began to reverberate through the countryside, startling into flight a flock of crows sitting on a nearby tree.

"This is Deputy Hill of the Dorsetville Police. You are being advised to stop and surrender the vehicle. Move over to the side of the road. I repeat, move over."

The teenage driver floored it.

"Okay, if that's the way you want this to play out," he said. No one messed with Deputy Hill and got away with it.

Up ahead lay a mile-long stretch of road that ran straight down to Sam Rosenberg's place. As soon as they reached it, Hill planned to gun the cruiser, swing it out in front of the RAV, and force it over to the side of the road. He nervously waited for the opening, adrenaline pumping like an oil geyser. Minutes later the road opened up. Hill stomped on the gas pedal. The big V-8 engine whined, accelerating easily, quickly sailing past the occupants in the RAV. He motioned them to move over. The driver nodded his head. He was caught and he knew it. Hill felt a sense of great satisfaction. Wait until he told the sheriff about this!

Then suddenly a family of deer began to cross directly in their path. Both drivers slammed on the brakes.

The RAV headed toward an open field, stalks of tall grass and pieces of blue-flowered chicory, daisy-white fleabane, and goldenrod catching in the side mirrors and windshield blades as they bounced along.

Hill fought to keep the cruiser from turning over, which meant he had to keep it on the road. Both the speed of his car and the steep decline propelled him like a launched missile. He was almost out of control.

Sam's place was directly ahead, and he could see the old Plymouth parked by the side of the road, looming larger and larger as he hurtled toward it. He stood on the brakes and smelled the combination of brake lining and rubber burning but knew there was no way to avoid Sam's car. Seconds before impact, Hill covered his face with both arms and screamed.

The cruiser hit head-on, causing the airbags to explode, driving his head back against the headrest. This was followed by a sudden jolt that jarred every bone in his body as the car lifted several feet up off the ground before slamming back down onto the ground. The police radio began to crackle.

Hill sat dazed, unable to move, as he watched a brown cloud of dirt and smoke begin to rise outside the car windows. He heard Betty's voice in the distance.

"Deputy, I've called the sheriff at home. He said to park the cruiser on the side of the road and don't move until he gets there. And, Hill . . . you might want to take a walk before he arrives. He sounded meaner than a junkyard dog."

$\mathcal{T}$WELVE

$\mathcal{S}$ome mornings it was better if one went back to bed and conceded defeat, Father James thought. Take this morning, for instance. At 6 A.M. George Benson came thundering into the rectory and dropped his toolbox onto the kitchen floor.

"I'm here to look at that hot water heater," he announced, loud enough to wake up the nursing home residents clear across the street. Father Dennis had called yesterday.

Father James closed the side windows. "Isn't it a little early to be making calls?"

"Early? I don't know about you priests, but we working men have things to get done. I've got a couple of jobs to estimate this morning and a new one starting over in Manchester this afternoon."

George looked around. "I don't suppose you have any coffee?"

"Not this early."

George bent down to pick up, his toolbox and grunted. "Things have sure gone to hel—" He remembered who he was talking to and changed course. "—to rot and ruin ever since your fired Mrs. Norris. Thought your new housekeeper would have been here by now." He was hoping for a breakfast invite.

"I did not *fire* Mrs. Norris. She retired." His stomach began to rumble. Why did this rumor continue to persist?

"That's not the word on the street."

On the street? George must be watching cop shows again. Father James decided to try explaining Mrs. Norris's absence one more time. "Taking care of the rectory had become too much for her and she decided to retire. I *did not* fire her, and I would greatly appreciate it if you would help to set the record straight *on the street.*"

"If that's your story . . . but I'm telling you, most folks aren't buying it." George thundered down the basement stairs.

Next, Father James popped into the sacristy before morning Mass to remind Father Dennis to pick up Ethel Johnson and Arlene Campbell for bingo that afternoon. The church ladies had arranged for someone to stay with Fred. Since Sam's car had been destroyed, both priests were doing double duty as chauffeurs for many of St. Cecilia's seniors.

"Is there something wrong with your hands?" Father

James asked, noticing the white cotton gloves Father Dennis was wearing.

"These? I'm wearing them to protect my hands." He saw Father James's confusion. "For the show. For close-ups," he explained.

Father James headed back to the rectory murmuring "Celebrities."

Later that morning, as he sat reviewing the week's bulletin, which was due at the printers that afternoon, a strange young woman waltzed right into the kitchen dressed in the shortest pair of shorts Father James had ever seen, and without a word or "how do you do?" starting filling the kitchen sink with hot water.

"Er . . . excuse me, miss? Who are you and what are you doing in my kitchen?"

"Didn't Viola tell you I was coming?" she asked. "No? Oh, well . . . she probably forgot. My name's Audrey. I'm Viola's younger sister."

Had he missed something? "And you're here because . . . ?"

"Odis is on a bender."

That certainly didn't make it any clearer. "I'm afraid I still don't understand."

Audrey left the water running and slid into a chair opposite the priest. "It's like this. When Odis is on a bender, he wanders."

He looked at her blankly.

"You know . . . takes off by himself. One time Viola found him in Newark."

"And what does that have to do with you being here?"

"I was told you men needing taking care of," she said with a sassy smile and a wink.

The wink unsettled him. "I appreciate you coming in for your sister, but I don't think it's necessary. We'll be fine until Odis gets over his . . . er . . . bender."

"That might be awhile."

"Excuse me?"

"You can never tell with Odis. Some of his benders last for a couple of weeks. Sometimes a couple of months." She leaned forward, her low-cut blouse revealing an ample bosom.

He carefully focused his eyes over her head.

"Viola told me about the state of things when she got here. She said, next to Odis and his beer buddies, you priests are the messiest men she's ever seen. So she asked me to keep things up. She doesn't want to start from scratch when she gets back. You know what I mean?"

"Well, yes . . . no. . . ."

Was that water he heard running? Did George forget to turn something off in the basement? And why were his feet wet? He looked down. A huge pool of water was now covering half the kitchen floor.

"Audrey! The faucet!"

Audrey shrugged, removed her strapless sandals, and held them high over her head before sauntering toward the sink as if she had all the time in the world.

"No big deal. You'll get used to it. I do that all the time."

Both Mrs. Norris and the Cliffords had arrived home on the same day, which was why the large round table in the center of the Country Kettle was flooded with photographs.

"This is me and my cousin Portance on the Lolita deck," Mrs. Norris explained.

"Who's that standing on her right? The guy looks like he's pushing ninety," Ben said, then leaned closer to study the photo. "And are we supposed to believe that jet-black hair is really his?"

"His name is Murray Crumkie, and he's a retired auto parts salesman." She hadn't particularly liked Murray, and Ben was right. That was the worse toupee she had ever seen.

Murray and Portance had met the first night out at the welcome cocktail party and were inseparable for the rest of the cruise, leaving her to spend most of her time aboard ship playing solitaire. Although she would never admit it to anyone, it had been the most miserable vacation of her life.

"I wonder if Nancy knows him," Timothy pondered.

"Knows who?" she asked.

"Murray."

"Why would she know Murray?"

"He sells auto parts. She owns a garage," Timothy said.

She snatched back her pictures and rolled her eyes.

"Where was this picture taken, Nellie?" Harriet asked, holding up a photo of the newlyweds in front of a white beach and swaying palm trees.

"Which picture?" Nellie adjusted her reading glasses. "Oh, that was just outside our room at the Radisson. We could see the entire ocean from our balcony."

"Not the *entire* ocean, dear," Harry teased, giving his wife a hug.

Nellie leaned against him and blushed. "Well . . . not the entire ocean, but our portion of it anyway."

"I tell you folks that if I had the money I'd retire there," he said as the photo was passed around. "Never saw anything so beautiful. And the food . . ."

". . . was wonderful," Nellie finished. "I'm sure we both put on ten pounds. How was the food on your cruise, Mrs. Norris?"

"Cholesterol rich," she said with distaste. "Cream sauces, deep-fried shrimp, and lobster. Even the vegetables were smothered in butter or sour cream. It's a wonder people survive any of those cruises with their arteries intact."

"Well, I hope you found something you liked," Nellie said.

"Steamed vegetables and fresh fruit were pretty decent."

"And boring," Timothy mumbled.

"Hey! The honeymooners are back!" Father James shouted as he bounded through the front door. Sam lagged behind. "Now things will get back to normal around here."

Father James greeted Harry with a bear hug. "Missed you, old buddy."

"You missed my home fries," Harry joked.

"And, Nellie . . . you look wonderful. Apparently salt air, sandy beaches, and marriage agree with you." He walked over and gave her kiss on the cheek.

"It was a wonderful honeymoon, Father. In fact, Harry and I have decided that we're going back every year for our anniversary."

"I think that's a wonderful plan. And how was your vacation, Mrs. Norris?" he asked, pulling up a chair alongside her. "Sam, come sit here. There's plenty of room."

"Restful," Mrs. Norris said, collecting her photographs. "It was nice to have someone wait on me for a change."

The innuendo was not lost on Father James. "I'm sure it was. I'm glad you had a nice time and got some well-deserved rest."

Wendy stopped to pour him a cup of coffee without asking.

"I heard you hired Viola Tunis to replace me," his former housekeeper said. "Quite an interesting choice for a housekeeper."

He was not about to let her know that Viola had been his *only* choice. "She does a good job," he said in defense of his decision, not adding "when she shows up."

"I've known Viola since grammar school," Mrs. Norris offered. "I hope she has better success as a housekeeper than she's had in love. She's never been very bright when it came to choosing men. Too bad Charlie's mother put the kibosh on their romance. At least with him she could have stood a chance."

"Her and Charlie?" he asked. Well, that explained the cold reception the mailman had received.

She nodded. "That's before you came here, of course. They dated all through high school, but when he was getting ready for college, his mother put a stop to it. Said some pretty unkind things to Viola, and that was the end of that.

"So, on the rebound, she marries the first bum who comes along. Some guy from Waterbury she met in a bar. He wasn't much different from Odis. She used to chase him around the state too, trying to keep him out of trouble.

"Then, out of the blue, he sobers up and gets a job,

hauling freight. He stays sober for nearly a year, but then one day he goes off the wagon and gets behind the wheel of a sixteen-wheeler."

Mrs. Norris made certain everyone else was engaged in conversation before adding "He's the one who was driving the rig that killed Harriet's daughter-in-law and granddaughter."

Father James grew pensive. How strange and interwoven our lives could sometimes be.

"But then Viola goes right off and marries another drunk," she added. "Some people never learn. And now I hear that her sister, Audrey, is taking her place at the rectory while she's chasing Odis all over the state."

"Let's just say that she's trying," Father James replied.

Mrs. Norris took a sip of coffee, then whispered, "Be careful around that one. Audrey will try to seduce anything in pants."

"So what happened this morning down at State Farm?" Timothy finally asked Sam.

Father James had driven him over to the insurance office to file a claim.

"They offered book value," Sam replied.

Those around the table grew quiet. An awkward pause followed.

Finally Ben asked the question that was on everyone's mind. "So, how much is book value?"

Sam sighed. "Three hundred dollars."

Timothy leaned over to Ben and whispered, "I guess we'd both better learn how to ride bikes."

———

After Father James dropped Sam, Ben, and Timothy over at the cable station, he went to see Doc Hammon. The doctor had paused after Mass on Sunday and asked him to drop by his office. Today seemed as good a day as any.

"Come in and close the door, Jim," the doctor said. "You've come at a perfect time. I'm finished for the day. Take a seat. Can I get you anything?"

"No thanks, Doc. I just came from the Country Kettle."

"Let me guess. Harry just got back, so you had a plate of home fries and a pot of coffee."

"Two plates and maybe a little more than a pot," Father James confessed, smiling a devilish grin.

Doc massaged the area over his left eye. He was getting one of his headaches, something that happened lately more often than he liked. His practice was getting too large. He needed to hire an assistant.

"You wanted to talk with me?" Father James prompted.

"Yes, I have two small patients who need our help."

"What can I do?" he asked without hesitation.

"I take it you know the Kilbourne twins?"

He nodded.

"Both of them have developed a serious eye condition. Without immediate surgery, the girls will go blind."

"Dear Lord!"

Doc continued. "The problem is . . . Valerie hasn't any medical coverage, and hospitals and surgeons won't take them on as patients without it."

"Even when the girls have something as serious as this?" Father James asked in disbelief. What happened to compassion?

"Even then."

Father James sat further back in his chair. "How much will an operation like that cost?"

"Around sixty thousand . . ."

Father began to whistle.

". . . each."

"Good Lord. Where does that leave Valerie and the twins?"

"Pretty much out in the cold, or deeply in debt for the rest of her life—that is, if a bank would even loan her the money." Doc leaned back in his chair. "Do you know Sirius and Judy Gaithwait?"

"Sure, they attend St. Bartholomew's. Sirius grew up in that parish."

"Their little boy, Joey, was born with a defective heart valve. Highly treatable but expensive. The Gaithwaits didn't have health insurance either, so it was the same scenario. The surgeon and the hospital refused to operate until they saw the cash. They wanted seventy-five thousand dollars up front."

If only people world learn to ask for help, he pondered, the folks in Dorsetville would have gladly pitched in. "Mind if I ask how they managed?"

"Mortgaged their home to the hilt," Doc told him. "Judy was just in the other day with a severe case of poison ivy. I hadn't seen her for a while, so I asked where she's been hiding. She said they had to stop having yearly exams and visited a doctor only when absolutely necessary. They're still trying to pay off the mortgage and save for Joey's college. It's not likely they will ever get out from under that mountain of debt."

I must give them a call, Father James thought.

The buzzer sounded.

"Excuse me, Jim. Yes, Shirley?"

"Doc, it's Mrs. Gallagher," she said over the intercom. "The Gallagher boys have another rash. She wants to know if you would stop by on your way home."

"Tell her I'll stop over in about an hour. Oh, and Shirley, ask her to check their room for chocolate wrappers. That's usually the cause."

Father James stood up. "I'd better be going. Thanks for letting me in on this. Our parish will help Valerie and the girls anyway we can."

"There might be a *personal* way you could help."

"Anything I can do, you know I will."

Doc leaned forward. "There's a free clinic in New York City, one of the few that is equipped to handle the girls' problem. Unfortunately, they will only take city residents. Doesn't your friend Monsignor Casio live there?"

"Yes, he's the pastor at St. Timothy's."

"Think he might be able to pull a few strings?"

"I don't know, but I'll give him a call."

"Make it today, Jim. These girls don't have much time."

It was a little after noon and Stephen could hear the muffled strains of Audrey's soap opera from downstairs. Chester had sent the crew home earlier. He had the rest of the day off. The retirement home's attic had turned into an oven, which even three mammoth exhaust fans borrowed from the fire department couldn't relieve. The wall thermometer continued to register 105 degrees.

Six crew members, George's assistant, and an electrician had worked through most of the morning as the temperature baked them like so many loaves of bread. By ten o'clock, tempers flared and men became careless. One of the guys had come close to cutting off his thumb with a skill saw. Then Chester arrived, took one look around, and sent everyone packing.

"Go home. If you guys stay here much longer, someone's going to die of heatstroke."

Stephen was glad for the extra time to spend working on his drawings even if it meant a reduced paycheck this week. He had hoped to buy some new tubes of paint, but now it would have to wait. The cost of art supplies still amazed him. Eight years ago, he could have purchased a tube of crimson red for under ten bucks. Now it cost $48.

The small air conditioner he had bought at Stone's Hardware and stuck in the back window was struggling hard to keep up with the soaring temperature outside. Maybe he should trek down to the river for a swim. Come back later when things cooled down. Barry Hornibrook had carved out a nice little town beach by his hotel complex. But Stephen was still uncomfortable taking his shirt off in public. His chest bore several ugly scars, souvenirs from his stint in the pen.

Instead, he took a cold shower and sat around in his shorts. He hated being idle. It gave him too much time to think, especially about Valerie. So far their paths hadn't collided, for which he was grateful. He still didn't know what he would say when they met. But he knew it was just a matter of time. This was a small town.

He must have fallen asleep on the cot he had found when clearing out the attic. When he awoke, the sun had shifted to the back side of the house, making the room almost bearable.

He grabbed a glass of cold tap water from the bathroom downstairs, and glanced around the studio at the drawings that lined every bit of wall space. Since he had started drawing again, he hadn't been able to stop.

To the untrained eye, many might have appeared incomplete, in need of some final touches. But these were never intended to be finished pieces; they were studies Stephen had done to help hone his rusty skills.

Along one lower portion of a wall, he had tacked several sketches of the town's storefronts. Working with architectural subjects helped him to sharpen his use of perspective, the method through which artists achieved the sense of dimension.

Included in this category were renderings of the Country Kettle, Stone's Hardware, and the old Palace Theater. He had also drawn the Congregational Church but had abandoned his effort to sketch St. Cecilia's after several hours' worth of revisions. He was doubtful if even Michelangelo himself could make that strange, misshapen church come to life.

But for the most part, Dorsetville had provided a wide array of interesting subjects. One of his favorite trips had been inspired by Father Keene, who told him, "There's a spot in the woods just behind Platt's farm. It lets you get a glimpse of what God sees when He looks down from heaven."

Father Keene's description sounded too good to be missed, so one sunny Saturday afternoon, Stephen borrowed a bike from one of the nuns across the street and set out to follow the priest's rather vague instructions.

"Turn off where the Bee Brook runs underneath the road, then head up toward the big gray barn until you see the gnarled oak . . ."

Fortunately, Father Keene hadn't mentioned the herd of cows that he would have to navigate around, or the horseflies that would stick to him like glue for the better part of the climb up the steep mountain ridge. If he had, Stephen might have skipped the outing. He hated flies, and the closest he had ever come to a cow was a New York strip.

But when the woods gave way to a small meadow and he spied the church steeples rising through the trees in the distance, he understood Father Keene's love for this secret place. With little effort, Stephen filled two entire sketch pads.

Landscapes, however, covered only a small portion of the walls. Most of the space was devoted to portraits, his first love.

Stephen felt that a person's entire life could be found written across their face. Laugh lines, jowls, sagging eyelids all told a story, and he had learned to read them well. Gallery owners and art critics would someday talk about the effortless sense of clarity he brought to his paintings that allowed viewers to experience more than just color, shape, or design. His mastery allowed them to glimpse the subject's soul.

One such portrait showed Fred and Arlene Campbell at a church picnic. Seated behind them were a young mother and a two-year-old son. Stephen used the juxtaposition of the subjects to portray the circle of life. The young mother nourishing the child. The older wife nourishing the man who appeared to Stephen to be slowly reverting back to a child. It was a powerful piece.

He had also captured Lori and Bob Peterson in pen and ink at the same function. The scene showed the young couple walking past a mother pushing a baby carriage. Lori's hand rested protectively on her stomach as she gazed at the infant.

But not all of his work was meant to be ponderous. Stephen also liked to exhibit a playful sense of humor, like the painting of Sheriff Bromley as he viewed the police cruiser his deputy had totaled being carted away to the salvage yard. It made Stephen laugh every time he looked at it.

A storm was brewing over in the west. The room grew suddenly dark, and he switched on a table lamp. Resting alongside was his sketchbook. Valerie's face gazed back at him. She had become the first image he saw upon rising each morning, and his last before slipping off to sleep. How much longer could he go on hiding from her? It was time he either confronted her or packed up his belongings and went back to New York.

"Valerie," he whispered. "If only I knew for certain that you would believe me."

THIRTEEN

A summer's storm was gathering; the kind that shook the valley with thunder and slashed the skies with spears of lightning. Its precursor, a damp, sharp wind, had begun its course down the mountain, winding its way throughout Dorsetville. Women scurried to pull in lines of wash that snapped in the stiff breeze like canvas sails on a ship.

All along Main Street, business owners hustled outside. Harry was the first to hit the sidewalk with an awning pole in hand. With one eye to the clouds gathering above the town's main thoroughfare and another to the awning, he began to wind back the canvas briskly. A few summers ago a similar storm had galloped in one afternoon and taken the last one in its wake.

Three doors down, the sisters at Second Hand Rose rolled in the two racks of summer skirts. The sales sign that read "This week only . . . two for $9.99" blew off in a sharp gust later to be discovered, wet and sodden, by Roger Martin as he jogged up the steps to the town hall.

Mr. Yokohama and his family cowered behind the bamboo shade to his Japanese restaurant, occasionally peeking out to watch Gus Dinova haul several large tarps outside with the help of two stocky teenage boys. Just as Gus tied the last cord to the base of the large fruit bin, the heavens opened. Within minutes the sidewalks were drenched, sending the few shoppers who had ignored the ominous cloud cover scurrying to safety.

Those inside St. Cecilia's, however, were mostly unaware of the weather change. The church's thick stone walls kept the sound of the pounding rain outside and the air conditioner working overtime to keep pace with the rising humidity masked the rumbling of thunder.

At the front of the church knelt Harriet and Ethel, who had come to storm the gates of heaven on Sam's behalf.

Ethel leaned over and whispered into Harriet's ear, "Are you sure it's proper to pray for a car?"

Harriet held tightly to her rosary and made the sign of the cross before answering. "When the multitudes needed to be fed, Jesus gave them food. When the disciples needed to pay their taxes, He provided a coin. In God's eyes, a need is a need."

Lori sat quietly, staring at the altar, her very soul filled with torment. She was angry with God, yet where else could she go for comfort? He alone held the answers she sought.

No matter how much Father James or her husband tried to console her, she still couldn't bear to think of the lifetime of pain her unborn child—a son, the tests had revealed—would have to endure. Wouldn't it be better if he had never been conceived?

And in the darkest moments of her despair, in the silent, secret recesses of her innermost thoughts, she contemplated abortion. She always had been against it, had even helped gather petitions for *Roe v. Roe* to be repealed. She felt that God's word was quite explicit when it said *I knew you from your mother's womb.* In God's mind, a soul, a life, was formed the moment of conception. Abortion was murder, pure and simple. But in this case, wasn't it more humane? How could a mother consign her child to a lifetime spent in a crib or, worse, in an institution? How could God? Where was the humanity in that?

Where was God in all of this? What was His purpose? Why would He allow her innocent baby to suffer? If only she could understand, she might come to terms with her child's infirmity, find the courage to go on.

She prayed day and night for insight, for illumination. Why, why, why? echoed through her mind even though she knew that God did not owe her an explanation. As Father James often said, we are but servants; God is sovereign.

She knew she had no right to ask God to explain. He needn't be accountable to her, but she could not stop asking in the hope that He would give her the glimmer of insight she needed in order to find her way through this dark valley of fear and dread.

She removed a missalette from the back of the pew

and turned to the day's reading. It was the story of a blind man whom Jesus healed and His disciples' response. His followers had sought to understand the reason behind the man's infirmity.

"Rabbi, who sinned, this man or his parents that he was born blind?
"Neither this man nor his parents sinned," Jesus said, "but this happened so that the work of God might be displayed in his life."

She closed the book and looked across the sanctuary, lost in thought. It gave her courage to think that even the apostles had asked Jesus to explain why some are born to suffer.

She read the text again.

Jesus stated that the man's blindness was to showcase God's glory. Without the infirmity, there was no reason for the miracle, a miracle that would give people hope and belief in God's infinite compassion down through the millennium.

Slowly her doubts and fears began to give way to insight.

What if God planned someday to use her baby's handicap to bring others to a stronger place of faith? Was there a more precious gift anyone could give the world?

It wasn't that long ago that Lori had sat in this same pew and prayed that God would send her hope, hope that a bone marrow donor match would be found in time to save her husband. And God had answered that prayer in the most miraculous way, restoring her faith, allowing her to appropriate the miracle that was needed.

Was it possible that through her child's infirmities,

others would receive a similar hope? Did this mean that God someday might wish to heal her son by way of an instantaneous healing or through a medical discovery that would restore him to health? Anything was possible with God, wasn't it?

Suddenly she was reminded of a sermon Father Keene once had preached. He said that all adversity contained seeds of greatness and that every trial, every heartache, every disappointment or loss, when planted in the fertile soil of God's love, possessed the ability to grow into mountain-moving faith. And through the witness of that faith, others received hope.

Father Keene had said, "We are all born to do our Father's work here on earth, which is to share our faith in Jesus Christ. We do this through the witness of our faith and its power to overcome the world.

"So, when you experience any of life's trials, don't run from them," Father Keene had admonished. "Instead, stand firm and face it squarely, asking 'How have you come to enrich me?'"

Lori pondered these things in her heart, and slowly a spiritual shift began to take place in her soul. Her child was not a victim, a helpless cripple. He was an instrument of God's grace.

A new confidence began to grow. A conviction that somehow God would use this child to enrich His world.

Valerie lowered the riser and knelt to pray. A conversation she had just overheard at the Country Kettle deserved a special thank-you.

Valerie had been seated in a back booth, hidden behind the classified section of the *Dorsetville Gazette* as she searched for a part-time second job, when she happened to overhear Betty Olsen and her sister-in-law, Shirley, in the next booth.

"Did you hear about the Kilbourne girls?" Betty asked.

"Yes, isn't it a shame? Their poor mother must be out of her mind with worry. Imagine—it will cost tens of thousands of dollars for the children's operations."

"My Joe says he's going to talk to his buddies over at the Rotary. Take up a collection," Shirley said.

"And I was wondering if some of us could get together and run a raffle. I know the quilters will donate one of their quilts."

Valerie had been so overcome with gratitude that she could no longer see the newsprint through her tears.

Now, seated at the back of the sanctuary, Valerie bowed her head and prayed.

Dear Father,

I just wanted to stop by and say thanks. Thanks for choosing me to be the mother of my girls. Thanks for my job. And thanks for leading me to this special little town filled with such good friends.

She paused, wondering if it might be improper to attach a request along with a prayer of thanksgiving.

And if it's in the cards, someday would you let me find a wonderful father for my girls? Sometimes it's awful tough going it alone.

Father James often visited the sanctuary in the afternoon. A special kind of quiet filled the church this time of day.

Unlike the early morning, when the atmosphere held a hint of anticipation as the day stretched ahead filled with challenges and a sense of wonderment prevailed—how would God meet a need?—in the afternoons the church exuded a sense of serenity.

Father James slid silently into a back pew that was partially obscured by a large column, affording him some privacy. This was his time to reconnect with God, to lift up his concerns, his failings, and to receive a fresh in-filling of His grace. He called it "filling up the well." It was also the time that he interceded on behalf of the many friends, parishioners, and good people he knew who needed God's special attention, such as the Campbells.

Yesterday he had driven the couple home after the dentist. It was becoming more and more apparent that Fred's growing dependence on Arlene was taking its toll. He tried to offer his assistance, but Arlene insisted that she was quite capable of handling things herself. There was nothing left that he could say. Instead, he must wait to be asked for help.

Next, he prayed for Lori seated a few aisles over. She was having such a hard time coming to terms with her child's condition. He prayed that God would offer her His special peace.

Valerie Kilbourne sat a few aisles behind her. Father James knew the burden this young single mother was carrying, and he beseeched the Lord on her behalf. Afterward, he planned to pull her aside and let her know that she was not alone. The entire community was pulling for her. He had also phoned the Gaithwaits to let them know they, too, were not alone, their neighbors were here to help.

He had also found time to place a call to Monsignor Casio, as Doc Hammon had requested. His old friend was more than willing to lend a hand.

"It might take time, Jim," Monsignor had stated. "I'll need to find the right city bureaucrat who can override the clinic's policies."

Father James told him that time was the one thing the girls didn't have.

The soft sound of the women praying the rosary at the front of the church made him think of Sam, no doubt the subject of their prayers. They were not alone in their petitions. It seemed most of Dorsetville was praying right along with them.

It wasn't hard to envision Sam plying the back roads in his gold Plymouth Duster as he delivered noontime meals and chauffeured his friends. In fact, Father James truly hadn't realized just how much people depended upon Sam until now.

Besides the meals program and driving the St. Cecilia's crowd to and from church, Sam apparently took people to Mercy Hospital for tests when they needed a ride; volunteered twice a week as head cashier for the hospital cafeteria; worked with the Salvation Army with their ongoing clothes drive; helped to distribute food boxes for the local food bank; and had on more than one occasion fetched an overdue library book when someone couldn't get into town.

Father James closed his eyes and in the silence of his shepherd's heart laid the burdens of his people at the foot of the cross, placing special emphasis on the Kilbourne girls' need of an operation, Lori's unborn child, and Sam's need of a new car.

"Father, are you busy? I have your church bulletins, hot off the press," Valerie said, stepping inside the rectory.

"Come in. I was just going to make a sandwich. Would you like one?" Father James offered.

"No, I'm not that hungry." She hesitated, uncertain. "Besides, I can only stay a minute. Sister Claire is watching the girls."

"How are they? I've been praying up a storm on their behalf," he assured her.

She smiled. "I'm glad to hear it. I've been praying quite a bit myself. In fact, I've been talking to God a lot lately."

He smiled. "That's good to hear. God never turns a deaf ear to a mother's petition."

She settled into a kitchen chair. "You know, before I moved here, I must confess that I never *really* believed in God. I had a hope that He existed, but no real belief."

Father took a loaf of bread out of the bread bin. "And now you do?"

She nodded.

"What changed your mind?"

"The people who live here."

Something inside her was different, Valerie thought, stepping onto the rectory's front porch and into the sunlight. She felt lighter, as if the heavy burden she had been under for weeks had suddenly lifted. It made no sense. The problems confronting her daughters still existed, yet it was as if this time her prayers had connected, forging a new certainty that God had heard her petitions; everything was going to be all right, somehow He would work it out. She needed only to trust and wait patiently for His promise to appear.

These thoughts, however, were in direct contrast to her rational mind, which had already unleashed a flood of arguments before the seeds of faith could take root and grow.

The money needed for the operations just doesn't fall from the sky. . . . Time is running out. . . . You can't afford to wait on God for an answer. . . .

For just a moment, she faltered as the first tremors of doubt threatened to displace this newly sown faith. It did seem rather irresponsible. How could she just wait and do nothing? The doctors said that every day the girls' surgery was delayed, more of their eyesight would be lost.

A cloud slipped over the sun, shading the pathway in partial darkness.

"O Lord, I want to believe. Please help my unbelief," she prayed, echoing a petitioner of Jesus some two thousand years ago.

She hurried the rest of the way down the flagstone path, as if she could somehow outdistance the doubts that nipped at her heels. Head bent, intent only on her footsteps, she increased her speed while trying to coax back the assurance of God's love she had felt only seconds ago.

Suddenly a figure loomed in front of her. There was no time to get out of the way. With a bone-crunching thud, she plowed straight into a man whose arms were filled with cartons of painting supplies.

"Ouch!" she screamed as she tumbled onto the flagstones, skinning a knee.

"I'm so sorry, miss. I didn't see you," the man explained. "Are you all right?"

"No, I'm not," she snapped. Why hadn't he watched were he was going?

The sun suddenly appeared, creating a sharp glare. Valerie shielded her eyes with a hand in order to see him more clearly. He bent to offer assistance.

"Stephen?" she asked incredulously.

Later that week, the first heat wave of summer idled into Dorsetville, immobilizing its citizens who, as New Englanders, were unaccustomed to such tropical temperatures.

Nights seemed the worst as the humidity sealed the valley like a cork in a bottle. Youngsters exchanged their soft down mattresses for sleeping bags out under the stars. Grown-ups who were fortunate enough to have summer porches set up their beds in the screened-in area. Others consigned themselves to restless nights under the full power of one of Mark Stone's fans; still, sleep was mostly elusive.

But the hot, clammy temperatures weren't the only thing keeping a lot of Dorsetville citizens awake this night. The citizens of this small country town had a lot on their minds.

Sam lay awake wondering how he was going to get the large, white-paneled van Nancy had loaned him to deliver the Meals on Wheels up Mrs. Gildersleeve's steep, twisting driveway without landing in a ditch.

———

Sheriff Bromley was thinking about Hill's annual review, wondering how he could get him transferred, preferably to another state.

Lori fanned herself with the new *Parenting* magazine as she looked at the nursery walls, wondering if the lime green she had originally chosen wasn't a mite too bright and what the cause of the strange pain she sometimes felt in the lower portion of her groin was.

George Benson was soaking his feet in a bucket of ice water as he studied the two replies he had received from his personal ad. Neither one seemed very promising, Should he run it again? he wondered. And should he use the bottle of black hair dye he had bought at the pharmacy over in Woodstock? The girl had said it was guaranteed to take ten years off his age, which he figured would be a good thing, should he ever get a reply that was worth responding to.

Emily Curtis was trying not to disturb her husband as she tossed and turned in search of a comfortable place. They really did need to get an air conditioner. She had seen one advertised over at the new Wal-Mart by Hartford for $99, which was definitely within their budget. But she knew that her husband would never approve the purchase.

"If it can be bought in Dorsetville, then that's where we should buy it," he always said.

Of course, he was right, but the one at Stone's Hardware cost $285, which was definitely *not* in their budget.

The digital clock on the nightstand read 1:50 P.M. She was never going to get any sleep at this rate. She turned over again to face the back of her husband's pajama top.

Of all the nights to suffer from insomnia, she sighed. *The Fat Friar* aired tomorrow, which meant she had to get up early and prepare three versions of everything that was to be featured on the show, including three recipes of the Last Rites Chili.

Next, her thoughts drifted onto new menu ideas. She and Father Dennis had been discussing a seafood soufflé that they planned to feature on an upcoming show. But neither could decide on an accompanying sauce. Father Dennis was leaning toward a wine sauce, which she felt was used so often that it had become boring; she thought a cream sauce would be nice. Father Dennis, however, felt it would be too heavy.

She had just begun to sink into a wonderful state of drowsiness when a sudden thought whizzed straight like an arrow through her mind, returning her to full consciousness.

Why, that was it! The recipe for the sauce that she and Father Dennis had been looking for. It was simple yet elegant, understated but sensational. It was truly inspired.

Before it could fly away, she went in search of a pen and pad, careful not to disturb the sleeping reverend.

Nancy Hawkins also had been jarred awake by a truly inspired idea. She had figured out how to help Sam.

It would take some time and manpower, but she was certain she could get volunteers to help. As far as materials, what she didn't have in the shop, she'd get donated. She'd hand Father James that job. No one in town could turn him down.

She sat up in bed, turned on the light, and tried to pull out her nightstand drawer in search of some paper. It stuck. She gave it a hard yank and it came crashing to the floor. She swore under her breath, got out of bed, and began to dump the scattered contents back inside. Bottles of old nail polish clattered, pens banged against the wood, an old set of keys crashed.

Meanwhile, her husband blissfully slept on. Nancy always said, "Don could sleep through an atomic blast."

Over at the rectory, Father Dennis also was having a restless night. From 1 A.M. to 2 A.M. he read. From 2 A.M. to 3 A.M. he plumped pillows and pulled the bedsheet up and down. By 3:15 A.M. he conceded defeat and went in search of a cool drink and a piece of chocolate.

He felt his way down the back staircase, trying not to disturb Father James. The pastor was still a little miffed at him for having left Arlene Campbell stranded at the hair salon. Father Dennis really couldn't fault him for being angry. After all, he had promised to be there at exactly three o'clock.

But then he and Emily had gotten into a discussion on menu suggestions for several upcoming shows and had hit upon an idea for a seafood soufflé, but neither could decide on the sauce to accompany it. Before he knew it, it was four-thirty and he was in big trouble.

Father James had been waiting for him when he arrived back at the rectory. Wearing a scowl that made the young cleric's stomach sink right to his toes, Father James called him into his study. Father Dennis had stepped over the line.

"When you asked to do this show, I made it perfectly clear that our parishioners and their needs must always come first," he said between clenched teeth. "You agreed. You also agreed to pick up Arlene Campbell at the hairdresser's two hours ago. Now, because of your ir-responsibility, Fred was left alone for nearly an hour. Anne Rivers was watching him, but she had to leave at three-fifteen to meet her kids at the bus stop. Arlene tried to call, but you had turned off your cell phone—"

"Carl doesn't like us to get calls at the studio," he tried to explain, but even to his ears it sounded rather lame.

"Then you had better find another way to have emergency calls transferred while you're there."

"I'm sorry, Father James. I just lost track of time."

"I'm not the one you should be asking for forgive-ness."

Father Dennis hung his head. "I know. I'll call Arlene and apologize."

"Yes, you should. She was nearly frantic with worry by the time I got there. But she wasn't the one I was re-ferring to."

He tried to think who else he might have offended.

"You need to beg the Lord's forgiveness," Father James reminded him. "This is His flock which He has entrusted into your care and you've really let Him down today."

Father Dennis left his office feeling like pond scum.

Father James was right. Maybe he had become too preoccupied with the show, he thought, turning on the kitchen light and pouring himself a glass of iced tea. Maybe he should quit. After all, his first duty was that of a priest. Still, he did enjoy the excitement, the fun of being in front of a camera. He even enjoyed the fan mail. It was nice to know that others thought of you so highly.

He grabbed a handful of Oreos and sat down at the table, then began to sift through the pile of mail. Four fan letters and an *Epicurean Classics* magazine. As a form of penance, he put the letters aside although he longed to read them and began to leaf through the magazine.

A full-page ad on page 58 announcing an upcoming cooking contest drew his full attention. It was being sponsored by the magazine, and finalists would be invited to the celebrated cooking school on the Hudson River for a cook-off. A panel of celebrity chefs would determine the winner.

Sipping his iced tea, he read along until he reached the list of prizes. Aga stove, deep-freeze refrigerator, Chrysler Town and Country minivan. He nearly choked. A minivan? A vehicle? It was just what Sam needed and what the entire town had been praying for!

If he could win the contest, Sam would get a new car, Father James would see the importance of him continuing the show, and he would still get fan mail!

But what recipe should he enter? Which one stood the best chance of winning?

The first rays of morning sunlight had just begun to filter through the kitchen window when Father Dennis made his decision. He would enter a seafood soufflé. Now all he had to do was find the perfect sauce.

Mrs. Norris watched a light in the rectory go on while waiting for the teakettle to steam. Who was up at this hour? she wondered. She pulled the curtain aside and spied a large shadow pass the kitchen window. Father Dennis. Probably raiding the refrigerator again.

She let the curtain fall back into place and went back to making her cup of tea, bypassing the boxes of herbal choices for a can of Earl Grey. Caffeine was bound to keep her awake for the next three days, but what did she care? It wasn't as if she needed eight hours of sleep anymore. She no longer had to get up for work.

As much as she hated to admit it, she had come to despise retirement. She missed the activity next door, the sense of purpose her job had given her. All she seemed to do now was to wander aimlessly about. She shopped, she went to lunch and played canasta, and that was about it.

There was no sense in going back to bed. The sun would be up soon. She would have a cup of tea and piece of whole-wheat toast, then start right in on making her blueberry preserves. There was a basketful of blueberries on the back porch that she picked yesterday over at March Farms. They wouldn't last forever.

Mrs. Norris planned on putting up three dozen. A dozen for her and two dozen for the church's fall Pumpkin Festival. They always sold out. In fact, some folks called the night before just to reserve a jar. That's because her preserves tasted as they ought. Not like the store-bought stuff that tasted like thickened fruit juice.

She walked into the living room, her slippers flip-flopping on the polished wooden floors. Now, where did she leave the television remote? She found it wedged between the sofa cushions. Several quick surfs around the channels proved her theory that idiots and teenagers had taken over television programming. She switched it off, picked up the copy of the *Dorsetville Gazette* lying on the coffee table, and read the front page.

Seemed Roger had announced he was running for mayor again. So what else was new? And the Salvation Army was having another revival series on the green. She hoped they were a little quieter this time. Last revival, some dang idiot kept blowing a trumpet every time someone said "Praise the Lord." She was glad she was a Catholic. It was a much quieter religion.

She paused at the personals.

> *DWM fifties and fit. Still has his own hair. Looking for a mature, independent woman. Must like Elvis Presley movies.*

Viva Las Vegas happened to be one of her favorites. She sipped her cup of tea. Maybe she should answer one of these personals. A male companion might make retirement a whole lot more appealing.

She read through the entire male section. It was slim pickings. The man who liked Elvis Presley movies seemed the most interesting.

The full morning's sun had filtered through the sheer curtains. She switched off the lamp and wondered how someone went about answering one of these things.

Valerie never got to sleep. Her meeting with Stephen played again and again and again in her mind.

After the immediate shock had worn off, she was filled with an almost uncontrollable sense of rage. She scrambled to her feet and let fly all those years of suppressed anger.

"What happened to you? I waited and waited. You disappeared without a word of explanation."

Stephen just stared, uncertain how to begin.

"Well?" He owed her an explanation.

"I got an offer that I really couldn't refuse." That was the dumbest thing I have ever said, he thought. She deserved something more than a line from the *Godfather*.

"And so you just left. No word. No good-bye." Hot tears slid down her cheeks. "How could you just leave like that? I spent weeks trying to find you. No one seemed to know what happened to you. I was crazy with worry and kept thinking that you must have been in some terrible accident, lying in a hospital at death's door. It was the only reasonable explanation I could find for you not coming back."

He took her arm. "I'm so sorry if I hurt—"

"*If? If* you hurt me?" She snatched her arm free. "Don't you know how much pain I was in after you disappeared? You said that you loved me and that we would always be together. You asked me to marry you after graduation. You promised we would always be together. Happily ever after, remember? I loved you, Stephen, with all my heart and soul. How could you just leave without a word?"

His eyes filled with tears. He shook his head, thrusting his hands into his pants pocket in resignation. "I'm sorry. I should have told you the truth from the beginning. If you'll give me a moment, I'll try to explain."

"You needn't bother, Stephen," she said, dusting off her skirt. "I think that eight years is a little too late to be explaining things."

She raced into the street unmindful of George Benson's van. He had to run up onto the sidewalk to keep from hitting her.

"Are you nuts, lady? Trying to get yourself killed?" George screamed.

She raced home, even forgetting to pick up the girls from Sister Claire's. The nun would call to remind her later. Her hands shook so badly, she could hardly turn the knob to the front door. Once inside, she locked herself in and finally let the tears, the hurt, and the anger flow freely.

The phone had repeatedly rung that night until finally she took it off the hook. She never wanted to speak to him again.

FOURTEEN

"Audrey, will you come in here?" Father James called from his study. Audrey was dusting outside in the hall, dressed in her ubiquitous short shorts with a bikini top that left little to the imagination.

"Yeah?"

"Can you tell me why my pencil sharpener is full of this pink goop?"

She sauntered into the room then bent over to study his sharpener, her ample breasts spilling onto his desk. He leaned as far back in his chair as he could without breaking through the dining room wall.

"That stuff?" she asked. "It's lip liner."

Why was he always befuddled whenever he dealt with her? "What's lip liner doing in my pencil sharpener?"

"I had to sharpen it somewhere. You can't get a proper outline without a sharp point."

Lord, give me an extra helping of patience. "When is your sister returning?"

"Hard to say." She slithered into the chair opposite his desk and got comfortable. "Yesterday Viola found Odis over in Danbury. That's where a bunch of his old army buddies live," she explained. "He was tanked to the gills."

"Maybe it's time that Father Dennis and I started to look for another housekeeper. Perhaps the timing of this job is all wrong for Viola, you know, with the added pressure of keeping tabs on Odis and all."

Audrey shrugged her shoulders, which did some amazing things to the part of her anatomy encased in the very tiny top. Father James studied the ceiling.

"It's okay with me," she said. "But it's going to make it really hard on Viola. Last time he went on a binge, he tore right through their savings in about two weeks."

He sighed. As much as he would prefer a house-keeper who actually showed up everyday and didn't send her scantily clad sister in her place, Father James thought it best to practice the Christian charity he so often preached.

"All right. Maybe we can wait another week or two and see if your sister's life settles down. But in the interim, I think it best if you . . . er . . . not feel it necessary to take her place."

Why was he sweating?

"If I leave, Viola will quit."

He locked onto her face. "Why?" His eyes involuntarily slid down to her breasts. He forced them back to the ceiling.

"Pride. As long as I'm working in her place, Viola feels she's keeping up with her obligations. If you let me go, she'll see you holding this job open for her as a form of charity, and Viola doesn't take charity."

"I see." He was befuddled again.

Nellie finished reading her newest manuscript, *The-I-Don't-Know-Whos*, to the Kilbourne girls for the third time.

"Read it again," they pleaded. The girls seemed enthralled with the tale of creatures that could be seen only by children and who were responsible for stealing one sock out of every pair.

"Can we draw the pictures for your book?" Linda asked hopefully.

"Illustrate it? Why, sure you can," she told the girls as the seed of an idea was born. Why hadn't she thought about this before? Their mother was a talented children's artist. The beautiful mural she had painted for the Congregational Church's Sunday school rooms attested to that. Nellie would talk to her publisher.

"Will we get paid for this?" Leah, the practical one, asked.

"Leah, it's not polite to ask for money," Linda said, poking her twin in the ribs.

"You will be paid with cookies and hugs," she told them, kissing each on the top of her head. The girls giggled.

While the girls labored over their drawings, Nellie

went inside to assemble a tray of lemonade and cookies, occasionally glancing out the kitchen window to check on their progress. Both girls were bent over their artwork, nearly nose to nose with their drawings. It was enough to break her heart.

It seemed as if everyone in town was working hard to help Valerie and the girls. Doc Hammon had opened a medical fund over at the Dorsetville Savings and Loan. She and Harry had made the first, albeit anonymous, donation, the entire royalties from her last book.

Bake sales were conducted every Sunday after Mass spearheaded by the Henderson sisters; Matthew and his friends ran a car wash over at Nancy's garage on Saturdays; Carl Pipson was planning a telethon over at the station; and there wasn't a person in a fifty-mile radius who hadn't been approached to buy tickets for a raffle being run by the Clothesline Quilters. The first prize was a handsome log cabin quilt.

Still, they were a far cry away from the amount needed for the girls' surgery.

Nellie checked her watch. It was nearly three o'clock. She had better start to get ready for her appointment with her agent. They planned to review a new book proposal.

Ethel Johnson would be arriving shortly to pick up the girls and take them to her house. But she had to leave at five o'clock to attend her niece's housewarming party over in Manchester. Lori Peterson had offered to swing by after work and take the girls to her house. There they would stay until Valerie arrived at six. It certainly does take a whole village to raise a child, Nellie thought.

She paused outside the kitchen door to watch the girls, their small hands so busy at work, and prayed that

God would send the help they needed before it was too late.

When the twins arrived at the Petersons' Stephen was just packing up to leave.

"Why did you paint the room over again?" Leah asked.

"Mrs. Peterson wanted a color change," Stephen answered.

"I'm glad," Leah said. "I didn't like the other one."

Stephen broke out into a smile as he went about packing up his things. "You girls here for another sleepover?"

Linda shook her head. "No, we're just staying until our mommy gets back."

Leah whispered something into her sister's ear. Linda grew serious as she studied Stephen's face. Finally she nodded at her sister and smiled. The girls stepped farther into the room.

"Elmo, you stay there," Leah commanded the Petersons' dog, who stood between her and Linda. Then she turned to Stephen. "Our mommy is very pretty."

"And very nice," Linda quickly added, pushing her glasses back on her nose.

"I'm sure she is," Stephen said.

"I bet if you asked her out, she would say yes," Leah offered.

"You could take her to a movie," Linda quickly inserted. "She really likes the movies."

"Movies, you say? I like the movies too." What were these two little minxes up to?

The twins edged closer.

"Then you'll ask her out?" Leah asked.

"For a date?" Linda clarified.

"Maybe she wouldn't want to go out with me," he teased.

"Oh, she will," Leah offered. "She has to get married."

"Oh?"

"Yeap, she caught the bridal bouquet at Mrs. Clifford's wedding," Leah said.

"Do I smell paint?" Valerie asked, stepping inside the Petersons' home.

"We had the nursery repainted," Lori explained.

"You sure it's good for you to be breathing in those fumes?"

"The painter left an hour ago. I have windows open upstairs. We'll be fine," she said, placing her hands over her abdomen.

"Hi, Mommy," the twins called from the top of the stairs. "Can we sleep over?"

"No, you can't," Valerie said.

"Pleasssseee."

"It's time to leave. Say thank you to Mrs. Peterson and then hop into the car. I have to get to Dinovas' market before it closes."

The girls thundered down the stairs in protest. Elmo gave chase, barking with excitement.

"Hush, Elmo," Lori said.

"Thank you, Mrs. Peterson," the twins chimed in unison.

"You're welcome, girls."

Valerie watched her daughters bound outside into

the yard like frisky puppies. When she turned around, she noticed Lori wince in pain.

"Have you called Doc Hammon about that?" Valerie asked.

"It's probably nothing," Lori said, brushing it off. "See, it's already gone."

"Just the same, you should have it checked out."

"You're probably right. I'll make the call."

"Promise?" Valerie asked with concern.

"Promise. First thing tomorrow morning."

Valerie gave her a hug. "Thanks again for everything."

Lori listened to Valerie's car head down the gravel driveway as she made her way upstairs. The house seemed unnaturally quiet after the children's clamor and Stephen's portable radio. For just an instant, she paused to close her eyes and drink in the welcome silence. Too bad it would be so short-lived. Bob was expected in about a half an hour. Maybe she would call the Japanese place in town and order in tonight. She really didn't feel like cooking. But first she needed to take a peek at the nursery. Other than a cursory look as Stephen was leaving, she hadn't had the chance to give it the once-over. She hoped this color choice would be infinitely better than the last.

She paused briefly at her daughter's room and tried not to become distracted by the clutter left in the wake of the girls' playtime. "When you've finished picking up this mess, will you come downstairs and help me set the table for dinner?"

"In a minute," Sarah answered, in that distracted way

children have of answering parents when their attention is elsewhere. She was seated among a clutter of Barbie dolls, absorbed in dressing Ken for a night out on the town.

"Make that a short minute." Sarah's "minutes" had a way of stretching out indefinitely.

The nursery was sandwiched in between Sarah's room and the master bedroom. Lori opened the door and was overcome by the odor of fresh paint. For a moment she felt nauseous. Lately it seemed as if everything made her stomach sick, even the smell of coffee, which was something of a dilemma considering she worked in a place whose coffee was famous for miles around.

Ignoring the queasiness, she bravely sallied into the room and was pleased to find it had been wonderfully transformed. Gone were the Popsicle green walls, replaced by a soft lemon yellow that lent the room a warm, sunny atmosphere.

Fortunately, the color change had not necessitated Stephen painting over his mural. Through some alchemy, he had managed to blend the new color into the scene. She touched the wall lightly, marveling at Stephen's mastery of detail. The texture of the string in Pooh's hand; the fur that seemed so real she found herself running her hand over it, half expecting to find it real. Once again, she wondered why such a talented artist was working as a mere construction helper and moonlighting as a house painter.

A robin flew past the window and brought her thoughts back onto the room. "The baby's bedroom," she said softly.

How long had it been since she and Bob had referred to this room as such? Sarah was growing so quickly. Lori had nearly despaired of ever holding a newborn again.

She ran a loving hand over her stomach. How could she have ever contemplated an abortion? The thought still filled her with guilt. She had confessed it to Father James.

"We cannot control the birds that fly over our heads," the priest had said. "We are responsible only for those we let nest in our hair."

She closed her eyes and tried to imagine her son's face. She wished Bob hadn't been so insistent that she not tell him the sex of their child. She also would have liked to have shared her choice of names. She wished to call him Ephraim.

"So what do you think of the new color, Ephraim?" she whispered, her heart flooding with love at the sound of his name. How her arms ached to hold him for the first time. The thought brought tears to her eyes.

She pulled her thoughts away from her unborn child and glanced down at her watch. Six-fifteen. Bob would be arriving shortly. She'd better get hustling. There was a load of wash that needed to be put in the dryer and a basket of clothes that needed ironing.

Lori closed the door to the nursery, forcing away thoughts of new curtains and layettes as she headed toward the stairwell. The strange pain had returned, but she was only slightly concerned. After all, Doc Hammon had said she was healthy as a horse. Still, Valerie's words of concern made her veer to the safe side. What if something was wrong? Lori made a decision right then to call for an appointment first thing tomorrow morning.

She had just stepped onto the upstairs landing when the pain shifted, wrapping its tightening grip around her entire abdomen. The swiftness of it caught her off guard.

She grabbed hold of the banister for support and let out a deep moan.

"Mommy, are you all right?" Sarah asked, rushing into the hallway, Elmo close on her heels.

She had broken out in a cold sweat. "I'm feeling a little sick, honey," Lori said, trying to downplay an inner alarm. Something was terribly wrong. "I think I'll go lie down until Daddy gets home. You go downstairs and wait for him."

Sarah hesitated.

Lori forced a smile. "I'm all right, honey. You go downstairs and wait for Daddy. Take Elmo with you."

She waited until Sarah had descended the staircase before heading toward her bedroom. She tried to quiet her fears. Maybe it was just a strain. After all, she had put in a full eight hours at the bakery, then come home and cleaned the kitchen. Bob was right; she really had to slow down.

She felt as if she were walking on the sharp edge of the pain as she made her way toward the bed. It was hard but bearable. Perhaps if she moved slowly, it would ease up, go away. Perspiration dripped down her back. Then, like a hammer blow, the pain intensified, forcing her to her knees. She stuffed her hand into her mouth to stifle the scream, not wanting to frighten Sarah. If she could only make it to the nightstand, she could call 911 for help.

She clawed her way along the carpet. The pain had shifted again. Now it came from inside her womb, a tearing, searing pain. This time she could not contain the scream. She cried out, falling across the bed, just as something hot and molten gushed between her legs.

Sarah thundered back up the staircase, Elmo barking

as if an intruder had broken in. Her daughter crashed into her room.

"Mommy . . . what's wrong?" she cried, voice filled with terror.

She found her mother lying sideways across the bed, her knees tucked tightly underneath her chin. Something had stained the bedspread red. Sarah broke out into tears. Her mommy was dying. What was she supposed to do?

From downstairs she could hear her father's voice calling. "Hey . . . is anybody home?" Elmo charged out of the room to greet him.

Sarah would have rushed to join her canine friend, to find comfort in her daddy's arms, but a small orb of bright light that had begun to take shape by the side of her mother's bed drew her attention. She remained riveted in place as if her feet had been nailed to the floorboards.

The white light rapidly increased in size until it encompassed most of the room and from its center two large shapes began to take form. Sarah's heartbeat increased like that of frightened bird's.

"Fear not," a voice said from within the white light. Two men the size of giants now stood by her mother's bedside. They wore silvery tunics that shimmered like diamonds, and rays of light pulsated from their heads.

"We are the angels of the Lord," they told her." "We have been sent to take your brother, Ephraim, back to God's throne."

Sarah was too frightened to move, let alone speak. Instead, she watched transfixed as one of the angels reached down over her mother, took hold of a baby, and lifted him up into his arms. Sarah looked on with awe. Where had the baby come from?

Then just as suddenly as the angels had appeared they vanished, leaving only a memory in their wake.

As soon as Father James got the call, he had raced right over to Mercy Hospital. Bob was standing in the emergency room waiting area when he arrived. One look at his distraught face told the priest that Lori had lost the baby.

"I'm so sorry," he said with compassion.

"It was a boy." Bob said, trying to hold back the tears. "I just found out that we would have had a son."

Father James placed a hand on his shoulder. "What can I do?"

"Will you come and bless his remains?" Bob's voice choked with grief.

They walked silently down the long corridor.

"Do you have a name for the baby?" Father James asked, slipping on a stole.

Bob turned, tears freely washing over his face. "Lori just told me a few minutes ago. She had wanted to call him Ephraim."

They paused outside the hospital room door.

"And, Father, we've decided not to tell Sarah that the baby was a boy. At least not now. She had her heart set on a baby brother. We think it might be too hard for her to accept his loss."

"I understand," Father James said, and then slipped inside the room to offer a last blessing for this tiny little soul.

$\mathcal{F}$IFTEEN

$\mathcal{F}$ather James was staring into his mug of coffee, as if he could somehow lose himself in its inky depths.

"I'd ask you if you wanted another cup," said Wendy, "but looks like you're doing a fine job of nursing that one."

She neatly clipped her Mont Blanc pen to the rim of her apron pocket, dusted off a coating of crumbs on the red vinyl stool, and sat down beside him.

"So what's wrong?" she asked without preamble.

He shrugged his shoulders like a lost child.

"Of all the people who tromp in and

out of here each day, I'd say you were the least likely I'd peg to get depressed."

"I'm not exactly depressed," he hedged.

This response garnered a raised eyebrow.

"Okay, I might be a little down," he conceded. "I've got housekeeper troubles."

"So I've heard," Wendy said.

"You have?"

"Everybody has."

"Oh, brother." What made him think he could keep a secret in this town? He tried to explain.

"You see, I hired Viola Tunis, who is a great house-keeper—that is, the few times she actually showed up. The rectory was neat, the kitchen spotless, the wash and ironing done to perfection. She also put together a mean grilled cheese sandwich in a pinch. But she has—er—personal problems that prohibit her from coming to work as regularly as she should."

"Odis," Wendy said sagely, removing a pack of cigarettes from her apron pocket.

Father James grinned, thinking how God often sent help through the most unlikely sources. This morning he had asked God to send a sounding board. He needed to work things out about his housekeeper. Wendy, however, would definitely not have been his first choice. But since she was here . . .

"Yes, Odis. Anyway, she sent over her younger sister—"

"Audrey."

"You know about Audrey too?"

"The entire town knows about Audrey," Wendy said, searching the other apron pocket for a book of matches. "So why don't you just fire them?"

"It's not that simple."

Wendy looked at him with an expression that could have stopped a New York mugger dead in his tracks. "Of course it's that simple! When you don't show up for work, you get fired. Just because Viola sends her sister to take her place doesn't mean that she shouldn't be fired for not showing up for work."

"But Viola needs the money," he explained. "Odis is drinking away their savings."

"And how did that become your problem?"

He had no answer.

"Listen up. You hired a woman who doesn't show up for work. Fire her. Then give her the phone number for ALANON. Tell her to get a life because she can't save Odis until she first saves herself."

Wendy turned to another waitress who was pouring water over a teabag. "Hillary, I'll be outside having a smoke if you need me." Wendy paused briefly before taking off.

"I had an uncle like that," she told him quietly. "My aunt did the same thing Viola is doing. Chasing him all over town. Paying his bar tabs. It only made things worse. Had she made him confront his drinking problem and take responsibility for his own life, he might not have died from cirrhosis of the liver in his late forties.

"You're not doing Viola a favor, Father James, by letting this go on. In fact, your misplaced sympathy is only fueling the problem."

He thought about this for several minutes. "Okay, even if you're right, I can't just abandon them. It's doesn't seem Christian."

"The Book of James says 'each one is tempted when by his own evil desire he is dragged away and enticed,'" she quoted. "These people are responsible for themselves. They've made the choice to live this kind of lifestyle, and allowing Viola to keep her job and show up whenever it suits her fancy means you're subsidizing that choice. So, as I see it, you're not being a good Christian by helping them. You're being a doormat. There's a difference. Now . . . I'm going outside for a smoke. Anything else I can help you clear up?"

"No, I think that about covers it."

"Good."

He watched her disappear wondering what shocked him more, that her advice was straight on target or that she could quote the Bible.

He went back to his coffee, thinking Wendy is right. It's time to give Viola and Audrey their walking papers. In fact, he would do it this very afternoon.

He fished in his pocket for some change, placed it on the counter, then went to pay his tab. Mrs. Norris was ringing up an order. Harry had hired her to help out while Lori was out on sick leave. The Petersons were much in everyone's prayers this week as the young couple tried to come to grips with the loss of their unborn child.

"One ham and cheese sandwich with extra mayo, three-fifty," Mrs. Norris was saying. "Plus two custard doughnuts, seventy-five cents."

Father James stood behind the man who was waiting for his order. Funny, something smelled like fuel oil.

"Throw in a malted, will you, Mrs. Norris?" the man said.

The voice sounded familiar, but whom did he know with pitch-black hair?

"One dollar," Mrs. Norris said. "Hillary, will you fix a malted to go, please?"

"That's five dollars and twenty-five cents, George," Mrs. Norris said, hitting total. The cash drawer sprung open with a clang.

George?

George counted out the change, grabbed the takeout bag, and spun around, nearly colliding with the priest.

"Hi, Father."

Father James was speechless. Not only had George dyed his hair black, he had restyled it into a circa 1950s DA.

"Needed something to tide me over to lunch," George explained, holding up his takeout bag. "Well, I'll be seeing you."

He nodded dumbly as George headed toward the door.

He was still in a state of shock when he heard Mrs. Norris's voice. "I *said* that will be a dollar seventy-three, Father. Father James?"

He passed her a five-dollar bill without turning around. His eyes were still riveted on the back of George's head.

"Here you go, Father. Don't you want your change?" his former housekeeper asked.

"I'm sorry, I wasn't paying any attention," he said, turning to face her. And for the second time in less than five minutes, he was stunned into silence.

Mrs. Norris was wearing metallic blue eye shadow and lipstick the color of the underbelly of a flamingo. He couldn't stop staring.

She nodded toward the door. "Did you see George's new hairdo? Someone should tell him how ridiculous he looks."

———

"Wendy, I'm going back to the bakery. I've got to get that cake ready for the garden club."

Mrs. Norris headed through the archway that separated the restaurant from the bakery, noting that the front display cases were nearly empty again. How was that possible? She had baked an extra batch of crème de menthe brownies and a whole tray of éclairs. How did Lori do it six days a week? she wondered, sliding the empty trays out from behind the glass case. Keeping the bakery stocked, she had discovered, was a lot harder than she would have ever imagined.

Lori's name made her thoughts turn naturally to the young mother. Poor girl. Trouble just seemed to find its way to that family's door. She would make certain to swing past their house on the way home and drop off the roasted chicken she had prepared earlier and some fresh dinner rolls. Maybe she should ignore her rules against giving sugar to children and include a few cookies for Sarah.

Her mind was preoccupied with this and other thoughts as she walked into the back kitchen and slipped the used trays into a large rubber bin. Peppy, the dishwasher, would be in later to gather them up. Tightening her apron strings, she scanned the large metal shelves in search of the ingredients to make a lemon buttercream icing for the Garden Club's cake. Someone would be by to pick it up later. Suddenly she broke out in a wide smile at the incongruity of all of this. Here she was a woman who had sworn off sugar and sweets, working in a bakery. Truth was, she loved it.

The other waitresses were busy on the restaurant side, setting things up for the supper crowd, so she had the kitchen all to herself. Without distractions, she quickly began to load the mixing bowl with butter, cream, and vanilla while her thoughts wandered back onto Lori. She personally knew the pain this young mother was going through.

Like Lori, Mrs. Norris had lost a child to stillbirth. It was a little girl. Even after all of these years, the memory of that loss was difficult to relive. Especially hard was the moment when she had been refused the right to hold her dead child.

She had pleaded with the nurses as they took her daughter away. They said it was best this way, but what did they know? When she cried even the louder, they had sedated her.

Three years later she and her husband were blessed with another little girl. They named her Jenny. One day when she was six years old, Jenny followed some neighbors' kids down to Fenn's Pond to watch them ice skate. No one saw her fall through the thin ice at the edge, and by the time they discovered her body, it was too late.

This time Mrs. Norris insisted that she be allowed to hold her daughter one last time. The ambulance personnel had tried to dissuade her, but Sheriff Bromley shoved past them, lifting Jenny's lifeless body off the stretcher and gently laying the child in her arms. At that moment, she had looked into the sheriff's eyes, surprised to see a depth of grief that had matched her own.

Painful memories, she thought, but thankfully they had grown easier to endure with each passing year.

She assembled the cake quickly, taking an inordinate amount of pleasure in the task. She had almost forgotten the joy of working with her hands, making meals and desserts that gave people pleasure, not to mention the many blue ribbons they had won over the years at the country fairs. It certainly gave her more satisfaction than the new health food regimen she had adopted that leaned heavily on fiber and tofu. Where was the joy in that?

Last week Harry had asked her to make a pot of her famous Mulligan stew for his lunchtime customers. She almost feared she had forgotten how, but as soon as she started browning the meat, it all came back. And much to her delight, Harry sold the whole batch by noontime.

The sun streamed in through the window and the muffled voices in the restaurant drifted in through the kitchen doors. Mrs. Norris felt a new sense of contentment. She loved working again, the sense of being needed. Of course, when Lori came back, she would have to give this all up. She tried not to think of that or of how much she hated retirement. As her grandnephew often said of things he disliked: It sucked.

Instead, she centered her thoughts on the man she had recently met through the personals. He called himself Hound Dog. She signed herself Betty Crocker, and they had been corresponding for several weeks. Receiving his letters had become the highlight of her days.

Through them she had learned that he had no children but wished it could have been different. He liked to listen to Frank Sinatra in the evening, but Elvis Presley kept him company during the day. He claimed to have every record the King had ever made and believed that he really hadn't died but was living in a remote cabin somewhere in Montana.

He also wrote that he had never missed a single

episode of *Wheel of Fortune* (Mrs. Norris's favorite game show) and felt that Vanna White had past her prime and really should be replaced.

Mrs. Norris was a little put off by this comment, feeling women shouldn't be judged by their age, but it had gotten her to thinking about her own looks. Since she had worked in the rectory for all these years, she was accustomed to doing no more than washing her face each morning with Ivory Soap and lathering on some Pond's Cold Cream at night. After all, who was she suppose to impress, the priests?

But things were different now, so last week she decided a change was needed and had driven all the way to the Danbury Mall to have one of those makeovers at Macy's. The girl had done a real nice job, which she tried to duplicate each morning. She was still having trouble with the eyeliner. She felt it made her look like a raccoon, yet she perservered hoping she would get better with practice.

Mrs. Norris began to put the finishing touches to her cake, quickly transferring her thoughts back to the task at hand. It needed to be perfect. Rochelle Phillips, the garden club's recording secretary, had a sister who was a professional caterer. Rochelle was certain to look at it with a critical eye.

Mrs. Norris hummed as she piped icing around the top edge, then piled strips of lemon peels coated in crystallized sugar onto the center. It took her thirty minutes to finish the cake, but when it was done she surveyed it with pleasure.

"You haven't lost your touch, Margaret," she told herself, then carefully shifted the cake into a baker's box, tied it with a string, and carried it to the front of the bakery. While there, she moved some things around in the display case, wondering what to bake tomorrow. Pies seemed like a good choice. She could call March Farms and have them send over an order—peaches, blueberries. Men customers especially liked pies, so what she didn't sell here, Harry could use for the restaurant. The town crews would devour them in no time.

Thoughts of men and their food preferences brought her back to Hound Dog, who had once written about his fondness for johnnycakes, which happened to be one of her specialties. Recently he had been pressuring her for a date. Should she agree to meet him? She wondered what he looked like. Was he tall, dark, and handsome? She always imagined him with tender blue eyes, a sweet smile, and perfect, courtly manners.

But before she could fantasize any further, a member of the garden club arrived to pick up the cake.

"Sarah!" the twins shouted together from across the street. But Sarah didn't seem to hear them as she followed her father inside the rectory.

The girls turned back to their yardwork, a chore they hated.

"I thought Mommy said she was coming out to help us," Linda whined, dumping most of what was in her arms into a large black plastic bag held by her sister.

"She has to wash some stuff out of her hair first."

Linda gazed toward St. Cecilia's Rectory. "Do you think Stephen really lives at the rectory with Father James?"

The girls had begun today's chores in the front yard in hopes that Stephen might walk by and they could introduce him to their mother.

"Sarah said he did."

"What if he doesn't walk by?" Linda continued.

"He will," she said confidently.

"But what if he doesn't?" Linda wanted to know.

"Then we'll walk over and get him," Leah said in exasperation. Just then she spied Stephen walking out the rectory's side door.

"See, I told you," Leah said triumphantly.

The girls shouted in unison. "Hi, Stephen! Over here!"

From overhead, the fire siren sounded, its high-decibel pitch drowning out their voices. The girls covered their ears with their hands.

"Go get Mommy," Leah shouted to Linda, watching Stephen head toward Father James's Jeep. It looked as if he were going for a drive.

"Hurry!" Leah shouted. "I'll stop him when he passes by."

"Mommy, you need to come outside."

"Why? Is your sister in trouble?"

"No, we want you to meet someone."

"Who?"

"A man?"

Oh, no, not again. Valerie wished she had never caught that bridal bouquet. Last week the twins had suggested she date the exterminator, a kid barely out of high school with an advanced case of acne. The week before that it had been the butcher over at Grand Union, who smelled like raw meat.

At this moment, Valerie had no patience for their matchmaking.

"I'll be out as soon as I can."

"Mommy, please. You need to come out *now*!"

"Go outside and wait. I'll come out when I can."

"But, Mommy . . ."

"Outside!"

Valerie stared into the mirror at the face of a stranger. The color on the dye bottle had said "Satin Blonde," which the picture suggested would be a soft, beige blonde not unlike her own hair, the perfect shade for getting rid of a little gray.

But what she was now staring at was definitely not blonde.

She was now a redhead, and not just a simple, subtle, sultry redhead but an orange, Jeffrey the Clown kind of redhead. All she needed was a polka-dot suit and size-twenty shoes, and she could join the circus.

A light knock sounded on the bathroom door again.

"Mommy, *pleeaasse* come outside. There's a very nice man who wants to meet you."

"Darling, I'm not meeting anyone for the next six months," Valerie told her.

Linda raced back outside and found her sister sitting on a large pile of leaves with a look of utter rejection.

"What happened?" Linda asked.

"Stephen went the other way."

———

Father James listened attentively as Sarah concluded her story about the two angels she had seen.

"I didn't tell Mommy," Sarah said. "I didn't think she would believe me."

Father James studied her face intently. It was an extraordinary tale but the strangest thing was, it had the ring of truth. For instance, most children Sarah's age would have described angels as effeminate beings with long flowing hair, wearing diaphanous gowns; instead, she had described the angels of the Old Testament—beings of superior strength and stature whose awesome presence elicited fear.

But how was he to counsel her? What was he to say? He closed his eyes for just a moment and lifted a prayer for wisdom.

Sarah continued, "Why would God let me see the angels and not my mommy? It would have made her less sad if she could have seen them take my baby brother to heaven."

Brother? How did she know the child had been a boy?

He tried to answer her query. "That's one of God's many mysteries. I don't know, my child. God's ways are often not our ways. We can only accept the grace He supplies and not try to reason why."

Sarah pondered this a moment. "Then should I tell Mommy what I saw? Should I tell her that the angels took Ephraim to heaven to be with Jesus?"

The hairs along the nape of his neck stood straight up. There was no way Sarah could have known the baby's sex or his name unless . . .

He leaned forward and took her small hands into hers. "Yes, Sarah, I think you need to tell your mother what you saw."

Sixteen

❈

Father Dennis's confidence was slipping faster than spaghetti off a plate on a downhill slope, under the scrutiny of the PBS television crew who stood ready to film the cooking contest finals.

There were cables strung across every section of the floor, taped down with duct tape. Banks of overhead lights showed so brightly that they could have easily guided a 747 through a dense fog; and workers called "grips" moved counters, chairs, tables, and scenery across the set in a dizzying dance. Father Dennis had made the mistake of placing his cup of tea on a counter to tie his shoes; when he stood up, it had disappeared.

Most unsettling, however, was the director named Tray, an acne-faced youth who looked as though he had just graduated from high school and who possessed an ego that far exceeded his present standing among television notables. In fact, he had been given this job only because his father was a prominent sponsor of the show.

Tray sauntered over toward Father Dennis, followed by a retinue of assistants, all holding fast to every word he spoke as though they contained the secrets to life.

Tray eyed the nervous priest with indifference. "I suppose by your drab black garb, you must be Father Dennis?"

The priest nodded.

"All right then," he sighed, as though all of this was getting to be too much. "Let me explain how this is going to work. Your segment will begin with an introduction. The announcer will tell the viewers a little bit about you . . . blah, blah, blah. When he's finished, you will walk out from there . . ." He pointed to a curtain strung across the back of the set. "Then travel this way and stop when you hit this spot." He indicated a piece of blue tape on the floor.

"*Then* . . . you will look up into the camera, smile and announce the name of the dish you have chosen to prepare . . . which is . . . which is???" He snapped his fingers. A young girl rushed over with a clipboard.

"Saintly Seafood Soufflé," she filled in.

"Saintly Seafood . . . yes . . . whatever, and then after that announcement, you will move over to this spot"—another piece of blue tape—"to begin your cooking presentation. Got it? Fine. Now who's next . . ."

Father Dennis watched him sail on, wondering which blue tape he was supposed to step on first. The one to the right or to the left? He could feel himself beginning to hyperventilate.

"You're not listening," Emily said, elbowing him in the ribs.

Listening? To what? The only thing he could hear was the pounding of his own heart.

"Remember to pour the heated cream into the egg mixture slowly, or it will curdle," she cautioned. "And don't let it boil once you've added the cheese because it will separate and look just awful."

"Yes, yes . . . you told me. Add the cheese. Heat the cream . . ." Father Dennis was watching the crew position cameras. Airtime was quickly approaching.

He wasn't ready. Maybe if they allowed him to use cue cards or a teleprompter. He glanced up at the sound booth. Timothy and Ben waved through the glass as though they were having the time of their lives.

What had made him think he could pull this off? This wasn't some local cable station. This was *the* Public Broadcasting Network, which meant the entire country would be watching, including all of his relatives. Even his Aunt Marge, whom he feared a little less than God but more than Mother Superior, would be there, glued to the television set. After today he might never be able to go home again. It would be too embarrassing.

God forbid he should forget the blue tape on the floor or wreak havoc with the studio's high-tech kitchen. He did have a tendency to set things on fire. And what was the difference between convection and conventional ovens? Oh Lord, he had forgotten.

He looked at the three cameras; their lights had begun to flash. Airtime was less than five minutes away.

He felt faint.

Emily was speaking to him but he couldn't quite catch what she was saying; something about clarifying butter—or was she clarifying what she had just said, which he hadn't heard? He watched her lips move, but for some reason the words just shot off into space.

Oh, why had he allowed himself to get into this mess? He vaguely remembered it had something to do with helping Sam get a new car.

"We're beginning our countdown. Airtime in sixty seconds," someone announced.

His mouth felt dry and his heart was pounding like the pistons of a train racing down a mountain pass.

"You all right, Father?" one of the cameramen asked as he settled himself atop a tall swiveled chair. "You look a little pale."

"Fine. I'm fine," he lied, running a finger along his white collar. "Could you turn up the air conditioner, please?"

Someone bumped him. "Sorry."

It was Wolfgang Puck. He was talking on his cell phone . . . "Tell Miss Roberts that she cannot serve cold crab with that wine and that *no one* is serving lamb anymore. Really! Some celebrities!!!"

Wolfgang was one of the celebrity chefs enlisted to judge today's contest. Julia Child had arrived earlier with her retinue and was now seated at the judges' table.

Tray, who had donned a set of earphones and a look of super-hypertension, suddenly waved Father Dennis to move over and stand beside the other finalists.

"We're going live in fifteen seconds. Quiet on the set!" the boy wonder shouted in a nasal voice. "Now . . .

let's see . . . who's demonstrating first? It looks like it's Father Dennis. When the announcer is through with your bio, I want you to take a step forward, hit your mark, run through what we rehearsed, then slide over to your next mark and begin your presentation. Everyone clear on all of that?"

Mark? What was a mark?

"Ten, nine, eight, seven, six, five, four, three, two, one . . ." The camera's red light came on.

The director pointed to Father Dennis, who suddenly couldn't remember why he was here. The announcer read his name. He nodded and tried to smile but found that, for some reason, his lips wouldn't move. The announcer finished. Silence fell like an iron curtain across the set. The judges stared, waiting for him to begin. The director was madly waving his arms in a propeller motion.

Oh yes, the competition, Father Dennis remembered. He was demonstrating how to make . . . ???? Something to do with lobster.

A hand reached out from behind the curtain and gave him a shove. He fell forward, almost landing head-first on the cooking island.

The director held on to a tight smile and increased his hand motions.

Father Dennis looked up at the cameras and saw everyone he had ever known throughout his entire life, staring back at him.

He opened his mouth to speak, to say something brilliant and witty and . . .

. . . hiccuped.

———

Sam looked at his watch. It was nearly two o'clock. The cooking competition should be over by now. He wondered who had won.

Timothy and Ben were all excited about watching a professional camera crew at work, and had talked about nothing else for days.

"Maybe we can pick up some pointers," Ben had said hopefully.

"Make some contacts," Timothy added.

Sam had hidden a smile. What did they think? That someone might actually ask them to join their crew?

But, as much as he would have liked to have gone and been in on all the excitement, he had a commitment to maintain. Shut-ins depended on him to deliver their meals, and volunteers like him were not easy to come by. Of course, it would have been easier if he still had his Plymouth, but what he had recovered from the insurance would never replace it.

Instead, he now delivered meals in whatever vehicle was available from the generous folks in Dorsetville. On Mondays Sam drove Roger Martin's Chevy Suburban, which made Sam feel as though he were a good ten feet taller than anyone else on the road.

On Tuesdays it was the Rabbi's wife's Ford Escort. A cute little car that was great on gas, but a little small. Sam's hip usually bothered him the night after he drove it.

On Wednesdays Sam drove Harry's paneled van with extreme caution. Visibility was limited, and Sam was often reduced to reliance upon angels as he backed out of driveways or tried to park.

Thursdays he drove whatever Nancy had down at the repair shop. Last week he had driven a 1985 Lincoln

Town Car, the size of a city bus. This week it was a small-bed Nissan pickup truck, which he felt necessitated making frequent stops every few miles to check that none of the meals placed in the back had bounced out along the way.

Fridays either Reverend Curtis loaned him his yellow SUV or Sam used Father James's Jeep; the vehicle had to be large enough to accommodate dozens of extra meals, since deliveries were not made on the weekends—a fact that the seniors bemoaned, for they missed the companionship.

Now weekends were also tough for Sam. Without a vehicle of his own, he had to rely on others for rides to Temple or to go shopping. If he wanted to go for an ice cream cone, he had to arrange it in advance. Trouble was . . . he never knew when he might feel like an ice cream, or one of Harry's cheeseburgers, and somehow planning for these things took away their pleasure. For the first time, he understood how Ben and Timothy must feel.

For weeks, he had reworked and reworked his budget. He called his tax accountant, hoping to find some new deductible that might provide some extra cash. But no matter how he played it, his retirement funds were not going to cover the purchase of another car. Even a used vehicle (one that would not break down as soon as it was driven off the dealer's lot) didn't come cheap these days. Most cost upward of $12,000.

Still, Sam hoped for a miracle. He believed fervently in miracles, having experienced one personally as a youth in Nazi-occupied Germany. Only a miracle could have saved him from the concentration camp.

So he prayed to the God of Abraham and even lit a

candle over at St. Cecilia's under St. Anthony's statue. Ben and Timothy took great stock in this saint's power for intercession, so Sam figured it couldn't hurt.

In just a few hours Lori would have to get up, shower, and get dressed. Mass was being said for her baby at three o'clock. But she didn't want to get up. She couldn't endure the looks of pity worn like black armbands, or people's attempts at consolation. Nothing could soften the grief she felt.

Well-meaning friends had tried. Valerie had brought casseroles. Harry dropped off a family meal each night on the way home. Harriet had sent a long letter describing the loss of her grandchild and the discovery that God did not abandon those in grief, but was everpresent.

Others brought paperback books with titles such as *Heaven's Harvest* and *Handling the Loss of a Loved One*. Still others, prayer cards.

And then there were those who said things like *It's better that you lost your baby now, than to carry the child through to term . . . Think of all the children waiting to be adopted in foreign countries . . . This may be a blessing in disguise. Imagine all the suffering this child is being spared . . . You're young. You can have another baby.*

But she didn't want another baby. She wanted this one. Why didn't they understand that she had lost a child, not a mass of cells that could easily be replaced? Her baby was dead. She would never hold that infant in her arms, sing him lullabies, watch him sleep. Her baby was DEAD.

She looked outside. The dark clouds that had circled for most of the early morning were giving way to sun.

She had hoped that it would rain hard and torrential, keeping people at home. She wanted to grieve in private. Why couldn't they understand that?

But she knew that she couldn't stay in bed forever. Sooner or later, she must get up to confront the nursery next-door with its freshly painted walls and soft satin coverlets, waiting for the arrival of a child who was gone forever. If only she knew that he was with God, safe in His care, perhaps she might be able to endure his death a little better. If only she knew that his life had not been in vain, perhaps then she could find peace.

She tried to slam the door on thoughts of God. He didn't deserve her worship or her praise. Mostly, He didn't deserve her allegiance. He had taken her child when He could have prevented his death.

She had fought so hard to come to terms with her child's handicap and to find the importance of this little life. She wanted to believe . . . with every fiber of her being . . . in a compassionate God, even though everything around her had spoken otherwise.

And then, when she had come to the end of her faith, He had spoken through a parable. Led her to the story of the blind man and hinted that this child, too, would be cause to give God glory. His life would not be wasted.

But where was the glory in a grave? How could God be honored by her baby's death?

She glanced over at the nightstand clock, noting that she really should begin to get ready. Even if she no longer called God her friend, both Sarah and Bob needed the comfort of this Mass. For their sake, she would go along.

Sarah's voice sounded at her bedroom door. "Mommy, can I come in?"

She felt a new lump in her throat. Her dear Sarah had witnessed it all. The bloodstained sheets. Her cries of pain. The fear in Bob's eyes; he later confided that he had thought Lori was dead. As a mother, she feared for the impact that this trauma might have had on her daughter.

Bob had already spoken with Doc Hammon, who'd suggested a counselor. They had chosen Father James, and Bob had brought Sarah to the rectory on Saturday morning. When they returned home, Sarah told her father she wanted to speak to Mommy alone.

But Lori had been putting it off, almost fearing what Sarah might ask. How did you explain a miscarriage to a ten-year-old without instilling more fear?

She still wasn't ready, yet she knew it couldn't be put off forever. Sarah needed comforting as much as she did.

"Come in," she told her daughter, trying to screw up her courage.

Sarah, usually so bold and loquacious, entered the room hesitantly.

Lori patted the empty place alongside her. "Here, come sit with me."

Sarah carefully climbed onto the bed, as though her mother were made of fragile glass that might shatter. Neither spoke for several seconds.

Finally Sarah asked, "Does it still hurt?"

"No, not anymore," Lori answered. *Except for my heart*, she wanted to add. She took hold of her daughter's hands. "Sarah, I know that what you saw the other day might have frightened you . . ."

Sarah suddenly came alive and she asked excitedly, "Did you see them, too?"

"See who, darling?"

"The angels."

Angels? Had she heard correctly?

"They stood right there," Sarah continued. "Right next to your bed. Didn't you see them, Mommy?"

Lori wasn't certain if her daughter was telling a tale, or if this was some type of coping mechanism that she had devised. She decided just to follow along. "No, dear, I didn't."

Sarah looked down at the bedcovering. "I wasn't going to tell you about the angels. I didn't think you would believe me. But Father James said I should."

"And I'm glad that you did, sweetheart," Lori said, pulling her daughter close, drawing comfort from her nearness. "If you say you saw angels, then I believe you."

Sarah pulled away. "You should have seen them, Mommy. They were this tall." Sarah stood on the bed and expanded her arms to encompass most of the other side of the room. "And they were wearing shiny shirts and had great big arms, bigger than anything I've ever seen before. Even bigger than the muscle man we saw at the circus that time."

Lori was amazed at the depth of her daughter's imagination as she reached up and gently pulled her back onto the bed. "And what did the angels do?"

"First, they told me to 'fear not.' I guess they knew I was really frightened."

"I guess you would be," Lori agreed. "And then what happened?"

"The angel that was standing next to the bed bent down and picked up my baby brother in his arms . . ."

Brother? Neither Bob nor she had yet told Sarah the sex of the baby. Maybe it was a wild guess on Sarah's part. After all, there were only two choices.

"And then the angels told me that they were taking Ephraim to heaven to be with God. Isn't that a pretty name, Mommy?"

Lori couldn't stop the tears from cascading down her cheeks.

The Mass of the Angels, which is conducted in memory of the loss of a child, was scheduled for Sunday afternoon at 3 P.M. By two-thirty, the entire church was packed. Most everyone in town, regardless of their religious affiliation, was in attendance to offer the Petersons their support.

Sarah sat on Lori's right side, gripping her hand and occasionally smiling up into her face. She was happy that her mommy didn't look so sad anymore. Father James had been right. She was glad she had told her about the angels. Now Mommy knew that her baby brother was with God in heaven.

Father James stood at the podium and looked out onto the congregation, offering a silent prayer that the words he had come to share would give comfort.

"You have all come here today to offer your condolences. To show the Peterson family . . . Lori and Bob and Sarah . . . that they are not alone in their grief.

"I am certain that you all have offered prayers on their behalf since hearing about the death of this child. Many, I wager, have prayed that their grieving hearts be mended. Some . . . that they might find peace.

"Yet I wonder how many have prayed that God

would answer the question that is paramount on our lips: 'Why?'

"Why has this happened to this young family? Haven't they suffered enough over the last few years? Why couldn't they have been spared this burden? The worst possible loss that any of us could ever experience is the loss of a child. And it is to this issue that I would like to address my comments.

"Why would God take this child, a child that we have not seen, yet we have loved? Whom we have not met, yet we now mourn? Who is this child?

"First, he is a child of God. It does not matter that he was not born before he was taken. The Psalmist tells us that 'God knew me in the womb'; therefore we are confident that this child is known by God.

"Next, we acknowledge that the conception of this child was a miracle. Doctors had told this young couple that they could not bear children after Bob's illness. The chemotherapy had killed any chance of that happening. Yet God is not bound by man's laws or man's science. He proved that by allowing this child to be conceived, and to grow and experience life inside the mother's womb.

"But why would God, who created this precious life against all odds, then elect to take him home? Wouldn't it have been better never to have allowed this baby to be conceived?

"The Apostle Paul writes in Romans, 'For we know that in all things God works for the good of those who love Him, who have been called according to His purpose.'"

Father James thumped the Bible for emphasis.

"But how can a child's death be used for good? What

possible glory could our Father derive from such a tragedy?"

He pointed to the crucifix. "What possible good was derived from that?

"Now, I'm certain that you would like me to give you a definitive answer to that question, something that you can use to neatly gather up all of life's tragedies, tie them up with a string and toss them into a box labeled 'One Size Fits All.' But I can't, and neither can anyone else, because God will not be boxed in by man.

"We do not know why this child was taken. But what we do know is that God has promised to turn this to good, and we can be confident that He will honor His Word because, as is written in Hebrews. 'It is impossible for God to lie.'

"We all know the story about the Garden of Eden where man was given a beautiful garden where all of his needs were supplied and where he enjoyed full fellowship with God.

"But then one day the devil showed up whose main purpose is to instill doubt in God's Word. And how did he get Eve to doubt? He enticed her to use mortal reason to define Godly actions.

> The woman said to the serpent, "We may eat fruit from the trees in the garden, but God did say, 'You must not eat fruit from the tree that is in the middle of the garden and you must not touch it or you will die.' "
>
> "You will surely not die," the serpent said to the woman. "For God knows that when you eat of it your eyes will be opened and you will be like God knowing good and evil."

Father James glanced up from the text and reiterated, "'And you will be like God knowing good and evil.'

"You will be able to reason. You will be able to take an incident like the death of an unborn child and figure it out. But mortal minds cannot know the mind of God, so what happens when we can't understand why a loving God would allow something like this to happen? We begin to believe Satan's greatest lie . . . that God mustn't be very loving. Or He doesn't exist. If He did, He would never allow bad things to happen to good people.

"But God's actions are not governed by mortal reasoning. Our finite minds can only see a small fraction of the plans He has for all of us; not just for us as individuals, but as God's extended family, which He governs through grace.

"God's grace is one of life's greatest mysteries. The Bible says it cannot be earned. It is a gift, a gift that God extends to help us during these times of turmoil, doubt, and fear.

"How do we enter into His grace? By taking God at His Word. God has said that He will turn all things to good and therefore we must trust Him, push aside human reasoning and stand on faith. Pure and simple.

"Easy to do? No, because it defies the facts. But He has asked us to walk by faith, not by sight, and this is the only way to full fellowship with God."

Father James paused and allowed this thought to settle over the minds of his congregation.

"What is the purpose of God taking this child? As I said before, I don't know the mind of God. But this I do know: that He is faithful, and perhaps . . . just perhaps . . . one of the gifts this tiny unborn child had come to bring was the gift of unquestioning trust in God. And if that was the gift this child bore, then his life, no matter how short, was not in vain.

"Let us pray . . ."

It was a sober, reflective group who slowly made their way toward the back of the church. People were taking their time, offering the Petersons their personal condolences. Some commented that Lori appeared less pained. There even seemed to be a sense of peace about her.

"Valerie, is that you?" Harriet asked incredulously as they stepped outside. "That's quite a new hair color you're sporting."

"I was trying to economize," she laughed.

"You poor dear." Harriet gave her a hug. "Well, don't you worry. That's the good thing about hair. It grows."

"I don't know what's taking Mommy so long," Linda told Stephen, standing on tiptoe to peer over the crowd.

"She's probably talking with somebody," Leah said. "But she'll be here soon."

"I'd like to wait and meet your mother, girls," Stephen told them. "But I've been invited to the Hendersons for lunch and it would be impolite to be late."

He was also calling to deliver a painting which the sisters had purchased. It was a small, intimate portrait painted from a faded photograph of a young man who had once courted Ruth.

"If they offer you a piece of cake, say no thank you," Leah wisely offered.

"Oh, there she is!" Linda shouted. "Mommy! Mommy. Oh darn, she doesn't see us."

Stephen looked at his watch. "I'm really sorry, girls, but I must be going. Tell your mom maybe next time we'll meet."

"No wait!" Leah shouted. "I'll go get her. You make him stay right here," she told her sister before taking off in a run.

Her mother had stopped to talk with Mrs. Norris. Leah nudged her way in-between the two women and grabbed hold of her mother's arm. "Sorry, Mrs. Norris, but my sister needs her."

"What's wrong with your sister?" Valerie asked, as Leah pulled her through the crowd. "Be careful. You're going to run someone down."

"Nothing's wrong with her. It's just that we want you to meet someone," Leah said, angling her way forward. "He's very nice. And he wants to take you to the movies."

"Oh darling, not again! Listen, I've told you and your sister a hundred times, just because I caught a bridal bouquet doesn't really mean that I will get married next."

"Here she is, Stephen," said Leah breathlessly.

"This is our mommy," added Linda proudly, although she wished her mommy still had her pretty blonde hair.

Valerie glanced over at the illuminated clock sitting atop her nightstand. It read three-thirty, and still she could not get to sleep. She was going to be useless today at work. She turned on the light, grabbed one of those literary tomes she had pulled out of the library that were guaranteed to induce sleep. Twenty minutes later, she was still wide awake as her thoughts continued to slip off the text and onto this afternoon's meeting with Stephen.

With her constant worry about her daughters' medical condition, and working extra-long hours, she hadn't given much thought to the likelihood of the girls meeting up with Stephen. She should have. Dorsetville was a very small town. The chances were good they would eventually meet.

Not that she would have tried to prevent it. After all, he was their father even if he didn't know it. Which brought her around to wondering why she hadn't introduced them to each other today? Was she trying to punish him, or was she fearful that he might disappear on them as he had once done on her?

She threw back the covers, lowered her feet onto the wood floor, and reached for her robe. She might as well get up, go downstairs. She was certain there would be no sleep for her tonight.

The meeting between her daughters and Stephen had given her quite a shock. What had she told him as she hurried the girls away? She vaguely remembered saying something about having to get home for a long-distance phone call, under her children's barrage of protests.

It wasn't fair, she thought, flicking on the kitchen light. She already had enough to worry about. Doc Hammon had left a message this afternoon. The new tests showed that Leah's retina was separating faster than they had anticipated. Time was of the essence and their last hope, through Father James's friend Monsignor Casio, wasn't panning out. Apparently, he was not having any success at finding a city official who could override the residency requirements for the New York clinic. Fundraising was going well, but they would never collect the amount needed in time. Valerie was exhausted with worry.

Maybe she should put a moratorium on all of this stuff with Stephen. Work it out later. She reached for the coffee canister.

But why was she really so hesitant to tell him? Was it unforgiveness for what he had done? She had been so terribly hurt and frightened.

She watched her reflection in the kitchen window. But they had been twenty-year-old kids. What did they really know about commitment? Sure, they had made some wild promises, but at that age who didn't? Did she really want to hold him to an oath made so long ago? And in truth, he never knew she was pregnant. Maybe if he had, he might never have left. She felt her anger begin to mellow.

In the predawn light, she acknowledged the truth that she had been running from for eight long years. She was still in love with him. She always would be.

As if on cue, the phone rang. She knew it was Stephen, and this time she would answer it.

"I saw your light," he explained. "I couldn't sleep."

"Me neither."

An awkward pause followed. Finally he said, "May I come over? I have something I want to tell you."

She hesitated only briefly. "And I have something to tell you."

$\mathcal{S}$EVENTEEN

$\mathcal{T}$he gently rolling
country lanes had
taken on the soft muted light of eventide
as Mrs. Norris steered her car toward
Woodstock. She drove by rote, having
plied these roads since she was a youth,
knowing every twist, bump, and turn
along its way.

As a child, it had taken her forty minutes to walk from town to old Mrs. Stenson's place along the next bend in the
road. Mrs. Stenson sold fresh eggs. About
a half mile further down had stood an old
tar-paper shack where she, Harriet, Arlene, and Ethel used to gather as children
on hot summer days.

It had been well hidden behind an

overgrown cluster of lilac bushes. Sunlight filtered in through the old boards and bugs flew in by means of the shattered windowpanes, but they loved it. To this day, whenever she smelt moss or newly turned earth she thought of that cabin shrouded in dark shadows, and of the long summer days they had spent conjuring tales of the people who might have once lived there and the ghosts they had left behind. It had been their secret place, and they had met there everyday throughout the seemingly endless summers growing up, until one day Ethel refused to return and would never say why. Over the years, they had stopped asking. But the cabin was gone now, felled by the 1950s hurricane that had ripped through the valley.

The road took a sharp turn as it traveled up from the valley floor and passed by March's Apple Orchard. It had been run by the March family for several generations and produced crisp, juicy apples—Pippins, Cortlands, Northern Spy, Baldwin, and Macouns—that tasted of New England and which could be found in every pie that had ever won a blue ribbon at the Goshen County Fair.

Tom March was standing on the back panel of his pickup truck, a sprayer in his hand, as Mrs. Norris passed by. She honked her horn. Tom turned and waved.

As her car climbed the mountain, heading toward the turnoff, she wondered what in blazes had possessed her to agree to this meeting with "Hound Dog"? Why couldn't she have just left well enough alone, enjoyed the mystery of it? Instead, she had agreed to meet at Bertha's Barbecue Pit for dinner. She was to be carrying a copy of the *Dorsetville Gazette* under her arm. He was to be wearing a red and white checked shirt, string tie, and cowboy hat. She had recently learned that Frank Sinatra and Elvis were not his only favorite singers. He also liked Willie Nelson.

She waited at the stop sign before turning onto Route 7. A sixteen-wheeler carrying a bed of new Toyota Camrys was headed toward Woodstock. She let it pass before pulling out.

She was exceedingly nervous over this meeting. Heck, it had been forty years since she had last been out on a date, and that had been with her late husband, Bill. There hadn't been a man in her life since.

Thoughts of her Bill made her consider the prudence of this meeting. Did she really want to get entangled with another man? She enjoyed the relative peace and tranquility of her life since his death. Not that she hadn't loved her late husband; she did, and was a devoted wife. But since his passing, she had come to treasure her freedom. Now she could come and go as she pleased, and no longer had to answer to anyone.

Bill had been a strong man in every aspect of the word. He was an ex-marine, and until the day he died he did fifty situps every morning. In all the years they had been married, Mrs. Norris had never once heard him utter a word of despair. Bill believed that you took what life gave you and you made the best of it. He held true to that philosophy even when they had lost their daughter.

Admittedly, at times he could be a little overbearing; younger women might say chauvinistic. But that was the era when gender lines were rigidly drawn. Men worked outside the home and women tended to the house and the children. Men held the purse strings and made all the major decisions, and women learned clever ways to get around them. It was totally unlike today, when men did the laundry and housework and women worked on construction sites and had their own bank accounts.

It wasn't until Bill's death that she had opened up her own checking and savings accounts. To those she had added a Christmas club and a few shares of stock. She was a financially independent woman and proud of it.

A large green road sign stated Northfield five miles, Woodstock ten. Her hands started to sweat. She wiped them on her skirt even though it was her best summer suit.

The first year after Bill's death, she was surprised to find that her thoughts centered less on bereavement and more on a new sense of freedom. She could eat dinner when she wanted. Now *she* controlled the TV remote. And when she wanted the girls in for lunch, she was free to set the table the day before, or rearrange the furniture to better suit her guests without any recriminations. When Bill was alive, he had forbidden her to entertain. "I don't like people in my home. I want my privacy," he had said.

But time had softened the edges on these memories and now often she felt the need for male companionship. She missed the sound of a man's voice calling her name with that special note of endearment, and secretly longed to be caressed, to be held, to be comforted by a pair of strong arms. Sometimes she felt loneliness begin to seep in.

Her work at the rectory had helped to lessen it some. The priests kept her pretty busy. It also gave her a sense of being needed. She missed her work, the way it had filled up the empty days. Now all she did was shop, play cards, and feel sorry for herself.

She had never *actually* meant to retire. All she had

really wanted was a sign of appreciation, a statement that what she did mattered. She figured the priests would make a big fuss over the announcement and beg her to stay.

Well, that certainly had backfired.

A car from behind flashed its lights, a signal she was going too slowly. She glanced at her speedometer. It read forty-five. The speed limit was forty. She looked up at the rearview mirror and spied a man with mirrored sunglasses and an impatient expression driving a stylish BMW. She pulled over. He sped by.

The right-hand turn that lead into Woodstock was coming up. She watched the road carefully while thinking that retirement had been the biggest mistake in her life. But it was too late. She had burnt her bridges. There was no going back.

She still couldn't get used to the idea that Father James had hired Viola as a housekeeper. What had he been thinking? Everyone in Dorsetville knew about Viola and her drunken fool of a husband, the fact that the sheriff had to pay a call on their trailer at least once a week for their disturbing the peace.

And that Audrey! Now there was a piece of work. *Taking over the housekeeping duties, my foot*, Mrs. Norris thought. She had seen the state of things on the day she had stopped over to deliver a jar of her preserves. The place was a pigsty. Dust an inch thick everywhere. The kitchen sink still filled with breakfast dishes at eleven in the morning. Apparently Audrey felt the only soap worth her interest was the kind she watched from ten until three o'clock each day.

The restaurant was just up ahead. Her resolve began to waver. Maybe she should just turn around, go home and forget this whole thing. What was she doing here anyway? Respectable ladies didn't meet strange men at barbecue pits.

She pulled into the parking lot and turned off the engine.

But on the other hand, what did she have to lose? She did enjoy his letters. He sounded like a nice, steady kind of guy. After all, it wasn't as if she ever intended to get married again. She just wanted company for an occasional dinner out or a movie. She wasn't interested in romance.

Oh, what the heck! She reached for her "Passion Pink" lipstick, applied a fresh coat, then slid the *Dorsetville Gazette* underneath her arm and headed inside.

"Welcome to Bertha's, how many in your party?" asked the perky teenage waitress. The music was so loud that it made Mrs. Norris's teeth chatter. She tried to shout above the din.

"I'm meeting someone here for dinner. He might have already arrived."

"What does he look like?"

"He . . . er . . ." How was she supposed to answer that? "Why don't I just take a look around and see if I can spy him?"

"No problem," the girl replied, already refocused on a couple with three kids that had just walked in.

Inside the restaurant the air hung heavy with the odor of barbecue sauce, onions, and beer. She waded in, feeling slightly embarrassed at being overdressed. The room was a sea of blue jeans and T-shirts bearing multitudinous sayings . . . "Looking for a husband? Mine's up for adoption." "Lyme Rock Road Rally Racers." "We love Grandma." "I raise German shepherds. My wife raises Hell." "National Rifle Association 2001 Convention."

Halfway inside the cavernous room, she spied him seated at a small table near the kitchen door, a lone man wearing a cowboy hat and a red and white checked shirt. His back was toward her and for a fleeting second she considered bolting back through the front door. Instead, she smoothed down her skirt, adjusted her jacket, and boldly walked in the direction of his table.

Her letters were neatly stacked by his elbow. She tapped him on the shoulder.

"Hello, my name is Margaret and I think you're here to meet— Oh my God!!! What are *you* doing here???"

"Mrs. Norris??!!!"

George Benson's jaw nearly dropped clear down to the floor.

Where was everybody, Sam wondered, hanging up the phone. Harriet's answering machine was on even though today was Friday, one of her busiest retail days. He left a message. "Call me."

Next he called Timothy but there was no answer at his house either.

He dialed Ben. His daughter-in-law, Julie, answered. "Ben's gone somewhere with Deputy Hill."

He asked her twice to repeat that.

Strange that no one was at home. Was there some kind of meeting he had forgotten about? He checked his calendar. It was blank.

He decided to call the rectory. Father James would

know where everyone had gone. He got the answering machine. "You have reached the rectory of St. Cecilia's Catholic Church. Our weekday services are at 7 A.M. and Sunday Masses are at 8:30, 10, and 11 o'clock. If you're calling about the housekeeping position, please come right over. The back door is open and you can begin immediately."

Sam glanced up at the kitchen clock. Two o'clock and he had nothing to do. He leaned over the kitchen sink and looked out the back window at a patch of prodigious weeds growing by the woodshed. He could put on an old pair of pants and tackle them, but somehow the thought of getting undressed, then dressed again, then hauling everything out of the shed to find his weeding tools, getting all hot and sticky, seemed like too much trouble. He turned his back on the window.

He wished Ben or Timothy was around for a game of cards, but lately it seemed that they were never home when he called, or they were on their way out the door and couldn't talk. Probably busy at the television station. Carl was putting together a new show to replace *The Fat Friar.* Father Dennis had called it quits after the humiliating scene at the cooking contest.

"I think it's time I went back to being just a priest," he had told the station manager. "There are many ways to feed God's people, and so I think I'll put down my apron and start serving generous helpings of God's love instead."

And from what Sam heard through the gossip mill, Father Dennis had returned to his duties with great enthusiasm. Some said it was just like when he had first come to St. Cecilia's, full of fire and passion.

"Sure keeps a body awake during Mass," morning attendees attested.

Sam heard several car doors slam outside. Who could that be? He opened the door and stepped out.

His entire driveway was flooded with people.

"*Surprise!!!*" they all shouted.

Harriet was standing next to Arlene, who was holding tightly to Fred's hand; the Petersons stood beside them with Valerie and her twin daughters and the young man who was staying at the rectory. Father James and Father Dennis were also there.

Mrs. Norris, Mother Superior, Sister Claire, and Father Keene were all clustered by the rose of Sharon with the Henderson sisters. Ethel Johnson stood nearest the back porch and gave Sam a big kiss on the cheek. Honey barked her approval.

"What is all of this?" Sam asked, confused.

Nancy Hawkins stepped forward and took his arm. "No questions. Just come this way."

Another crowd of friends, tightly packed in a circle at the end of the driveway, began to separate as Sam and Nancy headed in their direction. Sam recognized Rabbi Tantembaum and his wife with several of the women from Hadassah; Mrs. Hopkins, the director of the Senior Center, George Benson and his assistant Ted. Chester Platt was there with what seemed to be his entire construction crew.

As they passed Roger Martin, he patted Sam on the back. "Congratulations, Sam."

Congratulations? Did he win something?

Reverend Curtis and his wife, Emily, were stationed along with several members of their congregation including Charlie Littman and Rochelle Phillips. He even spied Sheriff Bromley standing next to Deputy Hill.

"Okay everyone, back up!" Nancy shouted, and like

the parting Red Sea the crowd moved aside to reveal Timothy and Ben, seated atop the front fender of Sam's gold Plymouth Duster and wearing smiles as broad as a barn door.

"But how . . . ?" Sam stammered. He was speechless. "It . . . it . . . can't be."

"Sure it can, Sam," Ben said, sliding carefully to the ground. The sheriff reached out to help steady him. "Nancy got a bunch of us together and we all pitched in to rebuild her."

"She's just like new," Timothy added.

"Better than new," Nancy added. "We replaced the bashed-up fenders and side panels with some from the wrecking company over in Thomaston. George and Deputy Hill were in charge of that part of the job."

"Thank you," Sam whispered, overcome with gratitude. He ran his hand lovingly over the newly painted hood.

"I thought it was the least I could do," Hill said meekly.

Sam inched his way around the car and marveled. It looked like the day he had driven it off the showroom floor. It was a miracle.

"But how did you get the money to do all of this? It must have cost a fortune." Sam worried about these kinds of things.

"Everyone here helped," Nancy said.

"We ran a bake sale to help pay for the new paint job," offered Ruth Henderson, who was especially pleased to have been asked to run two bake sales in the course of one month, and even more pleased to have sold out each time, wildflower decorations and all.

"And the quilters auctioned a quilt on eBay. It

brought in twenty-four-hundred dollars," Marge Peale said proudly.

"Some donated their time," Nancy explained. "Others donated money. In fact, there isn't a person in town that hasn't pitched in one way or the other."

Sam felt his heart expand with joy. "I don't know what to say."

"You needn't say anything," Father James said, joining in. "It was our great pleasure. Somehow Dorsetville didn't seem quite the same without your Plymouth plying the back roads."

"It was like looking up into the sky and not seeing the sun," the rabbi added.

"Get in, Sam, turn over the engine. Let's take her for a spin," Ben urged excitedly, like a kid on Christmas who wants to see his best friend's train set clanging down the tracks.

"I'll help direct traffic so you can back it out," Deputy Hill offered. "Everyone stand back, now. Get over on the grass."

"Just make sure no one gets run over in the process," Bromley warned him.

Nancy opened the driver's door and handed Sam the keys. He hesitated for just a moment, trying not to give in to the heavy wave of emotions he felt. He leaned over and gave her a huge hug.

"Thank you, dear. You don't know what this means to me."

Nancy's eyes filled with tears that she brusquely brushed away. "Go on, now. Get in. Do as Ben says. Take her for a spin and be careful. We couldn't find another Slant Six so we put in a V-eight."

"Maybe we should have put in a heavy-duty seat-

belt for your camera equipment, Ben," Timothy joked. "All this engine power might take Sam some getting used to."

"Want to drag race when I get my rig finished?" teased Matthew, who had just bought an old Pontiac Firebird he was restoring.

"I think I'll just take things slow and careful and leave the drag racing to young bucks like you," Sam said. He gripped the steering wheel with two hands, feeling like he had just won the Lotto.

"And where do you propose to do that racing," Sheriff Bromley asked, glaring down at Matthew.

"Just . . . er . . . kidding, Sheriff," Matthew stuttered.

"Glad to hear it," Bromley replied.

Matthew slowly melted into the crowd.

"So, let's go for our ride," Ben said, impatient. "I could use a box of Efferdent. I heard Kmart is having a two-for-one sale."

"My pleasure," Sam said, and began to back out of the driveway under Hill's direction.

"A little more to the left, Mr. Rosenberg. That's it . . . eeeeassssse it out nice and slow. Give her a little more gas. That's it . . ."

"Oh for Pete's sake, Hill," the sheriff swore. "He's backing up a car, not a tractor trailer."

"Wait a minute!" Timothy shouted.

Sam slammed on the brakes, causing Ben to slide off the backseat and crash onto the floor.

"What in blazes?" Ben yelled.

"Maybe Father Keene would like to come," Timothy said. "It's been pretty hard on him being alone with all those nuns. He says a priest was never meant to live with women. It's unnatural. I think he could use a break."

Timothy leaned out the window. "Father Keene! We're going over to Kmart, want to come along?"

"Saints be blessed," he said, sprinting for the car. "I was waiting for an invite."

"Don't leave him at the store again," Sister Bernadette scowled. Last time they had visited Kmart, they had left him behind.

"Nuns," Father Keene said with contempt, sliding into the backseat. "One little mistake and they never let a man forget it."

Father James watched Sam's Plymouth disappear over the last rise in the road. It did his heart good to see these old friends independent again. He prayed that God would keep Sam and his car in pristine condition for many more years.

He also sent up a prayer of thanks for all the good people gathered here today. They sure had outdone themselves this time. Father James had always known that those who lived in Dorsetville were the greatest people on the earth. Their kindness to Sam only confirmed it.

"Father James," Valerie called. "We wanted to thank you and Monsignor Casio for all that you've done to help the girls get accepted at the eye clinic. We're all ready to leave for the drive down to the city now."

"My pleasure," he assured them. "Although we didn't have that much to do with it. Stephen's residency was the real factor, and since the girls are his daughters, they couldn't refuse to take them on as patients."

Father James still had to marvel at how God had worked this all out. The logistics alone were staggering.

And now they were on their way to becoming a real family. The young couple had already asked him to schedule them for prenuptial counseling. They planned to be married next spring. Just looking at them gave Father James great joy, and reminded him of one of David's Psalms . . . *In you they trusted and were not disappointed.*

"Tell everyone how grateful we are for all the money they raised," Valerie added. "We'll only use what we need. The rest we thought might be used to help others who haven't medical insurance."

Father James thought of the Gaithwaits. Maybe some of the money could be used to help them get out from under their crushing debt.

"I hope that you might consider making Dorsetville your permanent home," he told the young couple.

"We couldn't think of living anywhere else," Stephen told him.

"Daddy, can we wait in the car?" Linda asked, yanking on his arm. "Our legs are getting tired from standing."

"Sure, honey," he said.

"And Daddy, don't forget, you promised us ice cream," Leah reminded him.

"I won't." He watched the girls head out toward the car. "That's the first time they've called me Daddy," he said with a catch in his throat. "It sounded awful good."

Valerie squeezed his hand. "I kind of like the sound of it, too."

Mrs. Norris joined Father James as he headed back toward his Jeep.

"So, the old boys are back on the road again, hey," Mrs. Norris said.

He smiled, remembering the look on Sam's face. "It's nice to see a community pull together when someone is in need of help."

"I gave the money for the new radio," she said. "It has both FM and AM."

"That was very generous of you."

"Figured I didn't need to buy anymore makeup or stuff," she said. "I've grown accustomed to my face the way it is, wrinkles and all. No sense trying to camouflage it."

Father prudently kept his opinions to himself.

"I heard you finally got the pluck to fire that Viola," she said. "So, you're back to looking for a new house-keeper again."

"Yes, I'm afraid so."

"I suppose I could come over and help out," Mrs. Norris said, testing the waters. "That is . . . if you want me."

"You could?" he asked tentatively.

"Truth is, Father, I'm bored silly hanging around the house," she confessed. "Lori's back at the bakery, so I'm not needed there anymore. And there's only so much Bingo and shopping a woman can do before her mind turns to mush."

He laughed.

"Listen, I know that I've been a little . . . unsettled, these last few months, but I had some things I had to work through."

"I see."

She paused.

"You know I've given up all that health food stuff."

"I see."

"So, if you want me back . . . just until you can find someone else, of course . . ."

"Of course . . ."

". . . it has to be under one condition."

"What's that?" He eyed her suspiciously.

"That I would go back to cooking the old way. You know, lots of cholesterol-clogging meat products, cream, cheese. Enough pots of black coffee to send a colon into spasms."

Father James suddenly felt that Sam wasn't the only one who had been blessed today. He gave her a hug, and a smile as large as the Cheshire cat.

"So when can you start?"

READING GROUP
DISCUSSION QUESTIONS

1. Why do you think the author entitled the book *Grace Will Lead Me Home*? Can you think of some instances in which grace is exhibited by one character toward another? Which characters are ultimately led "home"?

2. After Sarah sees two angels, she is fearful that she won't be believed if she tells anyone. Yet her account provides the comfort her mother so desperately needs. What other characters take the risk of rejection by making themselves vulnerable? With what kinds of responses are they met? Are there times when it's better *not* to take those risks?

3. Wendy gives Father James advice about his housekeeper, suggesting that he has crossed the line between dispensing Christian charity and being a doormat. How does one differentiate between the two?

4. Doc Hammon speaks about the medical crisis in our country, which has occurred mainly as a result of increasing numbers of lawsuits. Where does one find a balance between justice and the abuse of one's rights? Does grace ever enter into the equation? If so, what are the connections between grace and justice and expoloitation?

5. Can the stolen mailboxes be interpreted as a metaphor for losing an opportunity to receive a message? How does this relate to the Campbells, who have had their mailbox stolen three times?

6. Both Valerie Kilbourne and the Gaithwaits encounter huge medical bills without having the resources to pay them. How do these two families differ in facing this trial? Why would one family seemingly find a solution to the problem and the other not?

If your church book group would like to find more discussion questions about Grace Will Lead Me Home, *please visit www.randomhouse/doubleday/readers*